PANGEA ONLINE

DEATH AND AXES

S.L. ROWLAND

ALSO BY S.L. ROWLAND

Tales of Aedrea

Cursed Cocktails

Sword & Thistle

Pangea Online

Pangea Online: Death and Axes

Pangea Online 2: Magic and Mayhem

Pangea Online 3: Vials and Tribulations

Sentenced to Troll

Sentenced to Troll

Sentenced to Troll 2

Sentenced to Troll 3

Sentenced to Troll 4

Sentenced to Troll 5

Path to Villainy: An NPC Kobold's Tale

Collected Editions

Pangea Online: The Complete Trilogy

Sentenced to Troll Compendium: Books 1-3

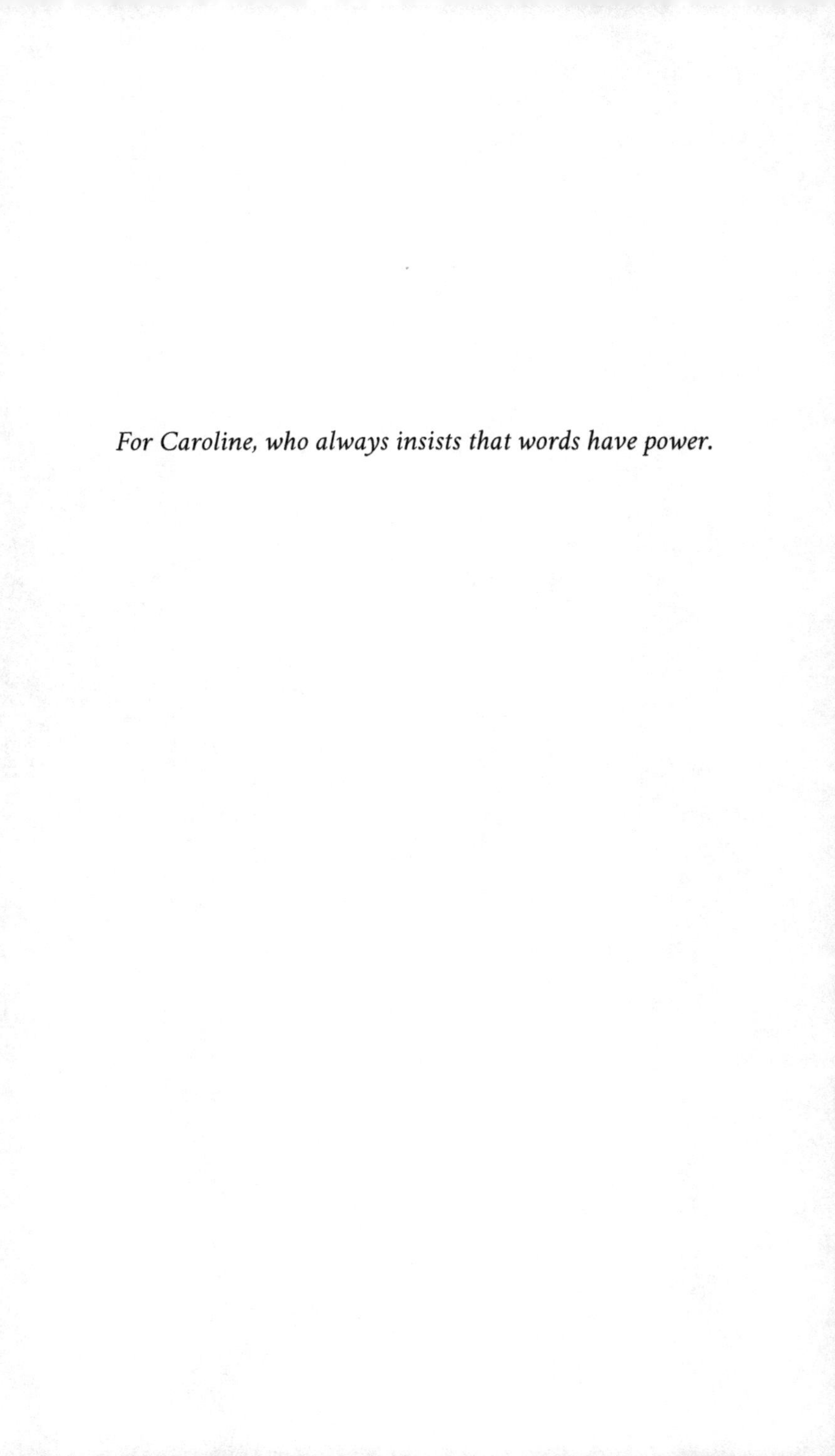

For Caroline, who always insists that words have power.

CHAPTER ONE

My life sucks.

I live in a place called The Boxes, which is a city of small, metal, living quarters stacked God only knows how high atop other metal boxes. A small window allows me to look out into the world. There's not much to look at, really. I watch the drones as they fly by, delivering food that will be dropped, sterilized, and then transported in an airtight chute to others just like me living in their own boxes. Across the alley, hundreds of other boxes litter the landscape. But that's about it. I don't know how many of us live here.

The Boxes used to be a large city called Atlanta. That was back before nuclear war wiped out a large portion of the population and forced those who had survived to live locked away from the toxins and radiations it left behind. I hear there are parts of the country where people can still go outside without masks. This isn't one of them. I haven't been outside in close to a year. Not since I turned eighteen and moved from the orphanage to my very own box.

Once I graduated, the orphanage couldn't house me anymore and sent me out on my own. They don't receive funding for me after I turn eighteen, so I don't really blame them. Mouths are hard to feed.

It's been so long since I've been outside that I've forgotten what fresh air smells like. My box smells like sweat and staleness. The sad thing is I don't even know what anything smells like in the game. You see, I'm a data miner. Now that I have graduated from my basic studies, I've been working eight hours a day swinging a pickaxe in the game, watching trails of data spring from the rocks and drift past me into the air. Data mining is a good profession for someone like me. It at least pays the bills and gives me something to do.

The mines I work in are designed after coal mines. Coal hasn't been used in centuries, but I guess the designers thought they were being cute. They love being cute. I've never actually been able to explore what the game truly has to offer. It takes money to do that. I can't afford even the most basic Worldpass, so the only places I go to are the mines and my home portal, a virtual home which is basically just as drab and boring as my box. But I do have free access to the web and am able to read about what others do in the game. I love watching streams of people as they go to the fantasy worlds and level up their avatars. There's something about the hero's journey that just resonates with me. Maybe it's because I'll never be one. In a fantasy world, I'd be the farmer tending his garden, not the brave warrior riding off to fight monsters and save the princess.

Data mining doesn't pay very well. It gets me three meals a day and this small metal box. That's about it. Oh, and I have my haptic suit. The designers send everyone a basic version the day they graduate. It's nothing fancy, but it gives me the in-game experience as if I was actually there. There are sensors so detailed that I can actually feel the handle of a pickaxe while I'm working in the mines. The headset I wear has better clarity than reality. Everything feels real, minus pain. They don't let you feel pain. Instead, your vision goes red around the edges, making it hard to see, and your stamina drops so it's harder for a player to move. I've never died in the game, but they say that everything goes black and you have a chance to lose your items.

The light flickers overhead, telling me it's time to power up my room. A stationary bicycle sits in the corner with a few wires that connect to a plug in the wall. I ride the bike for two hours a day and it powers my room for twenty-four hours.

Most of us in The Boxes don't have enough money to pay for power. I guess those in charge of the game realized this, so they started installing self-sustaining power sources in each box. They would never let my power go completely out. That would kill me. There is a grid that keeps the air purifier working, but for anything else, I have to power it myself. They do provide free internet, though. They make so much money from the game that they can afford to give it out for free. It makes people think they owe something to the game designers and therefore, when they have extra money, it all goes back into the game.

The game is called Pangea Online, named after the

supercontinent that existed before it all broke apart and gave us the world as we know it. I think it was their vision of bringing the world together under one game that sprouted the name. Before Pangea came along, everything people wanted to do on the web was segmented in different places. Now, it's all together. And it's all interactive.

Over ninety percent of the world's population spends time in Pangea Online. For those of us in The Boxes, Pangea is life.

Unless you're the uber-rich, most people no longer buy things for the real world. They spend their money on nice homes, clothes, and skills. All in the game. All virtual reality. None of it is real. And still, I have nothing.

They say that if you think you're crazy, then you're not really crazy. I wish that worked with being poor.

After charging up my room for the day, I strap myself into my haptic suit. I split my charging into two sessions, one before work and one after. It's less boring that way. The suit fits snugly around my body, capable of dispatching pressure at any moment so that I feel whatever is happening to my body in Pangea. There is a slight discomfort as the suit calibrates to my body. The suit can even warm and cool as I walk through different climates, not that everything in the mines isn't hotter than the bowels of hell. I put on my VR headset and it takes up the entirety of my vision, allowing me to experience the game as if I were really there. The only senses I can't experience are taste and smell. Considering where I work, I count it as a blessing. There is nothing worse than a hot fart in an enclosed space. I've experienced enough of those in my box.

I press my fingertips together and the blackness of my headset morphs into a three-dimensional world. The words 'Welcome to Pangea Online' appear over a blue swirling portal. If I were rich, I might see hundreds of portals in front of me, but since I am not, there is only the mines. I jump through the portal and dozens of worlds spin by me, offering glimpses of what else Pangea has to offer. Too bad I'll never see any of it.

The entrance to the mines greets me when the spinning stops. Tiny icons dot the edge of my vision detailing my health, stats, items, messages and a translucent map of my surroundings. There are hundreds of mines. I can see my destination as a flickering orange dot on the map. My inventory is scarce. All I have are my pick and my hard hat. I've always wondered what it would be like to hold a sword or cast magic, but I doubt that will ever happen. I focus on the pickaxe and it suddenly appears in my hand. I check the stats on it.

Item: Basic Pickaxe. +2 attack. *A pickaxe is a miner's best friend.*

I check my avatar's stats while I march to the mine I am scheduled to work in for the day. My class is Miner and the only ability I have learned is mining. My stamina has recovered overnight and I'll be ready to start swinging the pickaxe soon enough.

The thing about Pangea Online being a worldwide game is that all of the users are bound by the same constraints. Sure, money can buy you items to help your avatar seem more powerful than they actually are, but everyone is bound by two solid principles: stats and experience. Even mining grants experience. As you level up, each level grants a certain number of stat points to be allocated towards various attributes. There is **Strength, Agility, Vitality, Intellect, Dexterity** and **Stamina.** Over the past year of mining, I've put all the stat points I have accumulated into Strength. My avatar is far stronger than I could ever hope to be, but it allows me to gain more experience with each swing.

More or less, my character is modeled after me. Dark hair, pale features, and tall. The only difference being that I am thin and lean, like a cyclist, while my character is ripped like a Greek god from swinging an axe all day long.

My message icon blinks at me. I focus on the message and my inbox pops into view. It is a translucent gray and I can still see the world as I walk. The message is from Buzz. He works in the mines with me and is my best friend. His message reads:

Yo Esil,

Did you hear about the new tournament happening all over Pangea? A hundred thousand gold to the winner. Gah, I wish I could compete, but you know, work. See you in the mine.

-Buzz

Buzz loves watching people play games during his time away from the mines. It's practically all he does. He's never competed a day in his life, though. In fact, he's just as poor as me. He always talks about how good he could be if he took time off from work. He lives with his mom in a box not much bigger than mine. I only know because he let it slip one day that his mother had been sick. I haven't told him much about myself. Growing up in an orphanage is something I prefer not to talk about.

I send him a quick message that I haven't heard about the tournament and I can't wait to hear more. The game automatically translates my voice to text and sends it to Buzz.

He's waiting for me at the entrance to mine one-twenty-four. His avatar is not as big as mine. For whatever reason, Buzz elected to put all of his stat points into Intellect. In the rest of Pangea, it might be useful. He could equip magic items and cast spells, but there is no benefit to it here. Because of his buffoonery, Buzz is still level two after a year. On the other hand, with the additional experience my strength has garnered me, I am level four.

He wears a stained white t-shirt and jeans, the same as me. Starter rags for the mines. In one hand, he holds his pickaxe, in the other, his yellow helmet with a light attached to the front. A huge smile beams across his face.

"Another day in paradise," he jokes.

We walk into the mine and immediately I feel warmer. Green ones and zeros flutter past me as they exit the tunnel. Data. Someone has already started working. The mine is dimly lit by dangling light bulbs with glowing filament. A single pair of train-tracks leads us down the cavern. Walls as black as night surround us on all sides. This place would be hell for someone afraid of enclosed spaces.

At the end of the tunnel, Grayson, one of the longest tenured mine workers, is already sweating as he swings his axe. He enters in the morning with a gray beard, and by the end of his shift, he looks twenty years younger. No one knows how long he has been working in the mines, but everyone I've met says the same thing. He was here when they started.

"About time you boys showed up," he says. His voice is as gruff as the cavern, but there is a twinkle in his eye. When I focus on Grayson, his stats pop up to the side of my vision. He is level forty-five, practically unheard of in the mines. Over the years, he must have been able to save some gold, because he has a diamond-tipped pickaxe. What I would do for one of those.

"Good to see you, Grayson," I say. "How was your night?"

"It was good. I spent the evening on a beach listening to mermaids sing," he says between swinging the pick. Grayson is the only miner I know who has a pass to go to other worlds. I wonder if I work hard enough, will I be able to buy one someday?

"Why would you go to a beach when you could go into a gameworld?" asks Buzz.

He and I both begin working. Each swing of my pick sends bright green data fluttering through the air. It flows down the cavern, casting an eerie glow in the darkness. I have no idea what kind of data we are mining or where it goes. All I know is that this is my life. My dull, monotonous life.

Buzz keeps talking. "So, Esil, the tournament. How did you not read about it? It's the largest payout in game history. One. Hundred. Thousand. Gold." He enunciates every word for effect.

"I guess I missed it." Truth be told, I had spent the

previous evening watching a stream following an elven princess and her band of dwarven followers as they traveled through a mountainous pass overtaken by orcs. It had been an exciting three hours before I fell asleep. I much prefer watching people quest and explore in the gameworlds. I guess because in my own life, everything is planned out and routine, I like the freedom and adventure that RPGs bring. Buzz loves PvP games, where its player versus player. I think those are boring, it's the same goal every time.

"I thought it would have been your kind of thing. It's a quest this time. They say it will be three stages testing the most well-rounded players in Pangea. No max level players allowed. They haven't announced all the details yet, but I hear it is taking place over all of Pangea. There is all kinds of speculation on what the quests will be, but no one really knows. It's going to be epic! If I wasn't working, you know. I mean, just think of what we could do with that money. We'd be set for life."

"Pipe dreams," says Grayson. He wipes sweat from his brow and leaves a black streak on his forehead.

"You're such a downer," says Buzz.

"I'm a realist."

"This coming from a man who listens to mermaids singing on a beach in his free time," I say and they both laugh.

The day passes slowly, but Buzz fills us in on all the speculation of the upcoming tournament. I almost feel sorry for him, but then I realize that it gives him hope. The mines would be a terrible place for him if he didn't have hope of someday leaving them.

When a small ding alerts me that our shift is over, I

notice my XP bar is only a few points away from hitting level five. I've heard that at level five, you gain a few extra item slots in your inventory. Not that it would help me much with my two items, but it'd be cool nonetheless.

I would love to be able to allocate my points before the next shift, so I tell Buzz to go ahead and that I'll catch up with him later tonight after I power up my room.

Three XP stand between me and leveling up, so I swing faster. My stamina bar shrinks with each hit, but I'll have the whole night to recharge so I keep pushing. Data trails past me in a stream. I'm focused. The only thing that matters is hearing the chime telling me I've leveled up.

I'm one XP away when my stamina drops to zero. My swings move slower than they ever have. My arms feel heavy with each movement and I know my haptic suit is making me feel fatigued. With great effort, I take one final swing and watch my experience bar fill completely before resetting to zero.

A loud chime rings in my ear and a bright silver five sweeps across my vision. My inbox fills with notifications. I'll check them later when I get home. The last bit of data streams out of the tunnel and I am left in the dimly lit cavern once more. Out of the edge of my vision I see something shiny where I had just been digging.

A small handle protrudes from beneath the coal. I give it a hard pull, but it's lodged in place. I begin swinging the pick again and the green glow returns as data flies past. Piece by piece, I uncover what is hidden beneath the coal. As I expose more and more, I realize it's a chest. Each swing becomes harder. In my year in the mines, I've never heard of someone finding an item while digging. I can feel my heart racing in anticipation of what could be inside.

I give the chest another tug and it comes free. The chest is heavy. For a moment, I imagine gold beyond my wildest dreams inside. I place it on the floor of the tunnel. There are runes carved on the top of it in a language I can't read. I look behind me, making certain no one is watching. Then I flip the latch and open the lid.

CHAPTER TWO

A bright glow surrounds the chest and fills the cavern. It hurts my eyes as I stare into the chest, trying to make out what is inside. A piece of parchment rises from the chest and hovers in the air before me. It reads:

Congratulations, Esil! You have found a hidden chest. Make the most of its offerings and as always, never stop leveling!

-Pangea Online Developers

I have heard of the highly sought after Developer's Chests, but never in a million years would I have thought I would find one in the mines. Most people find them at the bottom of an incredibly hard dungeon, or at the end of a long quest.

I turn around and make sure no one is behind me. If living in the orphanage has taught me anything, it's to never trust anyone if you have something they want.

The glow of the chest fades and I can make out a few items inside. I quickly touch them and they all fly into my inventory. I nearly faint as I look through each item.

__Item: Worldpass Premium. Soulbound. Cannot be traded or discarded.__ Allows user to travel to any world free of charge.

Holy shit! The Worldpass is a game changer.

__Item: Dwarven Boots of Stamina. Soulbound. Cannot be traded or discarded.__ These ancient Dwarven Boots recharge 2% stamina every five seconds.

Even Grayson will be jealous of my new boots. The impact they can have on my work output will be astronomical.

__Currency: 1000 gold.__

My jaw drops wide open. This can't be real. Pangea Online is so popular that in-game gold is the most stable currency in the world. One thousand gold is more money than I have made this entire year. We are paid in silver and it takes ten silver to equal one gold. That amount of gold can literally change my life. What will I even do with so much gold? The gold, combined with my new Worldpass, means I can actually explore Pangea with my avatar instead of living vicariously through other players. Buzz is going to lose it when I tell him.

I stare at the items in my inventory. My head spins with possibilities of where I should go. The stream of the elven princess comes to mind.

I equip my new boots and immediately feel like I could work for hours. They gleam even in the dull light of the tunnel. The silver thread is beautiful and I worry that the coal will dirty them, but as I walk, they miraculously stay clean. I send Buzz a quick message on my way to the portal.

Buzz,

You're never going to guess what just happened to me. We need to video chat ASAP.

-Esil

I desperately want to explore Pangea, but my room is low on power. I've already stayed longer than I should have. Nothing would be worse than traveling to an exciting new destination and having my entire system power off. No, first I'll go home and charge my room, then I'll plan my next move.

I step into the portal that takes me home. Normally, I go straight through and arrive at my home portal, where I logout of the game. This time, I am greeted with hundreds of different portals to choose from. Dozens of open worlds where I could become a king or a warrior or spend my entire life devoted to singing songs to tavern wenches. There are shops and villages, each more interesting than the last. I want to see them all. Soon, I will.

My home portal is a dark gray room not too different from the box I live in. The walls and floors are bare. I've never had any extra money to spend on making it feel like home. It could use some artwork and a chair to sit in. Maybe I'll use some of my newfound gold to spruce the place up.

After logging out of Pangea, I open the sliding door to the chute where my food is delivered and take it out. I've heard stories of people who eat fresh food, but in The Boxes, all we can afford is processed food. It comes in a wrapper and is packed full of nutrients. It tastes like licking a dirty floor.

I spend the next hour on the bike charging my box.

My mind wanders, wondering where I want to go first. The premium Worldpass is something few people have. While it's true that most people are not as poor as those of us who work in the mines, most people still have to pay to travel. Certain worlds can be very expensive. Unlimited portals free of charge means I can go to a dozen worlds in one day. I can see all of Pangea.

Once I'm finished biking, I take a quick shower. The water is cold, but at least it's clean. I towel off and strap into my haptic suit. As soon as I'm online, my message icon blinks. I expect it to be Buzz, but it's the notifications from leveling up. I quickly scroll through them.

Congratulations on reaching level five! You now have a new stat point to allocate as you see fit.

Congratulations on reaching level five! Your inventory has been upgraded to carry more items.

I laugh to myself at that one. I've only ever had two items in my entire life. A new notification pops up as soon as I close my inbox.

A wide smile creeps across my face when I open it.

Aleesia is streaming live, would you like to join in? Y/N

The elven princess. I focus on the 'No' icon and close my inbox again. Any other time, I would be ecstatic to watch her stream, but not today. I jump through the portal and focus on the Mortican Mountains. Today, I'll be watching in person.

The portal empties me into the town square. I've seen it a hundred times through Aleesia's feed, but it doesn't compare to actually being there. Cobbled streets stretch out in front of me. In the far distance, I see the peaks of the Mortican Mountains with their snowcapped tops jutting above the nearby rooftops. To my left, I see an armor shop and beside it a blacks—

"Get out of the way, noob," a voice rumbles. A minotaur stares down at me, covered in bright blue chainmail that contrasts with his golden fur.

I jump out of the way, afraid of being trampled by his massive hooves. He pushes his way through the crowd and I can see his horns swaying back and forth above the sea of people.

The town square bustles around me. Dozens of players walk past, their nametags hovering above their heads. They distract me from how beautiful the city is so I focus my thoughts and they disappear. Elves, dwarves, humans and several other races all interact, buying and selling in the open market to my right. I even spot a gnome trying to fight his way through the crowd. It's amazing! I've only ever seen other humans in the mines. It takes gold to start a character with a race other than human. These people could be from anywhere across the globe. Pangea Online has the most state of the art language translators, allowing the entire world to interact in one place.

"Nice rags," someone yells at me as they walk past and I am suddenly aware that I'm wearing the same starter clothes I've had for the past year. Now that I have money, I should buy something new.

Up the street, I spot the tailor. A coat of arms hangs over the door with a needle and thread on a checkered purple and white background.

When I enter the shop, the tailor immediately scowls. The clothing that adorns the walls is of the highest quality. Richly dyed fabrics with intricate details of leaves or vines embroidered on the sleeves and collars. Stuff I could never have afforded a day ago. A green tunic with a black axe on the collar catches my eye.

"The soup kitchen is down the street," he mutters. The man has the hooked nose of a hawk and beady eyes. His hairline recedes and what hair he does have is slicked back.

I pull a few gold coins from my inventory and lay them on the counter. His lips curl into a devious smile.

"I'm sorry, sir. Where have my manners gone? How can I assist you today?"

For a moment, I contemplate leaving the store. In reality, no one still wearing their starter clothes would ever have the money to shop in a place like this, so I can't really blame the man.

"I'll take one of those," I say, pointing to the green tunic. I find a pair of khaki pants and a nice leather belt with a silver buckle shaped like a wolf. I check out the new clothing in my inventory.

*Item: **Green Tunic**. +0 armor. Not everything is about stats, you know.*

*Item: **Khaki Pants**. +0 armor. Not everything is about stats, you know.*

*Item: **Silver Wolf Head Belt**. +0 armor. Not everything is about stats, you know.*

The clothing adds nothing to my stats, but I don't care. For once, I don't look like a beggar.

The tailor starts to offer me a pair of boots, but then he sees the ones I'm wearing and his eyes go wide. I can sense the greed in them. He must want to ask me where I got them, but he's worried of overstepping his bounds again.

"That'll be two gold, please."

I hesitate to part with the money, but eventually slide it across the counter.

Exiting the tailor's shop, I already feel like less of an outsider.

I want to explore the town, but there will be plenty of time for that later. I set off for the mountains, taking in the shops as I go. What I'm truly excited about is leaving the town and exploring the countryside on my way to find the princess.

My inbox glows, indicating I have a new message. It's from Buzz.

Esil,

Sorry, but it'll have to wait. Mom is sick again and I need to make sure she's taken care of before I log back in. I'll catch up with you later.

-Buzz

I feel bad for Buzz. His mom has been sick for a while. When people get sick in The Boxes, they don't usually get better. Maybe I can use some of my gold to help her get the medicine she needs. I'll talk to Buzz about it at work tomorrow.

I push the thoughts of his sick mother to the back of my mind. Two guards stand sentry at the entrance to the town. Their steel armor reflects my green tunic and I can't help but admire how good I look. Such a stark contrast from the rags I am used to. The guards, along with the tailor and most of the shop owners, are NPCs—non-playable characters that the game designers implemented for tasks no one else would want to do. They nod at me as I walk past.

You are leaving the town limits and entering a PvP zone.

In town, players are not allowed to attack each other, but out here, I'll need to watch my back. Some jerk could cut me down while I'm not looking and guard over my tombstone, making it impossible for me to retrieve my items. There are penalties for killing other players who have not agreed to engage in combat, especially those with lower levels, but just like at the orphanage, bullies exist everywhere.

The landscape before me is the most beautiful I have ever seen. Lush fields and clear blue skies abound for miles. I take off running. My stamina bar drops slightly and replenishes with each step. With my new boots, I could no doubt run for hours.

A small dot on my map tells me an enemy is nearby. My first battle! Adrenaline pumps through my veins as I search for my opponent. I spot the bird-like creature crouched below a giant oak tree. When I focus on it, its stats appear to the side of my vision.

Lesser Harpy. Level 3. *Its bark is just as bad as its bite.*

I'm level five, so I should have no problem taking it out. I've seen harpies before on the streams, but seeing one in person is an awesome feeling. The creature is half bird, half human, with the body of a woman, but the legs of a bird. Sharp talons curl menacingly where fingers and toes should be. Wings sprout from its back, allowing it to hover slightly off the ground. It watches me warily as I approach. It lets out a raucous crow and digs its claws into the dirt, ready for battle. Feathers ruffle and then it attacks. The harpy jumps into the air towards me feet first. Its talons extend, ready to rip my body to shreds. I duck and roll to the right and it lands in the grass with a thud.

I equip my pickaxe from my inventory. The harpy jumps at me again and I swing my pick. It digs straight into the ground and a small stream of green numbers sprout from the earth. Why did I just use mine in the middle of battle? Claws connect with my chest and my vision goes red from the talons ripping through my flesh. My health bar shrinks by half. I try to swing for the harpy again and again, my pick digs into the earth. Green numbers flutter past my ear. My stupidity dawns on me. Mine is the only ability I know. Red fades from my vision just as the harpy attacks again. Its claws dig into my arm and blood stains the grass beneath me. My vision begins to darken at the edges. The harpy lunges for me once more and everything goes black.

CHAPTER THREE

The blackness slowly clears from my vision and I am back in the town square. My health has returned and my clothes are new and shiny again. I check my inventory. Everything is there except for my pickaxe and a tenth of my gold. A message flashes across my vision.

You have died. You now have one hour to retrieve your belongings before they become public property.

When you die in the game, there is a chance that any item not soulbound will be left behind. I need to get my pickaxe before the timer expires. I'll need it for work tomorrow. I could just buy a new one, but I would rather spend my gold on other things.

I still can't believe I went into a battle with no abilities. Most players go through a tutorial when they log into Pangea for the first time. When they choose their class, they practice the ability and learn a few basic attacks. Not in the mines. We just learn to swing the pick. That harpy, even though it was only level three, shredded me to pieces. I'll need to invest in armor at some point. That's the downside of putting all my stats into Strength. Which reminds me, I never sorted my stats from hitting level five.

I open my stat page. Currently, I have fourteen points put into Strength. Each avatar is given eleven points to start with and are awarded one stat point per level.

Stats:

Strength - 14

Strength determines how hard I hit and the max weight I am able to carry.

Agility - 0

Agility determines how fast I can move. It also has an effect on my dodge chance.

Vitality - 0

Vitality determines my total health points and HP regeneration.

Intellect - 0

Intellect determines how powerful my spells are, my mana points and mana regeneration.

Dexterity - 0

Dexterity determines my hit chance and how long it takes to cast spells.

Stamina - 0

Stamina determines how much energy I have available.

My first reaction is to put my new point into Strength and go all out. Now that I have the Worldpass, though, I want my character to be more balanced. I have no need for stamina at the moment with my new boots. I may want to invest a few points in it down the road, though. Intellect could be useful if I learned some spells and would be handy in the long run if I want to carry powerful magic items. Agility would complement my strength nicely. The battle with the harpy reruns through my mind and I decide to spend my point on Vitality for increased health. I'd rather not die again.

Down the street, I see a building with a sword and shield over the entrance. That's where I need to go.

Inside, two men fight in a ring with wooden swords. A variety of swords and shields line the walls. There are spears with intricate carvings and colored tips, bows and arrows with brightly colored fletchings, daggers. This place appears to have all manner of physical weapons. Another man stands behind the counter. He watches me from behind a fiery red beard. When I focus on him, I learn his name is Raibert. His gray nametag tells me he is an NPC shop owner.

"How may we assist you?" he asks.

"I was hoping to learn some combat abilities."

He interlocks his fingers together and gives me a wink. "Well, you've come to the right place. Lokston there is the best weapons trainer in town. What's your weapon of choice?"

The pickaxe is a great tool, but not a weapon. I need something that requires less precision but will still feel natural in my hands. I catch a glimpse of myself in the reflection of a nearby sword. The little black axe embroidered on my collar answers the question for me.

"An axe," I say.

He steps out from behind the counter and I notice he is wearing a green and yellow kilt. His legs are the size of tree trunks. I would not want to meet him on the field of battle. He leads me, past the ring where the two men continue to fight, to a wall adorned with an array of axes.

A double-edged battleaxe catches my eye. It's made of a dark black metal. The blade shimmers. I know that's the one I want before I look at the others.

"I want that one."

"You have quite the taste. That will set you back five gold."

I gulp at the thought. That's almost half a year's wages on an axe. I have an idea.

"Five gold? Throw in some free training and you've got a deal."

His eyes cut at me for a moment as he thinks over what I've said. I don't know if NPCs are allowed to haggle, but I give it a try anyways.

"Deal." He extends his hand and we grasp each other by the forearm, cementing our agreement.

Congratulations! You have learned the skill 'Barter.' May prices ever fall in your favor.

I place the gold in his hand and the axe appears in my inventory. It is beautiful.

Item: Meteoric Iron Axe. +10 strength. 10% armor pene-tration. *This double-edged axe was forged from the heart of a meteorite.*

When I take the axe in my hand, it feels natural, like I've held it my whole life. It reminds me of my pickaxe the way it fits my hand. I can't wait to take it to battle. That harpy won't know what hit it.

"If you wait until Lokston is finished, he'll teach you your ability."

I take a seat by the ring and watch as Lokston spars with a young man. The young man can't be much older than me. He is fast, but Lokston is faster. His swings blur through the air, making contact before the man has a chance to raise his sword in defense. I definitely came to the right place.

When their training is over, Lokston approaches me.

"Ready to learn to fight?" he asks.

I nod my assent and we step into the ring.

"I'm going to teach you three abilities. Two are basic and one is special. These will more than help you on your journey." Lokston grabs me by the shoulder and I feel an energy flow through me.

Congratulations! You have learned the basic ability 'Attack.' Knock them to the ground.

Congratulations! You have learned the basic ability 'Defend.' Try not to fall on your ass.

Congratulations! You have learned the ability 'Lunging Strike.' Effect: stuns opponent for .5 seconds. Cost: 50 mana. Cooldown: 10 seconds. They can't hit when they can't move.

We spend the next few minutes sparring with wooden weapons. There is no learning curve to my new abilities. Once I have learned them, they flow through my body with ease. Lokston presses the attack and I parry each blow with my axe, using its head as a shield. His blade lodges in the hook of the axe and I thrust, sending Lokston in retreat. I press onward, regaining lost ground. Time to test out Lunging Strike. I jump, axe raised, and come down in front of Lokston. The force of the impact immobilizes him. I attack. Even with my wooden axe, his health bar depletes by a quarter. When he rises to his feet, there is a look of surprise on his face.

"How do you hit so hard for one so weak?" he asks. I'm baffled by his question.

"I'm sorry, what do you mean?"

"Your level is weak, but there is a great strength within

you." He pats me on the shoulder. "We are done for the day. Come back and see me when you are in need of more training."

I can't shake Lokston's words once I leave his shop. What did he mean that I hit so hard to be so weak?

I can worry about that later. First, I have a harpy to kill.

When I find my way back to the harpy, a tiny gravestone marks where I died. The harpy sits atop the grave marker smirking, as if goading me to attack. I fully intend to wipe the smirk off its face.

I run full speed at the harpy and it hops off of the tombstone, letting out another shrill call. It hurts my ears, but I press on. I use Lunging Strike, coming down in front of the harpy and stunning it. One swing of the axe lops off its head. The birdlike body stumbles back and forth before falling to the ground. That was far easier than I had expected. I pick up the loot from the harpy along with my pickaxe.

*Item: **Rusted Chest Plate**. **+1 armor**. It's better than swiss cheese.*

*Item: **Dirty Boot**. Some things in life aren't worth having.*

*Currency: **8 copper***

I equip the rusted chest plate because it's better than nothing and toss the boot. The eight copper doesn't amount to much, but I add it to my inventory nonetheless. It takes ten copper to equal one silver and ten silver to equal one gold.

The Mortican Mountains stare at me from the distance. It will take me at least a few hours to journey there. I'll make the most of it and farm for experience along the way. Up ahead, I see a black bear walking through a clearing.

Black Bear. Level 4. *These normally docile creatures have a powerful bite.*

The black bear looks calm as it walks through the clearing and I almost decide to leave it be. The name of the game is leveling up, though, so I use Lunging Strike and momentarily stun him. The ability wipes out my mana. A quick attack drops three quarters of his health. The bear is tankier than the harpy and stronger, too. He swipes at me with his powerful paws and I lose half my health. My vision goes red, making it hard for me to focus on my attacker. I finally gather myself and it only takes another strike from my axe to send his health to zero. He drops fifteen copper and no items, but my experience bar takes another jump.

I make short work of two black bears, a harpy, and a large brown bear over the next hour before gaining another level. I put my stat point into Intellect. Lunging Strike is my best ability, but the mana usage limits its use to a max of two times per battle with my current mana pool. More points in Intellect should help with that. If I attack first, the half-second stun essentially allows me two attacks before I have to worry about taking damage.

After my latest battle with the large brown bear, my health is down to twenty five percent. I take a seat by an old oak tree and wait for my HP to recover.

Checking through my messages, I find the link to Aleesia's stream. A small feed pops up in the top left corner of my vision where she and her merry band of dwarves engage in a tumultuous fight with a group of orc raiders.

The dwarves, though they are short in stature, fight valiantly against their orc foes. They swing their axes and hammers in violent harmony. One dwarf stands near the rear, casting spells that rip the earth apart. The princess stands behind them, firing imbued arrows that explode upon impact. Orcs burst into flame while others stand frozen, overtaken by icy tendrils that crawl across their bodies like vines. She has a variety of magical arrows. A particularly devastating arrow launches from her bow and erupts into a volley of lightning bolts that zig and zag from one orc to another.

I close the feed and look at my map. I'm still a long ways off from her current location. A golden warrior gallops past on a horse as black as coal. I should really consider investing in a mount of some kind, though I doubt I could afford one even now. Mounts are expensive and hard to come by, but would shorten my travel time immensely.

By the time I reach the foot of the mountains, I am level eight. I invested my two new stat points into Vitality and Intellect and my avatar feels more balanced already. My inventory looks less and less like an empty closet as well. I now have plenty of rusted armor to sell when I return, along with a hefty supply of copper. The large brown bear even dropped a silver. I can't wait to see the kind of loot I'll be getting at higher levels.

A small hut sits near the entry to the mountain path. A gnome peers at me from behind a counter.

"Hello, traveler!" he greets me, "would you like to bind your soul here to reawaken upon death? Y/N?"

I think about it for a moment. It seems smart. If I die,

then I won't have as far to go to retrieve any supplies I leave behind.

"I have a question first. Is there a way I can get back to the town square without having to walk?" The only downside to being bound to a location so far away is that I'm hours away from my home portal.

"I can teach you to teleport. If you look in the bottom corner near your map, you will see a purple icon, focus on that for one second and you can teleport back to your entry point of any world you are in. If you are attacked or lose focus, it will cancel the teleport."

I do as he says and focus on the icon. My body starts to dissipate in front of me. I switch my focus back to the gnome and it stops.

Congratulations! You have learned the skill Teleport.

Now that's a heck of a skill! I wonder if I'll be able to use it in the mines at the end of a long day?

I bind myself to the hut and continue up the mountain. The princess and her group are close enough that I can see her icon on my map. The creatures I pass are above my level, so I try to avoid them. My only goal right now is to see the princess in person. A level sixteen mountain troll guards a nearby cave. I run past him and as soon as I do, he begins to aggro me. Once I am out of his attack radius, he turns and walks back to his cave.

The sound of metal clashing against metal and the roar of magics exploding echoes through the mountains, drawing me in. I know that I have no business involving myself in a fight with orcs two or three times my level, but I really want to impress the princess. I've watched her stream for so long that I feel like I know her. I don't think for a moment that she might not know me.

I reach the crest of the mountain and see the battle raging on the other side. I toggle on everyone's stat bars. They are all wounded. Aleesia's health is halfway depleted, her silver armor dented in places. Specks of blood taint her blonde hair. She attacks with an elven blade that catches the light with each strike. She moves with a grace I have never seen anyone else take in battle. I count eight dwarves among her group. Two of them are female, judging by the lack of facial hair, but that is really the only thing that distinguishes them. Many of the dwarves' health dwindle in the yellow or orange. One is in the red. Several orc bodies lay across the mountain pass. Many more have their health hovering in the red. It looks like the princess's company will win the day.

A loud roar echoes from behind me and everyone falls silent. The battle stops for a moment and all eyes turn toward the sound. Towards me. The rumbling of giant footsteps causes rubble to tumble down the mountain and I am afraid of what is about to appear.

Aleesia's eyes meet with mine for a moment. What's left of the orc forces abandon the fight and scatter down the mountain pass. All the while, the ground shakes more and more from whatever creature approaches. I turn my back to the dwarves and princess, readying myself for what comes next. I receive a notification, telling me I have a new message.

You have been invited to join Aleesia's party. Do you accept? Y/N?

I don't think twice before accepting. As soon as I join, I am able to hear their private chat.

"What the hell is coming?" asks one of the lady dwarves.

"Calm down, there is nothing that we cannot over-come together." The voice is Aleesia's. I'd recognize that voice anywhere. It sounds like music and I let it wash over me. "Welcome to our party, Esil. I hope you're ready for a fight. Though if I'm honest, you're a little out of your league here."

"I was born ready," I say. It sounds a lot cooler in my head than when I actually say it.

"For the princess!" one of the dwarves shouts. His long red beard is braided and he carries a warhammer engraved with a writing I assume is Dwarvish. He spins it in his hands and it begins to glow. Everyone around me begins to cast spells and imbue their weapons with what-ever magic they have. All I have is Lunging Strike, but I'm full on mana, so I wait.

A large, knotty head appears first. Giant, wide-set, angry eyes stare past me as it lumbers in our direction. I don't know how I made it past it this creature on the way here, but I'm thankful I didn't meet him on my own. I focus on his stats and feel my stomach turn.

Mountain Troll. Level 60. *Tough skin and a minuscule intellect make these creatures tough to stop.*

His gait is lumbering. Both arms drag low across the ground; one hand holds a large club bigger than my body. Drool drips down his chin and across his protruding belly. I look at the group I'm now a part of. Aleesia is the strongest, a level fifty-three archer. Most of the dwarves are in the forties, all warriors except for the one battlemage. And then me, a level eight miner. Normally, I think they could take it, but their HP is so low that the troll could take many of them out with a single hit.

A flaming arrow darts past me and explodes against

the troll's chest. He lets out a deep grunt of disapproval, but is otherwise unaffected. The dwarf with the warhammer charges. His hammer connects with an explosion of light and the troll stumbles to the right. When it regains its footing, the troll takes a hard stomp towards the dwarf, stunning him.

I have to protect him. I'm a part of the group, after all. I run towards the troll and use Lunging Strike. My ability has no effect and now I'm in his attack range. The only option I have is to attack. I slice at him with a hard strike and his health drops by a large sliver. I did more damage than the dwarf.

"How did you do that?" asks the princess, but before I can respond, I hear the crunch of bones beside me as the troll stomps the dwarf. I'm transfixed on the savagery when the troll swings his club and my vision goes black.

CHAPTER FOUR

I respawn at the base of the mountain. The dwarf I witnessed being pounded to a pulp must have been bound somewhere else because he is not with me. The gnome greets me with a hearty 'hello, traveler,' not knowing I just had my brains smashed in. I'm no longer in the group chat, dying must have kicked me out, but I can still see Aleesia's icon on my map along with a few other dwarves.

Even though I know I will probably just die again and it's time for me to go home and get some sleep for the night, something pulls me back up the mountain. I check my inventory on the way. My battleaxe is gone. Aside from my Worldpass and my boots, the battleaxe is my most prized possession. I can't leave without it. I've also lost just about every other item I've earned over the course of the day, including my pickaxe. Again. The only weapon I have is a rusty spear. It'll have to do until I can find my grave.

Up the mountain I run, my boots replenishing my stamina with each step. The small mountain troll comes after me as I pass by again and I almost laugh at its comparison to the one I just faced. The fact that I went after a level sixty mountain troll without a second thought was sheer stupidity. The smaller troll eventually turns around.

The sound of exploding arrows echoes the closer I get to the top. By the time I arrive, the troll is down to fifteen percent health. Only Aleesia and two dwarves remain. All of their HP bars dwindle in the red.

A new notification dings. It's probably Aleesia inviting me back to her group, but I don't check it. My grave is only a few yards away. Right underneath the troll. Blood has formed small puddles beneath its giant body. He's low on health, but still extremely dangerous. If I can get to my grave, I might have a chance at helping them defeat it.

I take off running for the troll. Halfway there, I launch the spear and it bounces off of his rock-hard head. It's enough to lower his health another sliver and divert his attention. When the troll turns to see the source of the irritation, I slide between his legs. I pick up my items and equip my axe, backing out of the troll's reach. The two dwarves give me a nod for my bravery and stand by my side. The princess stands behind us, an arrow notched in her bow.

I quickly open my messages and join their party.

"Thanks for coming back," she says.

"Glad to be back. Now, let's finish this." I thrust my axe into the air and the two dwarves do the same. It feels good to be a part of something. "Does anyone have any spells that can stun?"

"We all do, but trolls are naturally resistant to slows and stuns," says the dwarf to my right. She holds a small warhammer in each hand. I wish I had known that the last time, when I used Lunging Strike. "We'll have to beat it the old-fashioned way."

"I'll fire a volley of arrows as fast as I can and try to blind him. I need you three to finish him off. Do you think you can handle it?" Somehow, I feel the question is directed at me.

"We can do it," I say.

Apparently, the troll has had enough and is ready to end the fight as much as we are. It charges towards us. The two dwarves counter and I follow behind them. They each swing hard and take out a tiny sliver of health. A swing from my axe and another chunk of health disappears. I don't know how I hit so hard, especially against something so far out of my level, but I don't question it. I jump to the right, dodging the troll's swing, and the club rips apart the earth next to me. I attack again, slashing my axe against its massive thigh. The troll's health is down so low that a few more hits will kill him. I can't believe I'm about to have helped take down a level sixty troll. The loot it is sure to give will be epic. I look back to the princess and a giant hand wraps around my midsection.

My vision goes red and the crunch of bones makes my stomach turn. The troll's large, powerful hands crush me. He squeezes and my health drops to one bar. I can barely breathe from the pressure around my ribs. Everything is red and black. The troll squeezes again and I die.

After the blackness clears, I'm at the base of the mountain again. The gnome greets me with the same 'hello, traveler' as before. I check my inventory. I've lost my battleaxe and pickaxe again. Couldn't I have lost a rusty shield instead? I should really be getting home, but I can't leave those items. I'll just run up the mountain, grab my things, and teleport back home.

As I race up the mountain, I still can't believe the adventure I was just a part of. The princess has thousands of subscribers who watch her streams at any given time. I know most of them would be jealous of what I just did. I was in her private chat. Not for long, but I was there and it had been awesome. And when I attacked the troll the first time, the look she gave me…

Everyone is gone when I reach the area where the battle took place. A few gravestones mark the dwarves who died. I wonder how far away their last bind point was that they haven't made it back. Some of the grave-markers have already expired. I'm curious as to what kind of items they left behind. My curiosity is strong, but not so strong that I would betray those I fought beside. I was a part of their group, after all. Once I find my grave and equip my items, I focus on the purple icon and my body begins to disappear in front of me. The next thing I know, I'm back in the town square where I find my portal and go home.

My notifications ding and I see I have a new message. A smile spreads across my face when I read who the sender is.

Esil,

Thanks for your help with our raid today. I don't know how or why you were there when you were, but I doubt we would have won the day without you. If you are free tomorrow, I would like to meet you at the Lion's Head Pub. I have a surprise for you.

    -Aleesia

My heart threatens to beat out of my chest as I read through the message again and again. Princess Aleesia herself wants to meet me for a drink. I can't believe it!

I look through my other notifications for the day and I see a blinking tab I have never noticed before. It appears to be some sort of message request folder for people I have never met. There are over thirty messages in there, all from today. I filter through a few of them to see what they say.

"Dude, you have some major balls. Going against a level sixty troll at level eight. LMAO." I guess it is pretty amusing to an outsider. At the time, though, I didn't really think it through. It was all instinct.

"What are you, some kind of rich prick? You have to be to afford travel to the Mortican Mountains. I bet you paid to get on the princess's stream, didn't you, asshole?" I laugh out loud at this one. If he only knew.

"Hey man, how do you hit so hard? Please tell me your secrets."

They go on like this for a while. All of the messages are from viewers of the princess's stream who saw me and wanted to say hi. When I used my Worldpass to go to the Mortican Mountains, I didn't realize it was one of the hardest gameworlds to get into. A lot of people seem to be impressed by my strength. I'm sure I'm not the first person to ever put all their stat points into Strength from the start. I honestly don't see what's so special about it.

I log out of Pangea and get ready for bed. I have a wool blanket, a small strip of padding, and a flat pillow. It's not the most comfortable thing in the world, but it gets the job done.

Before I lay down for the night, I look out of the small window to my box. Most everything is dark, aside from the small lights of the drones as they fly by. They flicker like fireflies against the darkness. I can't remember my life before I went to the orphanage, but sometimes I dream about living in a place with flowers and clear skies and a big fluffy black dog. There's always a man, too. He picks me up and tosses me in the air and for a moment, I'm weightless. I'm not sure if the memories are real or not.

As I drift off to sleep, I keep replaying the day in my mind. It's only been one day, but I feel like my life has completely changed.

I wear my starter rags to the mines. I don't want to spoil the surprise before I have a chance to tell my story. Buzz is going to be pumped, maybe even Grayson, too.

When I make it to mine two-forty-six, where I am assigned for the day, Grayson is already hard at work. The trail of green ones and zeros glow past me as I walk down the tunnel. I wait for Buzz, but he never shows. When the alarm buzzes, telling us it's time to work, I send him a quick message to ask if everything is okay.

Quietly, I equip my dwarven boots and get to work. I

feel like I could swing my pickaxe forever as my stamina constantly replenishes.

Grayson and I work alone in silence for the first few hours. The only sounds we hear are the impact of our picks against the digital coal and the heavy breathing that goes along with manual labor.

My body moves mechanically, rhythmically swinging the pick and I lose myself in my thoughts. In just a few hours, I'll be meeting up with the princess for a drink and a special surprise. What could it be? Maybe she's decided to give me some of the loot from defeating the mountain troll.

"Hey, Grayson." I have some burning questions I hope he can answer for me.

"What's up, kid?" He takes a break from mining for a moment and leans on the end of his pickaxe. His gray beard is coated in soot.

"Have you ever heard of miners finding things in the mines?"

He raises an eyebrow at me. "Like what?"

"Oh, I don't know. Treasure, items, things like that." I can feel his eyes boring into me, searching for why I'm asking.

"What's prompted your curiosity?" He knows something is up. Maybe I should just go ahead and tell him. I elect not to. I promised myself Buzz would be the first to know.

"Just wondering."

"Hmmm. Well, every now and then something pops up. Usually, it's a piece of clothing, armor, maybe a weapon. But every few years, something good shows up."

"Is that how you got your Worldpass?" The question

pops out before I have a chance to stop it. Could it be that Grayson got his Worldpass and diamond pickaxe from a treasure just like me?

"What did you find, Esil?" He stares at me and I know he knows I found something. Grayson is a smart man. If he found a chest too, then he never told anyone about it.

"I'd rather not say." I expect him to probe me. To try and get to the bottom of my questioning.

"That's smart. Play your cards close. But let's say you did find something. Something valuable. Maybe even a little gold. I know you didn't buy those boots off a miner's wages. Be smart about it. Don't go blabbing your mouth about whatever you found. There are so many people who will take, take, take and never give anything back. Many of them because they don't know better. Some because they want to ride their way up, hanging on to your boot-straps. There is nothing worse than a man who has the means to improve his life for the long term and instead splurges on the now."

I'm shocked. Grayson has given me a lot to think about. I'm almost certain he found a chest too. I wonder what happened to make him so wary. Did he blow a chunk of gold that could have set him up for life? Does he have the Worldpass Premium like me? I want to ask him a lot more, but the buzzer rings, signaling it's time to go home. Grayson is out of the tunnel before I have a chance to catch up with him.

There will be plenty of time to talk tomorrow. For now, I need to get home. I have a date.

CHAPTER FIVE

The town square of the Mortican Mountains bustles around me just as it had the day before. I spot a few familiar faces on my way to the Lion's Head Pub. The golden minotaur has set up shop at the trading post with several weapons he no doubt won in battle.

I feel a little nervous at the prospect of a few minutes alone with the princess. Yesterday, I kept my cool remarkably well, but that was mostly due to the intensity of fighting a level sixty mountain troll. Today will be different. I will be forced to hold my own in a conversation, something I am not all that great at.

The dwarves surround the entrance to the pub, barring entry to several people before me. Above the entrance, a bright yellow lion head is carved into the wood. Its mane is a dark red and it almost seems to jump out onto the cobbled streets below. I wave at the dwarves as I approach. When the dwarves spot me, Ordin, the one with the braided red beard and massive warhammer, raises his weapon, calling me in his direction. He clasps his hand around my forearm and I return the gesture.

"Good to see you again, Esil." His voice is low and gravelly. "We owe you a great debt for your help yesterday. If you ever need anything, we will see that the debt is repaid." Several of the other dwarves nod in agreement. The female with the twin warhammers winks at me. Ordin steps to the side and gestures for me to enter. "The princess is waiting."

I walk into the pub. It's almost completely empty but for the princess sitting at a table in the back and a bartender behind the bar obsessively polishing a glass. I wonder what could be so important that the dwarves aren't letting anyone in.

The princess stands to greet me and I am momentarily taken aback by her beauty. For once, she isn't dressed for battle, but wears a shimmering green dress with lacy sleeves. A long necklace dangles across her chest. An intricately designed leaf pendant with a bright green emerald attached seems to radiate its own light. Her pointed ears peek through her long blond hair.

"Princess." I bow slightly.

"I actually prefer being called Aleesia. Please, have a seat."

I take a seat on the large wooden booth. The Lion's Head Pub is one of the most revered pubs in the Mortican Mountains. Many streamers come here to celebrate after a great victory or quest. Which makes it all the more impressive that the princess has the entire place to herself.

"Why do they call you princess?" I ask. As long as I've been following her, I've never been able to figure it out.

"My dad, he owns a castle on the other side of the

mountains. Someone called me a princess once and it kind of stuck. It sounds a bit pretentious to me, don't you think?"

I'm not sure if she wants me to answer, so I don't.

The bartender approaches and asks for our order.

"Two Fire Whiskeys," she answers.

He returns a moment later with two shots. A deep rusty orange liquid dances in the glass. Aleesia lifts her glass and we clink them together. I am unable to taste the fiery liquid, but a notification quickly pops across my vision.

Substance: Fire Whiskey. Buff: +2% attack for the next hour.

"Thanks." My body feels stronger as the fiery liquid pumps through my veins.

"Don't mention it. I wanted to thank you for your help yesterday. Myself and Glordin were the only two to survive the troll. I'm certain neither of us would have had you not been there. We both received a large amount of experience and rewards. I'll have the bartender give you a couple more on your way out. They can be quite handy in a bind. I also have something else for you."

She smiles at me and I can't for the life of me make out what it means. I think she is trying to read me. She brushes her hair behind her ear and I wonder if the woman behind the avatar does the same thing. For the first time in over a year, I find myself questioning what the person controlling a character is like. Everyone in the mines has the same story. We're all too poor and are just trying to survive. Sometimes I forget that there are people out there who aren't like us. That the people I watch stream every night are just as real as me and Buzz.

She pulls a leather pouch from her pocket and pushes it across the table.

"It dropped from the troll. I thought you might like it." Her smile curls up on one side of her lip and my heart beats a little faster.

I open the pouch and a small ring falls out. It is a dark purple, almost black.

Item: Vampiric Ring. Grants 2% lifesteal per attack. *To hurt thy enemy is to heal thyself.*

"That's amazing! Thank you." I add the ring to my inventory and equip it.

"With as hard as you hit, I thought it might be useful for you. Which brings me to the real reason why I wanted to meet you. There is no way in hell you should have been able to do that kind of damage to that troll. He was so far out of your league, yet you hit him harder than any of our group. How?"

Her smile disappears and is replaced by a stony expression. It was stupid of me to think she wanted anything other than information. For a moment, I feel like I am back at the orphanage, where people only took an interest if you had something they wanted. What interest could a princess have in a lowly miner like me outside of curiosity?

I sit in silence for a moment, not knowing what to say.

"What's wrong?" she asks. "I'm sorry if I offended you."

"It's fine. It's stupid, really. I guess I thought you just wanted to hang out and talk." I feel even stupider saying the words out loud.

"I did. I mean, I do. I just have never seen anyone so strong at your level. I was surprised is all."

"I don't have any answers for you. I'm just a poor boy

who works in the mines. Yesterday was the first time I've ever explored anything outside of the mines. I put all of my stat points in Strength starting out, but aside from that, I don't have any answers for you."

"Wait—what?" Her mouth hangs open in shock. "You're a miner? How they hell did you end up here? My dad says that the mines are for those who have no better options in life. He says that it's the developers' way of giving back to those less fortunate."

I suddenly realized she might be streaming all of this. There is no way in hell I want my personal history broadcast to all of her fans. I will not be someone else's source of amusement.

"Are you streaming this?" I whisper, leaning in close.

"No way. This is a private. Why do you think we have the place to ourselves? If you had some game-changing secret, I don't want the whole world to know."

I relax a little bit. Maybe she is just curious.

"There's no secret. I got lucky is all. There is nothing special about me."

"I'm not so sure about that." She winks and I feel my stomach churn. "Do you have any free time today? I was hoping you might help me with something."

"What is it?" And more importantly, why ask me instead of her band of dwarves.

"There is this dungeon I've been wanting to check out. I was hoping you might want to join me. I could help you level up, as a favor for yesterday."

"I think the ring is more than enough."

"Oh, come on. Let's have a little fun."

My inbox blinks and I check the notification.

Congratulations! You have received a new quest. The

princess Aleesia has requested your services with clearing a local dungeon. Reward: increased alliance with elves and 50% of loot and treasure. Do you accept? Y/N?

She has a Cheshire grin on her face when I accept.

The bartender hands me two more Fire Whiskeys before I leave. I add them to my inventory and turn to walk out the entrance, but the princess grabs my hand.

"This way." She leads me to a small exit in the back of the bar.

A white stallion is waiting outside the door. Aleesia gracefully climbs on its back.

"Where's mine?" I ask.

"Oh, come on. Just hop on." She smirks.

I'm not a prideful man, but something feels a bit off about riding on the back of a horse behind the princess. Nevertheless, I don't have any other options at the moment, so I climb on.

I've never ridden a horse before, so the sensation is not something I am accustomed to. My haptic suit does a great job of mimicking the galloping and I find my stomach churning harder and harder the farther we go. We race down the cobbled streets, the large beast parting the crowd under fear of being trampled. We pass the guards at the city gate and the horse speeds up. Golden fields stretch for miles and the mountains tower in the distance. I wonder where exactly this hidden dungeon might be. Just when I think I might hurl, we come to a stop at the edge of the forest.

Large oak trees with sprawling branches reach out of the forest as if trying to grab at passersby. It takes a moment, but then I realize the trees are actually moving. Small branches curl like gnarled fingers. A bird flies by and is plucked out of the air. A few feathers flutter in the air before the tree tosses the bird to the ground.

"What is this place?" I ask.

"The Guardian Forest. Most people stay away because of how dangerous the trees are, but I know a way in." She flashes me a devilish smile.

We climb off the horse and it takes off running back towards town.

"Do the dwarves know you left?" As long as I have been following her stream, I've never seen the princess traveling on her own.

"They do. The Angel Oaks have a terrible temper around dwarves. Even with my pendant, I'd never have a chance getting inside with them around." Aleesia pulls out the pendant that had been tucked inside her dress and it seems to glow even more than it did at the pub. She walks toward the trees and I am certain that she is going to be crushed by one of their massive limbs. The closer she moves, the emerald glows brighter and the trees move less and less. She motions for me to follow.

I'm hesitant to approach, but the limbs seem held at bay as I walk between them. The forest is dark once we pass the first few trees. The glow from the emerald shines a path before us.

"How did you find out about this place?" I ask.

"I've known about it for a while. I've just needed someone I could trust who wasn't a dwarf to help me get inside."

She's playing her cards close to her chest, but I can't really complain since she is splitting all of the loot and paying me for my assistance. Even if I die, I'll get paid if she completes the quest without me.

Small creatures scurry in the depths of the forest. The canopy is so dense that barely any light shines through. Occasionally, I see the glow of eyes in the distance. I focus on my axe and it appears in my hand. I hold it tight, ready to fight if the moment arises.

"There's no need for that yet. We are almost to the entrance." She puts her hand on my arm, gently pushing my axe down.

I still feel wary of the forest, but I follow her lead.

The glow from the pendant catches on something up ahead.

A bright white marble slab sticks out from the earth. It has Elvish runes engraved into it. The princess runs her hands over the runes and they begin to glow silver. They glow brighter and brighter until the slab begins to shake. Earth falls away and the slab rises higher into the air, pushed up by a large tunnel. I can see a set of stairs that lead underground. Into more darkness.

"How did you do that?"

"It's an elvish dungeon. Only an elf can open it."

"What did it say?" I feel like I am asking a million questions, but there is so much I don't understand.

"It said, 'Only two may enter. Only two may leave.'"

"What the hell does that mean?"

"I don't really know, but I'm guessing it means we both have to make it out alive. I hope you brought your big boy pants, Esil."

Great. I'm going into a two-person dungeon with monsters designed for a level fifty-four elf. I'm toast.

We walk down the stairs. Torches light the way. The corridor is tight, not much bigger than the mines. Spiderwebs stretch across the corners of the ceiling. The dull gray stones writhe beneath the dancing flames.

At the bottom of the stairs, I receive a notification.

Would you like to bind your soul to the Guardian Forest Dungeon? Y/N?

I've already agreed to help. I might as well bind here for when I inevitably die. I focus on the yes and a small dot appears on my map, letting me know where I am bound. I can see the corridor we just passed, but the rest of the dungeon is a blur. It must fill in as we journey through.

"Are you ready?" Aleesia asks. She has replaced her fine linens with battle armor once again. The silver armor has faint green hues that move in the torchlight.

"Let's do this."

As soon as I step past the bind point, a flaming arrow catches me in the chest.

CHAPTER SIX

My chest is tight and I find it hard to move. My vision goes red at the edges and heat pulsates around the wound where the flaming arrow struck me. My haptic suit is doing a great job of making me feel like shit. I yank the arrow from my chest. The arrowhead is coated in a thick layer of blood. I toss it to the ground just as another darts in my direction. I prepare to block it with my axe, but the air shimmers in front of me and the arrow comes to an abrupt halt and falls to the ground. I look to my right and see the princess with her arm extended, casting a shield spell where the arrow stopped.

"We need to find cover quick," she orders. "So we can find out what we are dealing with."

I pull a torch from the wall and attempt to cast light into the room. There is a small pillar not too far away. We both dive behind it, while flaming arrows whistle and clatter against the stone floor.

"Do you have any ranged weapons?" Aleesia asks.

"I have a rusty spear, but that's about it."

"It won't do. Looks like I'll have to take them out from this distance. Do you know any ranged spells?"

"I don't." I feel like an idiot saying it, but she is the one who invited me along. Without so much as a glance at my abilities. Yeah, I can hit hard, but I've only been questing for a day and here she is taking me into some unknown dungeon. If this ends badly, it is most certainly on her. Even if she is a princess.

"It's fine. I'm going to shoot an arrow in their direction, if you see a break, run and smash them. Got it?"

"Got it."

Aleesia nocks the arrow in her bow and pulls it back. The arrow begins to glow a bright red. Long fiery tendrils snake out from the arrow and curl around it. She steps around the corner and lets it fly. The cavernous room lights up before me and I can see five skeleton warriors. Two archers and three swordsmen. The arrow lands near one of them and bursts into a ball of fire. One of the skeleton archers runs towards it. The moss and ragged clothes that hang from its bones catch fire and the cavern is alight once more.

Now that I know how many there are, I take off towards them. Their positions show on my map in the bottom corner of my vision. The burning skeleton shoots a flaming arrow at me and I duck just as it flies past my head. My haptic suit warms around my left ear, letting me know how close the flames were.

A bright yellow arrow whizzes past me from behind. It lodges in the ribs of the archer and electric bolts charge out from skeleton to skeleton with a vicious crack, stunning them momentarily with each bolt. Their health bars drop by a quarter. I use the moment to check their stats.

Skeleton Warrior. Level 13. *These bony warriors are dying for a good fight.*

Level thirteen. Out of my league, but not so much that we don't have a chance. The princess could probably handle most of them by herself. I continue my charge towards the archer and use Lunging Strike. The blackness behind his eyes is dark and sinister. I stun him and bring my axe down hard against his shoulder. His bones clatter into a pile on the floor and my experience bar shoots up. I don't have time to check for loot. There are still four skeletons left.

The princess's arrows continue to barrage the skeletons, dropping their health in droves. The other archer collapses into a pile of bones. Three left.

The princess switches to her shortsword and we move in on the last three warriors together. She moves with speed and grace, slicing at the skeletons and parrying their blows far faster than I can. I attack hard, but not fast. The Vampiric Ring the princess gave me raises my HP by a fraction with each hit. If the skeletons were faster, I might be in trouble. In a few short seconds, their crumpled bones lay at our feet. A silver nine flashes across my vision, letting me know that I have leveled up.

"That was good." She smiles at me. "Here, let me help you."

She says something in elvish and then places her hand on the spot where the first arrow hit me. I feel my cheeks go red and wonder if my avatar's are as well. My HP begins to recover and I feel a warm sensation as her hand glows a faint blue. A moment later, I am fully healed.

"Thanks. That's a pretty useful ability."

"Yeah, how do you not know any spells?"

I decide to tell her the truth. "I've only been doing this for a day. I never had any money to travel outside of the mines until now."

"What changed?"

I'm not ready to divulge that much information, so I change the subject. "Shouldn't we go clear the next room?"

We pick up the loot before heading into the next room. I find some bronze armor and a few silvers. Nothing too exciting, but the armor is still better than the rusty breast plate I currently have. I switch them out and prepare for what might be coming next.

A few torches hang on the wall of the next room. Something scurries into the darkness and I briefly see a long furry leg.

"Is that what I think it is?" I ask the princess.

She shudders before responding.

"Spiders."

For a moment, I'm lost in my memories. I remember the orphanage. Before I moved into my box, I spent a long time at the orphanage. I don't really know how long. We would spend eight hours a day logged into the educational worlds of Pangea. They told us that a smarter world was a better world, but in truth, I think it only made us more aware of the lot we had in life. When we would log out, we would spend the rest of the day working. Sewing clothes, cleaning the dirty floors. At night, the spiders would crawl along the walls, their deep red eyes almost glowing in the night…

"I don't do well with spiders," I say.

"Grab a torch. They are terrified of fire."

The princess sends a flaming arrow across the room

and I want to run away. A dozen spiders now populate my map.

"Esil, they're not real. We can do this." She puts her hand on my arm and a little of the fear goes away. I've never had anyone comfort me, but it almost feels familiar.

She's right, after all. It's all virtual reality, as much as we might want to believe otherwise. The spiders can't truly hurt me.

I pull a torch from the wall. In my other hand, I hold my axe, ready for whatever comes. The princess has her arrow nocked. Flaming red tendrils reach out from the arrow. Something moves in the distance and she lets the arrow fly. It bursts into flame along its route, sending out fireballs that bounce around the pillars searching for targets. The arrow impales a large spider some fifty yards away and its legs curl up in death.

"Nice shot."

She gives me a smirk just before the spiders step out into the light. Eleven large, hairy spiders. Their milky white pincers click and their eyes glow a dull red, reflecting the flames from the torches. I am so not looking forward to this.

They surround us, moving faster and quieter than I thought possible. The princess and I stand back to back, all the while the clicking grows louder.

"I'm going to stun them. Hopefully my lightning arrow will set off a good chain. Then you hack them to pieces. Got it?" she says.

"Got it."

The next thing I know, there is a loud crack of lightning and I watch as the bolts dart back and forth, stunning each spider in turn. I take off towards the closest one and bring my axe down hard upon its head. Its legs immediately retract and its eyes gloss over. One down. I'm lucky this is only going to be a melee fight.

Just as the thought appears, a large glob of acid erupts from the mouth of the spider to my right. The acid sticks to my arm holding the torch and I lose all feeling. My arm freezes and the torch falls to the floor.

"Princess…" I call, but she is in the heat of her own battle, switching between her sword and bow. Several spiders lay crumpled around her. My only option is to fight with one hand. I have no idea how long my arm will be paralyzed.

I move in on the spider just as it launches another blob of acid in my direction. This time I duck and the projectile sticks against the stone wall behind me. I bring my axe down hard and the spider falls to the ground. Piece of cake.

Three spiders have me surrounded. I need to act fast if I don't want to become their next meal. The click of their pincers makes it hard for me to think. I have enough mana for two Lunging Strikes. I lunge at the closest spider and stun him. While the ability cools down, I attack the next closest and watch his HP drain to zero. I still don't know how I'm hitting so hard, but now is not the time to question it.

My haptic suit clinches around my arm and my vision goes red as the third spider digs its pincers into my one good arm. I jerk free and cast Lunging Strike. The edge of my vision is a dull flickering red as my HP continues to drop even after the spider has bitten me. The spiders must have a poisonous bite.

The first spider is no longer stunned, but I am able to

parry its bite. The sound of its razor-sharp teeth grinding against my axe hurts my ears. I swing hard into its head and a trail of green blood marks the floor, leaving only one spider left. I don't have time to find the princess, but she must be fine. She is nearly five times my level. The last spider arches its back in the air and spits another ball of acid at me. The projectile whizzes by and lands behind me on the floor with a splat. My vision still has hints of red from the poison, but most of my sight has returned.

I don't want to risk another bite, so I switch to the rusty spear for the added range. The spider scurries toward me, venom dripping from its teeth. I gather the spear in my hand, finding its balance, and let it fly. It catches the spider in the thorax just as it pounces in my direction. The force of the throw lifts the spider off its feet and carries it across the room. The spear lodges between the bricks of a pillar and the spider lets out a loud squeal before its legs curl up in its final embrace.

A slow clapping startles me from behind. I turn to see the princess, her hair slightly disheveled, wearing a grin.

"Very well done," she says. "If what you say is true, you've really got a knack for this kind of thing. We should do this more often."

My heart beats a little faster.

"First, we have to make it out of here. The rest of the way will no doubt get harder as we go along." I show her my arm. Feeling has returned, but the skin is inflamed from the spider's bite.

She reaches in her pouch and hands me a vial. A bright blue shimmering liquid swirls inside.

"Take this, it will restore your mana. Let me see your arm."

She places her hand on my arm and it begins to glow as before. The bite marks fade away and my HP recovers. I examine the vial in my hand.

Mana Potion. Restores 200 mana over 20 seconds.

"You should come well stocked next time."

"Hey, I didn't know you were going to bring me to some dungeon. How could I have prepared for that?" I thought we were going to talk and then maybe I would farm the countryside again.

She giggles and pulls her hand away. "You should always be prepared for adventure."

Maybe she's right. It's not like I don't have the money to stay well stocked with supplies now. I'll visit some of the local shops once we make it out of this dungeon.

I take the moment while my mana recovers to ask the princess about herself.

"So, princess, what do you do when you're not out questing with your dwarves?"

"Please, call me Aleesia. Save the 'princess' talk for the streams." She brushes her blonde hair behind her ear. "I'm in school. I want to follow in the family business and become a game developer like my father."

"Wait, your dad is a developer?" Should I mention the chest I found? Would he ask questions? Even worse, would he want to take it back? I decide against it.

"Yeah, he's worked for them for as long as I can remember. The company really takes care of their..." She stops mid-sentence, obviously remembering where I'm from. "Do you like it there? Working in the mines?"

"I don't know. Until yesterday, it's the only life I've ever known."

CHAPTER SEVEN

We gather the loot from the room before leaving. Most of the items are repetitive. Several hairy spider legs, venom sacks, a few health potions which I will undoubtedly need, and a handful of silver.

I pick up a torch and use it to light our way out of the room. Another set of stairs leads us down to the next level. I can hear loud grunts before we reach the bottom. Aleesia's hand grips me hard on the shoulder, stopping my progress. The voices beneath us echo through the dimly lit stairwell. Whoever they are, they are speaking a guttural language I do not understand.

"Goblins," she whispers in my ear and my entire body shivers. I wonder how she knows, but then I see she has her hand on her sword hilt. A barely visible glow appears as a fine line where the guard meets the sheath. Elvish blades glow in the presence of goblins. "Be careful as you go. They love to lay traps for unsuspecting visitors."

I slowly step forward and realize my foot is caught on something. Without thinking, I pull hard in an attempt to free my leg. The weight against my foot slackens and then I hear the whir of wire whipping through the air.

The whir continues for a moment, then a loud ringing fills its place. The sound of stone grating against stone comes from the stairs above and I realize we are trapped. How stupid can I be? I just set off their alarm.

Aleesia pushes me in the back, urging me forward.

"We'll die if we fight here. We need to get out."

The goblins seem momentarily shocked when I step out into the cavernous room. Their large round eyes are fixed on me with each step I take. Tufts of black hair jut out of their oversized pointy ears. Each one is clad in a mixture of ripped rags and dented bronze armor. A few wear jewelry made of bones. Some carry maces, others dull swords that serve better for blunt force than stabbing. Their skin is the same dull gray as the stone walls. One rides upon a grizzly gray wolf, the beast's ribcage showing through its matted fur. For a moment, they are silent.

The goblin riding the wolf, which I assume is their leader, bangs his mace against his dented shield and it echoes through the hall. I focus on his stats.

Goblin Rider. Level 25. *This goblin boss attacks with the fierceness of wolf and goblin combined.*

He is definitely the leader. The other goblins range from fifteen to eighteen. There must be at least fifteen of them. There is no way in hell we can take them all out, even if the princess is level fifty-four. It's just not possible. The room is too small and I don't have the defenses.

The wolf lets out a roar as it pounces across the room. Slobber drips from its gums as they pull back, exposing a long line of sharp teeth. The train of smaller goblins follows in its wake, yelling and clashing their weapons together.

"What do we do?" I ask the princess, because I don't have the faintest clue.

She moves past me in a blur. "We run!"

She glides across the stone floor, her movements full of grace. I don't understand how we are going to get past the horde of goblins that stand between us and the exit, but I follow nonetheless.

One of the goblins is an archer. His arrows cut through the air and the princess forces them to a halt with her shield spell. We are mere moments from being trampled when she reaches into her pouch and pulls out a vial as black as the night. She grabs my hand and smashes the vial on the stone floor. The next thing I know, the room is silent and color disappears from the world. Everything I see is another shade of gray. The flames on the torch I carry are different hues of slate and ash.

The princess continues to hold my hand. She uses her free hand to press her finger against her lips, signaling me to keep quiet. The goblins in front of us look around in shock. Their mouths move, but no sound comes out. It appears they can't see us. The goblin rider is furious and smashes his mace into a smaller goblin, drawing blood. The smaller goblin attacks the wolf's legs, causing the wolf to toss its rider to the ground. A scuffle breaks out amongst the remaining goblins and the princess pulls me around them, our backs pressed close to the wall. We make it out of the room into another corridor before she speaks. When she does, color returns to the world.

"What was that?" I ask.

"It's called Velvet Night and it's the rarest item I own.

Or owned, now, I guess. It's a one-time use item, but I didn't see us making it out of there alive." She smirks. "I thought I told you to pay attention?"

"I was," I counter. "I just didn't expect a tripwire in a dimly lit dungeon."

"What did you think it would be? Did you think it would have a bright yellow icon signaling 'don't step here?'" She laughs.

"Tell me more about this Velvet Night. What did it do exactly?"

"It's a beautiful item. It takes the user and up to two others to a lower plane of existence for up to thirty seconds. Essentially, it makes you invisible."

"And why did you waste it here? There has to be a million other places where you could have used that. I mean, this dungeon is below your level."

"Not everything is about level, Esil. I thought you of all people would understand that."

We walk down the corridor, the scuffle of the goblins echoing behind us. The hallway turns and leads into stairs that curl downward. I can hear a raspy breathing the closer we get to the bottom. My breath begins to smoke in front of me and my haptic suit does its best to showcase the cold. This must be the dungeon boss.

The princess stops and pulls several vials from her inventory. I recognize the Fire Whiskey, but not the blue or green bottles.

"I think this is it. I suggest you use any buffs you may have been saving."

"What do you think is down there?" I use my Fire Whiskey and check my stats. My mana and HP are both full. I put my new stat point into Intellect. If anything, I'll need the bonus mana for Lunging Strike. My current stats are:

Strength - 14
   Agility - 0
   Vitality - 2
   Intellect -3
   Dexterity -0
   Stamina -0

With the plus ten strength from the Meteoric Axe and two percent bonus from the Fire Whiskey, I'm hoping I can at least get in a few good hits before I die.

The princess looks determined. An aura of light surrounds her from whatever buffs she just took.

"Whatever we find at the bottom of these stairs, it has been an honor fighting beside you today, Esil."

Her words are touching. I almost wish she was streaming this so that all of her fans would know what she just said. Yesterday, I was nothing and today, I'm in a secret dungeon with one of the most popular streamers in Pangea.

"The honor is all mine, princess." I try to be smooth, but my words sound hollow in the cold stairwell. Aleesia does her best to conceal the laughter that bubbles on the edge of her lips.

When we step into the room, I am surprised. A frail old elf hunches in the corner. He wears a dark purple cloak that conceals his body and face. The only thing that dictates he is a male is the long gray beard that dangles across his chest. The cloak he wears is made of fine linen and embroidered with gemstones that gleam in the firelight.

A few small fires light the room. A podium holds an ancient book in the center of a circle engraved into the floor. Elvish runes run along the circles edge. Aleesia gasps when she reads them.

Her gasp startles the old elf. He raises his head and the space where his eyes should have been are dark, empty sockets that glow. When he steps into the circle, I can see that his eyes have been replaced with gemstones. They shine a bloody red. I focus on the old elf to find out what he is.

Elven Lich. Level 49. *This once great Elven Wizard bound himself to a dungeon so that he may never meet true death.*

"Welcome, Esil. I've been waiting a long time for you." A whithering old voice like dried parchment whispers in my ear. I look to the princess, but her eyes are focused on the lich.

"Who said that?" I ask.

The princess turns to me, confused. "Who said what?"

"You didn't hear that?" I ask. She should have been able to hear the voice from where she is standing.

"Pay her no mind," the voice beckons me. "You and I shall leave this place together. Only another elf may take my place. Free me from this crypt and I will make you stronger and richer beyond your wildest dreams. I have magics you could only dream of. All you have to do is subdue the elf."

The lich steps to the podium and turns the page of the book. He lifts his arms into the air and begins chanting in a language I don't recognize. A ribbon of light floats upward from his hands.

An arrow zooms across the room. I think it is going to hit the lich, but it explodes some ten feet from his position. The circle in the floor acts as a shield, blocking the princess's attacks. I can make out the shape of a dome surrounding the lich. Tiny magical veins almost invisible to the eye form a barrier between he and us.

The lich's words run through my mind. Riches and power. I know so many others from the orphanage who would betray the princess in a heartbeat. Perhaps she would betray me if she had the chance. But she has been kind to me as long as I have known her. I can't betray that trust.

"He wants me to attack you and take him out of here," I say. She needs to know what he wants if we are going to have a chance.

"Only two may enter. Only two may leave. It all makes sense now. He's offering you a dark quest."

Just as she says this, a notification pops across my vision.

Congratulations! You have been given a new quest. The Elven Lich has requested your help in escaping the Dungeon of the Guardian Forest. Reward: 500 gold and an unholy alliance with the dark. Do you accept? Y/N

Five hundred gold is a lot of money. And an alliance with the dark. No doubt he would teach me spells and abilities that could really take my game to the next level. But where is the honor in that? Just because we are in a game doesn't mean I can abandon everything I believe in. What do I have if not my honor?

The lich continues chanting and the light emanating

from his hands grows brighter and denser. After a few seconds, the light disappears.

Without warning, a beam of light smashes down from above, rooting me to the ground. A loud boom that makes my ears ring is the only thing I hear before I lose all sense of feeling.

"What is she to you?" the voice asks me. It's almost like he is inside my head. "She would betray you in a heart-beat. Join me. Fight for power and darkness." The words disintegrate inside my mind, littering their dark inten-tions in my head. The lich begins chanting again and this time, yellow light slowly rises from his fingers.

The princess fires another arrow and it bounces off the shield surrounding the lich.

"We have to break the shield. It's the only way we can defeat him." Her legs are still rooted, but she continues to fire arrow after arrow to no effect.

"How do I free myself?"

"You have to dodge his attacks. If you do, you can attack the shield. His magic is powerful and has a bonus effect on me because we are two sides of the same race, but it takes time and concentration for him to cast."

His beams continue to charge. Once they are ready to attack, I feel my feet free themselves. His spell has worn off. I jump to the right and do a barrel roll. A beam of light smashes into the ground next to me. I dodged it!

"Do not fight it. You will join me or you will die."

The princess is still rooted in place and now her health has depleted by a quarter. The root must last longer on her because she is quicker and more agile than me. The spells must get stronger with each turn as well, considering the damage she is taking. She continues her barrage of imbued arrows on the shield.

I need to break the lich's shield.

I run for the magical shield and begin attacking furiously. My attacks have no effect and all the while, the lich continues to speak into my mind.

The lich starts casting his next spell and a lilac beam forms in his hands. It will undoubtedly be stronger than the last. I continue to slash and stab at the shield to no avail. Just as his beams disappear, a small crack appears in the shield. I dive and roll, narrowly dodging the spell that rips apart the stone where I just stood.

The princess lets out an agonizing scream. Her health is down to ten percent and she seems barely aware of the situation. She is no longer shooting arrows, but swaying back and forth, still rooted in place. If I don't break the shield soon, she will die.

Our eyes meet for a moment. She gives me a knowing look and whispers something in Elvish. A weird sensation flows through my body before a notification runs across my vision.

Aleesia has cast Resilience upon you. You have increased attack speed for 20 seconds.

I don't waste any time before attacking the shield. My axe smashes into the invisible barrier and the crack widens, tiny webs stretching along its surface. I swing harder and faster with each blow.

The lich begins casting another spell. This time the beam is black. It draws in the light from the fires, devouring them and casting the room in shadow. I know that it will be the end of our quest if it lands on the princess. I am no match for the lich on my own. I decide to keep attacking and try to break the shield before he kills us both.

My stamina bar is low, but my dwarven boots replenish it before it can ever truly deplete. The cracks in the shield grow larger and wider. The black light disappears from the lich's hands and I brace myself for the incoming pain.

The shield shatters before me and I fall into the circle. I only have a mere moment before the princess will die. I toss my axe with as much force as I can muster and it flies across the circle, lodging between the jeweled eyes of the lich.

The beam of black light dissipates into the air above the princess, inches from her head. Her legs unroot and she falls forward to the ground.

The lich's jeweled eyes fall out of his skull and clatter across the stone floor.

Notifications ding and a silver ten flashes across my vision. I'll check them all later.

I rush over to the princess and she has a wild smile on her face.

"We did it! Well, you did it."

I help her to her feet and we walk to the lich's corpse.

"Shall we check our spoils?" she asks.

Gold is scattered across the floor along with the spellbook and the two jeweled eyes.

"You take the spellbook," I offer. I have a gut feeling that the spellbook is what she was after to begin with. "I'll take the jewels?"

"Works for me." She winks.

I pick up the items and add them to my inventory.

Currency. 500 gold.

Item: Jeweled Lich Eyes. *The eyes are the window to the soul.*

Another notification pops across my vision.

Congratulations! You have just completed the quest 'Guardian Forest Dungeon.' You now have an increased alliance with the elves.

Congratulations! You chose light over darkness, bonus 50 gold.

That's cool. I never knew you could be awarded based on the moral choices you make in the game.

"So, what does the spellbook do?" I ask.

"It's a new spell. I don't think I'm ready to use it yet, but maybe one day it will be useful. Thanks again for helping with this. I have something I want to give you." She presses her hand on my chest and recites a few words in Elvish.

Congratulations! You have learned the ability Resilience. Resilience increases the attack speed of you or an ally for 20 seconds. Cost: 50 mana. 20 second cooldown.

"That's awesome! Thanks. That, combined with my boots, means I can attack like a madman now."

"You're welcome, Esil. It's the only ability I am able to teach others, but it should come in handy for you. I should probably get going though. We've been here a while and I have homework for school."

We teleport back to the entrance and leave the dungeon. I sort through my notifications as we walk and notice I finally have a message from Buzz. It looks like he's ready to talk.

CHAPTER EIGHT

Buzz waits for me in our private chatroom when I leave the Mortican Mountains and return to my home portal. I'm still on cloud nine from my dungeon quest and can't wait to tell him all about the past two days. It's hard for me to believe that I've done so much in the past couple of days and Buzz has no idea.

Buzz's face pops up in a screen to the left of my vision once I arrive in my home portal. He's wearing his starter rags. The same ones I had until yesterday. He looks tired and I wonder if the avatar is mimicking his actual facial expressions. His face lights up when he sees me.

"Holy shit!" he practically screams. "Where did you get those clothes? And where have you been? Your status message said you were in the Mortican Mountains, but I know you don't have money to travel. What's going on?" His questions come out at a mile a minute.

"You're not going to believe what happened to me."

I spend the next thirty minutes telling him about the Developer's Chest, the Worldpass, my first day leveling up, Princess Aleesia, and the dungeon. Buzz is beside himself with excitement. It's great having a friend who is genuinely happy when something good happens to me.

"There was one really weird part," I continue. "Grayson knew something was up. He gave me this really cryptic advice. I think he may have found a chest a long time ago."

Buzz lets out a bellowing laugh. "You gotta be kidding me. What are the chances?"

I remember his message from yesterday and am suddenly ashamed I haven't asked him about his mother.

"How's your mom?"

His smile disappears.

"It's not good. She has a hard time moving, barely eats. They sent out a medical drone to scan her and that ate up most of our savings." His voice is overcome with emotion and I wish I was there to give him a pat on the back or a hug. His mom is the only person Buzz has in his life and she means everything to him. "The real shitty part is that there is a cure. We just can't afford it. She has maybe a year before her body shuts down and there is nothing I can do."

That's the problem with being dirt poor, when you barely get by as it is—there's no room for error in life. Maybe I can help.

"I can help. I have over a thousand gold. You can take it. Get your mom better." I don't even hesitate to offer the money. Buzz's mom is more important than anything I could ever want to buy. I've never had money and I'll gladly go back to that if it means getting her the treatment she needs.

Buzz's eyes go wide when I mention the amount of gold.

"Wow, Esil. I don't know what to say. That's very generous." His eyes blink in rapid succession, almost like he is holding back tears. "It's not enough, though. The treatment is expensive."

"How much?" I ask. I can go questing every day until I have enough to pay for it.

"Over eighty thousand for the initial treatment. Not to mention the medication she would need for the rest of her life."

Shit.

"It's okay, Buzz. We'll figure something out. You can't just give up."

"What can I do, Esil? The only thing I can do is go to the mines and work until I die. We're fodder for the system. Deep down, you know it. You know they probably don't even need us to mine data, but it's safer for them to lock the poor neighborhoods away under the pretense of work than it is to let us live on the streets. On the streets, we might realize how unfair everything is."

I've never heard Buzz sound so defeated. He is always the guy with a smile on his face and a laugh in his belly. I need to find a way to cheer my friend up.

"Hey, Buzz, do you think you could spare a little time to go traveling with me?"

"What do you mean?" he asks.

"I've got more money than I know what to do with right now. If it's not enough to help your mom, then maybe I can buy you a day pass and we can go visit one of your favorite worlds."

A smile starts at the edge of his lips and I think I might have cheered him up just a bit.

"Let's do it! Let's go to Steamworld."

You are now entering Steamworld. Steamworld is an alternate-future gameworld where steam-powered technology rules the world. This is a non-magic-based world. All magical components have been disabled upon entering Steamworld.

The portal drops us on a bustling city street that reminds me of photos of Victorian England I studied in school. Steam billows into the air from a hundred different sources. Whistles and the hiss of steam play across the airwaves.

Everyone that passes by looks so formal. The men wear three-piece suits and top hats. Monocles with tiny gears and multicolored lenses adorn many faces. The women wear corseted dresses that push their bosoms up to their chins.

"Man, oh man. I've died and gone to heaven," says Buzz as he ogles a woman in a purple dress. She has a red heart tattooed on her breast and a hefty supply of cleavage. She gives Buzz a wink as she passes by.

The streets are made of a dense inlay of bricks. A carriage pulled by mechanical horses parts the crowd. Tiny steam-powered mechanical insects flutter in the air near my head. I swat at one and the whole lot takes off. A bicycle with a large front tire and small rear tire zooms past me, narrowly avoiding my foot. The rider removes his hat and bows in apology, leaving a trail of steam in his wake.

Many of the people I watch wear jetpacks on their backs. Some have pipes that wind around their bodies. A street performer draws a crowd while he displays some sort of weapon. Fire erupts from the end of his hands in a large stream, propelled by the pack strapped to his back.

"Where do you want to go?" I ask Buzz. I paid for him to come here and I want him to have his fill. Personally, I much prefer the fantasy worlds, but there is a certain elegance to this place.

"Can we just walk around and explore? It's so crazy to finally experience something that's not a smoke-covered mine. I can never thank you enough for taking me here, Esil."

"It's nothing. I got lucky. It's the least I can do to share some of the fun with my best friend." I give Buzz a squeeze on the shoulder. Hopefully, I can make him forget about his troubles for a little while. "How about we get you out of those rags?"

"You don't have to do that."

"I know, but I want to. Let's find a tailor."

The tailor is tucked away between a weapons shop and a medicine shop. The weapons shop showcases a myriad of revolvers and rifles. There are more gearshifts, scopes, and types of bullets than I could have imagined. Silver and wooden bullets. One claims to explode into flame upon impact. A special section marked 'Rayguns' catches my eye before I see a dark gray werewolf sitting behind the counter. He wears a top hat and long coat. The tails of the coat hang low and his fur protrudes from the sleeves next to his razorlike claws.

We step into the tailor's shop and Buzz's eyes go wide. His short-buzzed black hair draws attention to the child-like wonder on his face. He sorts through rack after rack of clothing, piling up a large wardrobe he intends to try on.

In the end, Buzz looks more dapper than I have ever seen him. He chooses a pair of black and red pinstriped pants, a white shirt with a red vest, a bow tie, a pair of goggles with brass fittings, a belt full of pouches, leather bracers with a half-dozen buckles and a black long coat. He looks like a completely different person from the man I work with in the mines every day. He stands in front of the mirror for a moment, admiring himself.

When I step up beside him, I realize that I also look completely different in my green tunic and khaki pants. It's crazy how much can change in just a few short days.

I pay for the clothing, which sets me back nine gold, and we return to the street.

Far above us, a large zeppelin floats through the air. A banner hangs beneath it advertising Portigee's Emporium of Oddities and Eccentricities.

"I know what I want to do," says Buzz. He grins from ear to ear. "I want to play steamball."

"What the heck is steamball?" I ask.

"Oh, it's only the most popular game in all of Steamworld. I swear, Esil, sometimes I think your nose is so far up those elf butts that you forget the rest of these worlds exist."

"Shut up, Buzz." I give him a gentle push in the side. "Lead the way."

I follow Buzz down the crowded street. He knows where he is going and walks with purpose. I'm sure he's watched streamers walk through here a million times in his box late at night before falling asleep.

When we arrive at the arena, the stands are full. We have to put our names on the player list and wait for an open pitch. I use the time to learn as much about the game as I can. Buzz is more than happy to fill me in.

"Do you remember how before The Great War, people used to play a game called soccer? They called it the world's game. Basically, the goal was to kick a ball into your opponent's goal. That's kind of how steamball works, except the goals are three hundred feet in the air and everyone wears steam-powered jetpacks to fly around the pitch."

"That's it?" It seems like a simple concept.

"Yeah, if you score more goals than the other team, you win. Oh, and I forgot to tell you, the other team can attack you."

"What do you mean 'attack'?"

"Just like it sounds. If they are able to wound you, then it makes it easier for them to score. It's a bloody sport at times. And if they kill you, then you have to wait fifteen seconds to respawn, making the odds in their favor. Most games are five on five, but sometimes they will go bigger or smaller for certain events."

I watch the nearest game as it unfolds above us. Ten players zoom around leaving trails of steam, propelled by the packs they have strapped to their backs. A rather large man wears a pack with three canisters instead of two. He bobs along and I wonder if the packs have a finite amount of energy. Beside him, a wiry woman speeds by, carrying a brown leather ball. She has it tucked under one arm and fires a pistol with the other. A line of smoke erupts from the gun every time she fires and green lasers dart through the air. Two gnomes accompany her, one on each side.

They must be her escort, because one carries a large cannon that booms like thunder with each shot and the other carries a sword with a gun built into the blade.

The two gnomes wear large goggles that magnify their eyes tenfold. They look like large bugs fluttering through the air.

One of their opponents, a woman in a tight green corset, fires a rifle and the light beam that erupts from it knocks the ball from the wiry woman's hands. The ball tumbles through the air towards the ground.

Out of nowhere, a long hand swoops in and grabs the ball. The fat man that had been puttering along is still far away, but his hand is attached to his arm by a long retractable mechanism. He presses a button on his wrist and the hand and ball rapidly return to him. He tosses the ball to one of the gnomes and continues puttering along. I am completely immersed in the game when Buzz grabs me hard on the shoulder.

"We're up next," he says.

I follow Buzz over to a booth that rents jetpacks. There are over a dozen to choose from. Some offer faster top speed, and others, great acceleration or the ability to change direction quicker. I see the one with the triple canisters designed for those of the more portly variety. Buzz and I both pick the Steampack 2000, which Buzz says is the best all-around pack.

Item: Steampack 2000. Requirements: Stamina.

"Do we need ranged weapons for this?" I ask. Everyone I have seen so far has carried a gun.

"You don't need them, but they are definitely helpful in keeping the other team off your back." He shrugs, content to play the game even if he doesn't have all the pieces. Not today.

"Come on, Buzz. If we're doing this, we're doing it right."

His eyes light up when we walk over to the portable weapons shop. The weapons are housed in the back of a carriage. Dozens of firearms adorn the walls. Buzz immediately picks up a shotgun with a dragon etched down the side, named Firebreather. The stock is made of dragon bone.

"Esil, it shoots fireballs," Buzz says as he cradles the gun like a newborn child. "It. Shoots. Fireballs." The price tag is ten gold. I don't know if it's more for the design or the firepower, but I don't question it. I don't care if I blow every gold I have today, as long as Buzz has a good time.

I settle for a raygun with a rotating barrel. It shoots ray beams out of one barrel and a grappling hook out of the other. It might be useful in snagging down enemies. It costs six gold.

I remember my Barter skill and decide to test it out.

"Do I get a discount if I bundle these all together?" I ask the shopkeeper.

He rubs his chin for a moment before responding.

"I'll knock off one gold because I like your spunk," he says.

Congratulation! You have added +1 to Barter. A man who can trade can own the world.

Nice. I equip my new weapon to my inventory and check the stats.

Item: The Grappler. Raygun. +7 strength. Ability: Grapple, fires a grappling hook and attaches to the first object it

hits. 30 second cooldown. *"You'll not get away that easy, Bucko."*

Once our weapons are equipped, we take the pitch. I activate my steampack and slowly rise into the air. The basic speed doesn't use any stamina, but any time I speed up, my stamina bar drops a little. Three other players join us as we continue to rise to the two goals placed high in the sky. Two women and a tall lanky man are in conversation, talking about some quest they failed to complete.

"Hello," I say. "What's the plan? It's our first time."

"Great. Just great," says the man. He's wearing purple pinstriped pants and a green vest. Two revolvers with glass orbs attached to the hammer are strapped to his waist. A blue gas swirls inside the orbs.

"Be nice, Jayce," one of the women says. "We were all new once." Her corset is pulled tight, exposing her large chest. I take a glimpse but Buzz has no such tactfulness and stares openly. She gives him a wild smile before turning back to me. "Don't mind him. He's a little salty he failed his quest. Just have fun. Try and score, and me and my sister here will do our best to defend the net."

"What's your weapon?" I ask.

"You'll see soon enough." She winks. Her sister whispers something in her ear. They both giggle for a minute and Jayce rolls his eyes.

"What's this jerk's problem?" Buzz asks me. "It's not like this is ranked or anything."

"I don't know. Let's just have some fun."

A timer begins to count down in the center of my vision and the other team approaches from across the pitch. They look like a well-oiled machine with their matching outfits. Five men in brown and blue pinstriped suits fly toward us. Two carry revolvers, one has a rifle, one a long sniper rifle, and the other a shotgun. All of their weapons are ornately engraved and appear to be rayguns from the glass orbs attached to them.

I look behind me and see the woman and her sister holding two large cannons that hang by straps from their shoulders. Electricity reaches out like tiny tendrils inside of the large glass orbs attached to each. They must be packing some serious firepower.

The timer reaches zero and a brown leather ball falls from above. Buzz and two of our opponents rush towards the ball before I realize I should be joining.

Buzz flies forward like a maniac, laughing hysterically and firing his new weapon. Fireballs the size of my fist fly through the pitch like spilled marbles.

I focus and everyone's status bars appear over their heads. Our opponents are all named Mr. Wiggles, each with a different number one through five. One and two carry revolvers, three has a rifle, four is the sniper, and five has the shotgun.

The two women on our team are Hilda and Zelda. Zelda has the heart tattoo. Jayce passes me by and fires his weapon just as Mr. Wiggles1 picks up the ball. Blue lasers shoot out of his gun in quick succession, narrowly missing the man with the ball. Buzz continues to fly around the pitch, sending out a never-ending chain of fireballs. I wonder if the weapon uses mana or if the fireballs count as bullets? Either way, it doesn't appear to be stopping. I dodge a fireball at the last second and feel the heat across my face.

I'm amazed at the sensation my haptic suit is able to

provide. It feels like I am actually in the air as I float across the sky.

Mr. Wiggles1 passes by me and I aim my gun. The purple ray it fires hits him in the shoulder. His health drops by half and the ball falls from his hand. His teammates close in pursuit of the ball, except for the man with the shotgun who stays back to guard the goal.

A deafening boom stops me in my tracks and I see a giant ball of light floating across the pitch. It grows larger and faster the more it moves. I stand back, completely immersed in the orb that exits Zelda's cannon. The three Mr. Wiggles dive for the ball, oblivious to the orb approaching them. Mr. Wiggles2 catches the ball and raises it in the air just as the light swallows him whole. When the orb passes through him, all that is left is the ball, once again falling towards the ground. The other two attempt to fly away, but the growing orb pulls them towards it like it has its own gravitational pull. Seconds later, they disappear into the light before it dissipates.

"We've got fifteen seconds to score," yells Jayce. "Come on, noobs."

He picks up the ball and the two remaining Wiggles retreat in defense. Jayce fires off a few shots and fakes a dive. When he goes, our opponents move to block his movement. He tosses the ball over his shoulder to me and I catch it just as I ramp up my speed. I go high and see Buzz waiting by the goal. He has stopped firing his weapon and waves his hand for me to pass him the ball. I throw it hard and the ball hits him right in the hands. They are completely caught off-guard and Buzz tosses the ball into the goal.

1-0 flashes across my vision and then minimizes in the top left corner along with a timer on the game.

Mr. Wiggles1 respawns just as the ball reappears. He's the first one on it. He fires a shot that hits me in the shoulder. My vision goes red and my health is at fifty percent. He flies past me and another shot hits me in the back, this time from the sniper. I can barely breathe as my haptic suit clinches around my midsection. My health is down to ten percent. I need to take cover fast. All the leveling I've done the past two days hasn't helped with my defenses much. I focus on the opposing team and see that they are all level twenty. No wonder they damage so much. Buzz is lucky he hasn't been shot yet.

The sisters set off another loud boom when they fire their weapons. This time, two giant balls of light soar across the sky, but now, our opponents are ready for them and give them a wide berth. Mr. Wiggle1 does a barrel roll, dodging the long, slender beams of Jayce's raygun.

I push the speed of my jetpack and my stamina bar drops quickly. He is about to score unless I stop him. I activate Grapple and fire the hook. It catches Mr. Wiggle1 in the back and brings him to a halt, but not before he tosses the ball into the goal.

1-1 flashes across my vision. Jayce flies up behind the goal scorer and empties several shots into the back of his head as he struggles to remove my grapple. The body disappears and we have a momentary advantage. I retract my grappling hook and turn to where the ball will drop. Just as I do, a bright purple ray hits me in the face.

CHAPTER NINE

By the time the game is over, we have won five to three. Jayce and the two sisters were so good, it makes me wonder what kind of quest they were on beforehand. Buzz scored two goals and I doubt I could kill his happiness if I tried at this point. We still have a few hours before we need to log out for the night so we might as well make the most of it.

"Now that you've got a weapon, what do you say we go level up?" I ask.

We exit the city and head into the nearby village to farm whatever creatures this world has to offer. Mechanical rats and cats scurry between buildings. My message notification blinks and I focus on it. The message is from Aleesia.

Esil,

I had a wonderful time questing with you today. I do hope we can do it again sometime. ;-)

-Aleesia

Buzz must notice the smile on my face because he immediately starts teasing me.

"Someone's in love," he says. He draws out the final word way longer than it needs to be.

"We're just friends," I counter. "She's the only other friend I have besides you."

"Well, now that you've got the Worldpass, you should be able to make all kinds of friends."

There's no hint of jealousy in his voice, but I'm sure Buzz is worried we'll see less of each other going forward. Maybe I can buy him a basic Worldpass or something so that we can at least hang out outside of the mines sometime. I'm sure he would be much happier traveling around instead of surfing the web and watching other people live out adventures. I know it's selfish of me to think about the places I can go that others can't, but finding that chest was a gift and it feels wrong to not use it to the best of my ability.

We come upon an empty section of road between two Victorian Era houses. They are squat little things and nothing like the estates of the wealthy with their towers and turrets and large bay windows. Smoke billows out of the chimney of one house. A large metal monster blocks the road before us. I focus on his stats.

Mechanical Golem. Level 10. *Behold, the gears of war.*

The golem looks powerful with its long arms and broad shoulders. A bright light glows yellow in its chest and steam shoots out of two canisters on its shoulders with every movement. Its eyes are made of tiny gears that continuously turn. It's almost mesmerizing. When the golem beats its large hands on the ground like a gorilla, I feel the vibrations rattle through my feet.

"Ready for your first battle?" I ask Buzz.

He doesn't look the least bit nervous holding Firebreather. He raises one eyebrow and flashes me a wicked smile. He may be a little too cocky. After all, he is only level two and has put all of his stat points into Intellect. I'd hate to see him die in two hits like I did my first battle. The memory of the harpy ripping through my flesh is still fresh in my mind. At level ten, I'm sure I can handle it no problem.

"I'll let you take him on your own so you can get all the experience. Let me know if you need any help."

Buzz moves in towards the golem slowly. He pulls the trigger and a fireball blasts from his gun and hits the golem in the chest. The golem slides several feet across the road from the impact. A third of its health is gone. There is no way in hell Buzz should be that strong.

The golem rises to its feet and beats its mechanical arms against its chest. A loud ringing fills the area, making it hard to hear anything else. Buzz yells something, but I can't tell what it is. The barrels of his weapon smoke violently. He runs towards the golem and fires another shot. The golem loses another third of its health and is knocked off its feet, falling to the ground with a thud. Buzz shoots again and the golem falls apart into a pile of gears and metal plates.

"Ha ha, baby!" Buzz yells. "Level three!" He runs to the golem and picks up his loot. I try to catch up to him.

"You know that golem was level ten, right?"

"Yeah. So?" He doesn't see the point I'm making.

"Yeah, so do you think in all your infinite wisdom that a level two should be able to kill a level ten monster in three hits?"

His brow wrinkles for a moment as he loses himself in thought.

My mind runs wild itself. It can't be a coincidence that he and I both hit harder than we should. It has to be connected somehow. But how?

"You don't think it's a b—"

"Don't say it," I cut him off before he can finish the word.

If it is a bug in the system, then it could be bad. When it was just me, there was no way of knowing. I thought it was because of my stat points. But now that we know it's not just me, we will have to tread carefully. Pangea Online proudly boasts that it can't be hacked or cheated. Should I say something or file a report? If not, they might punish us. I might lose my Worldpass and everything I found in the chest. Or worse, we could lose our accounts. They might think we have abused the system. We would lose our jobs in the mines. That would mean getting kicked out of The Boxes. The only place lower than The Boxes is the streets. They say living a day on the streets is enough to drive a man crazy. After a week, the deformities start. The air does terrible things to those who don't wear the protective masks.

"But what if it is?" he asks, leaving the word unsaid so that there is no record of it.

"I don't know. Do you know any other miners who have been out into the rest of Pangea?"

"There's only one other person." I know the answer before he says it. "Grayson."

"Then that's where we need to start."

Going to the mines seems almost pointless with the amount of gold I have, but I need to talk to Grayson. Plus, if I stop working in the mines, then that means I have to find another place to live and even though I have more money than I ever have before, I don't have enough to live anywhere else for any extended period of time. So for now at least, it's back to the mines.

Buzz has the good sense to wear his starter rags to work, but once we are safely in our mine, he switches into his new threads. He looks out of place against the dark, sooty walls of the mine.

Grayson is already at work as usual, but he comes to a halt when he sees Buzz. His eyes cut sharply at me.

"What did I tell you, son?"

"I know what you said, but it's complicated." Grayson runs his fingers through his beard. "Buzz's mom is sick."

The hard lines of Grayson's face soften a bit.

"How bad is it?" he asks.

"Bad," says Buzz, looking at his shoes.

"I'm sorry to hear that. That's life in The Boxes for you. Shit always flows downhill. Best be getting to work."

The Boxes themselves are supposed to keep us safe. The metal walls and air purifiers keep the toxins at bay, but every so often, someone gets sick. I wonder if it is like this in the rest of the country. I wonder if Aleesia has ever had to worry about breathing tainted air. I've heard the developers all live together in a domed community somewhere in the Northeast.

We work in silence for several hours. Green ones and zeros flutter past me on their way out of the tunnel. It's dull, monotonous work and it only makes me long for the rest of Pangea. I don't know how I'll ever be content to spend a third of my day in the mines knowing that there is so much else out there.

When it is time for lunch, Buzz cocks his head and jerks it slightly towards Grayson, telling me without words that it is time to talk.

"Grayson, can I ask you something?"

He looks up at me, his face set in stone.

"I would tell you no, but I'm certain that wouldn't stop you. What is it?"

"Do you know of any other miners who have traveled to other worlds?"

"I have known several in my time. None in quite a few years, though."

I didn't expect that, but of the thousands of miners over the years, it only makes sense that some would have at least traveled to the cheaper worlds.

"Do you know if they ever battled?" I ask.

Grayson's eyes widen the slightest bit at the question and I know the avatar is mimicking the face of the man behind it.

"I can't say I do." His voice is flat. He's hiding something. Buzz decides to jump in the questioning.

"What about you? Have you ever fought monsters or anything while you were out adventuring?" he asks.

Grayson sits in silence with his hands interlocked and pulled up to his chin. I would wait him out, but Buzz is not as patient.

"Grayson, come on. Just tell us what you know. We both know you're hiding something."

Suddenly, there is fire in Grayson's eyes. For the briefest moment, I get the feeling he is about to show us something. But then the fire leaves his eyes and his face is expressionless once more.

"You don't know half as much as you think you do, boy. I'll tell you the same thing I told Esil. Keep your secrets to yourself."

The bell rings and we all go back to work.

No one speaks for the rest of our shift. The only sounds are the occasional grunt and the swing of the pickaxe. My mind drifts to what new world I might explore once I've powered up my room for the evening. When the bell rings, signaling that our shift is over, Grayson pulls Buzz and I aside.

"I'm only going to say this once. Stop asking questions. It will only lead to trouble. We have a gift here in the mines and most people don't know it because how bad we've got it. But if you're smart, you can get out of this place."

"Why are you still here then?" I ask.

"This is my purgatory."

CHAPTER TEN

After we go home, eat, and power up our boxes, Buzz and I plan to meet at The Haunted Forest. I bite the bullet and buy him a basic Worldpass. It costs me two hundred and fifty gold. This is one of the worlds that it allows him to go to, along with a handful of others. The Haunted Forest is actually a pretty cool place. Ghouls, ghosts, and every other manner of creepy crawlies haunt the forest, making it a destination for those interested in the macabre and who celebrate Halloween. We never celebrated holidays in the orphanage, not even birthdays, but I learned all about them in school.

The portal drops me in the heart of The Haunted Village. It is a raucous place with many people dressed in costumes and wearing masks. A large group of were-wolves stand on the steps of an old church howling at the moon and drinking an amber liquid. It is always night-time in The Haunted Forest, not that I would expect anything less. I pass by several shops on my way out of the town to where Buzz's location is marked with a blue dot on my map. One particular shop, Devilish Spells, has a cauldron bubbling on its banner. It catches my eye and I make a note to check it out later. Everything looks like it is on the verge of death, even the houses seem sinister with their slanted roofs, crooked gutters, and chimneys that seem to go just a tad too high in the sky.

While I walk, I sort my stat point from my quest with Aleesia. I add it to Agility. As soon as the point is added, I can feel my feet move a little faster. I figure the bonus to my dodge will also come in handy since I am still pretty squishy. If I can be strong and fast, that's a pretty deadly combination.

Buzz's maniacal laugh greets me before I turn the corner. He's locked in battle with a large vampire bat. He shoots fireballs from Firebreather, briefly igniting the night sky as the bat swoops down towards him. He dives to the side and the bat misses its attack, letting out a loud screech in frustration. Buzz lays on his back with a wild grin on his face. He sees me and gives a quick wave right before the bat attacks again. He stays exactly where he is with his weight pressed on his elbows and his weapon pointed upwards.

I'm worried he is about to be attacked, but moments before the bat is certain to sink its sharp teeth into his flesh, Buzz shoots a fireball, engulfing the bat in flames. It falls to the ground, leaving behind a silver.

"Works like a charm every time," says Buzz. "I just lay down and blast them when they attack."

Buzz has already hit level five. He must have been out here for a while already. I'm ready to do a little level grinding myself.

"How's your mom?" I ask.

"She was resting when I logged in. There's not much we can really do for her at the moment. The bad spells come and go."

I wish there was more that I could do to help her. Or at least make her last months more enjoyable. Maybe I could send some fresh food to them one day.

We follow a trail that leads into the heart of the forest. The branches of leafless trees interlock in a web above our heads and red eyes stare out from the darkness. I can still hear the faint howl of the werewolves back at the church, or perhaps these are new wolves in the forest. The moonlight cuts through the tree branches, giving us enough light to see the path. The wind whistles ominously as it cuts against the trees.

I hear a crunching sound in the depths of the forest and equip my axe. Buzz turns to face the sound. Several pairs of milky white eyes move closer. A dull groan overtakes the whistling of the wind. When the monster is finally close enough, its gray-blue skin almost glows in the moonlight. Its head is hairless and gaunt. A long pink tongue hangs from its mouth, whipping back and forth. Long pointy teeth salivate and the monster sniffs the air. Its claw-like fingers hang low beside its body with black nails that remind me of the harpy's talons.

Ghoul. Level 15. Undead and hungry, these ravenous monsters travel in packs and feed on human flesh.

I can make out the bodies of three ghouls. All level fifteen. There is the possibility that with our hidden strength, we could take them. Really, though, what do we have to lose?

"You take the one on the left. I'll take the other two," I say.

"Hell yeah, let's do this!" Buzz cocks Firebreather and steps up beside me.

I have my axe in one hand and a rusty, old shield in the other. I should really work on upgrading my defense items.

Buzz attacks first and hits his ghoul hard in the shoulder with a fireball blast. It stumbles back and lets out a high-pitched scream. It claws at the air and lunges for Buzz. The other two attempt to follow, but I attack them first. I hit the closest one with a Lunging Strike, momentarily stunning it. I follow up on its friend with a swing of my axe that takes out a chunk of its health. It counters with a claw swipe and grazes my stomach, causing my vision to go red around the edges. I've lost a third of my health from the attack.

The first ghoul attacks and I block it with my shield. Its claws grate against the metal with a screech. I cast Resilience and a rush of energy flows through me. Immediately, I feel like I can attack faster. The axe weighs almost nothing in my hands as I attack fast and furious. A hard swing cleaves the ghoul's arm from its body. Purple goo drains from the severed limb. My Vampiric Ring heals me slightly, but not enough to counter the damage I will take if this fight carries on much longer. I retreat from the two ghouls and wait for Lunging Strike to come off cooldown. As soon as it does, I stun the armless ghoul and attack the other. It lets out another screech and claws me before I can raise my shield. Red floods my vision. I am down to a third of my health. Another hit and I am done.

I attack the one-armed ghoul just as it becomes unstunned and lop off its other arm. It won't be much trouble for the time being. Quickly, I focus on my inventory for anything that might help me in this fight. I had completely forgot about the weapon I bought for steamball. I equip Grappler and fire off a few quick laser beams at the ghoul. Green streams of light zip through the night air. If I can't fight them up close, I'll stay far enough away and pick them off. I spend the next few minutes running away and shooting from a distance. When I have separated the two ghouls enough, I focus on the unarmed one. His health is almost gone and I think I can finish him off as long as he doesn't bite me. I switch back to my axe and use Lunging Strike. While the ghoul is stunned, a final blow sends its head rolling to the ground.

The second ghoul has closed the distance and is about to attack me. He's mid-swipe when I switch to Grappler and activate Grapple. I point at the nearest tree and fire the grappling hook. It hooks around the branch and then pulls me hard across the forest, leaving the ghoul swiping at air. After a few more shots and a Lunging Strike that empties my mana, both ghouls are dead.

I find Buzz leaning against a tree, covered in blood.

"Hell of a fight," he says, showing me his bloody ribs. "But I got the bastard in the end."

"Nice job! I need to heal for a bit. Those ghouls really got me good." The red still hasn't gone away from the edges of my vision. My health is just a little over a third. I'll have to be careful not to engage any monsters until I heal.

I sort through the loot the two ghouls left behind. There are several silvers and an old book lying on the ground. The book is vaguely similar to the one the princess took after our quest. I pick it up to have a look.

Item: Spellbook. Requirements: Level 10. Activate? Y/N

Awesome! It looks like I've got a new spell. I can't wait to see what it does.

Buzz and I both turn at the sound of galloping hooves up the trail. A skeleton horse barrels through the forest. His rider wears heavy black armor that clinks with each step. The armor is ominous with skull pauldrons and a breastplate engraved with two skulls facing each other. The rider's face is covered by a helm with two horns that curl around the side. Two orange eyes glow brightly beneath the helm. Skeletal fingers hold the reins in one hand and the other holds a broadsword that nearly touches the ground.

I focus on the man to find out who or what he is.

User: Ryken. Death Knight. Level 76.

I hope this guy isn't looking for trouble. He continues riding fast with no indication of stopping. It isn't until he passes between myself and Buzz that I notice he is being chased. A pack of wolves chomp mercilessly at the horse's heels as it runs past. Buzz and I both dive to the side. The pack of wolves chase the death knight as he rides away. All except one.

Worg. Level 57. These large magical wolves have a thirst for killing.

These aren't just normal wolves. They are highly intelligent and extremely strong. We are screwed.

The worg pounces on me before I know what happens. I can feel the weight of the creature pinning me against the hard earth. It's hard to breathe underneath its weight. The worg's teeth are bared and saliva drips across my face. Its growl vibrates in my chest as it presses me harder into the dirt.

The worg lunges at me and I prepare to die, but it is knocked to the side by a large fireball.

Buzz pulls me to my feet.

"Run!" he screams and we both take off after the death knight. Seconds later, the worg is on us. If it could chase a horse, what chance to we stand?

"We have to fight," I tell Buzz. "It's our only chance."

I turn to face the worg and prepare to use Lunging Strike, but my mana is only at twenty percent. Not enough. I plant my feet and cover my body with my shield. When the worg pounces on me, it sends me on my back with a thud and my vision goes red again. This time, the beast doesn't wait to attack. It lunges at my throat and my vision goes black.

CHAPTER ELEVEN

Buzz and I respawn in the village square. Buzz curses the bastard who got us killed.

"What a turd nugget. I've seen Ryken on a few streams here and there. He's really good, but come on. I mean really, what kind of a dick does that? I lost Firebreather and what few items I've looted. Now I've got to walk out there and get them back, all the while hoping those damn bats don't remember what I did to them. Ryken, wherever you are, you're a dick!"

I can't help but laugh at the situation. I lost quite a few items as well, but I still have my axe. We have an hour to reclaim our belongings and the spot where we died is about twenty minutes away. I take a moment to look through my inventory.

I had completely forgotten about the spellbook I looted from the ghoul. It's still in my inventory.

Item: Spellbook. Requirements: Level 10. Activate? Y/N

I focus on yes and a weird sensation flows through my

body. It's not like when I learned Lunging Strike. When that happened, I just carried on, feeling like I had mastered the ability. No, this is different. It feels like there are a million tiny vibrations happening simultaneously throughout my body. My vision goes white for a half a second before a notification pops up.

Congratulations! You have learned Mud Pits. Cost 100 mana. Creates a field of mud pits, slowing your enemies attack and movement speed by 50% for 20 seconds. Cooldown: 60 seconds.

Not bad at all. That would have been super useful for the worg that was chasing us. It's time to test out my new spell.

We're out of the town when I cast Mud Pits in front of Buzz. His gait slows and I pass him by. I find it hard to hold in my laughter as he looks around in confusion, oblivious to what just happened. He lifts his feet and a long trail of mud holds him in place before releasing his foot. This happens with every step until he is free of the pits.

"You asshole!" he yells once he realizes I cast the spell. He shoves me in the side a little harder than necessary. "That's a pretty cool spell, though. I can't wait until I find some. Do you ever think about specializing in a certain skill set?" he asks.

"I don't know. I'm pretty happy to learn anything at this point. I kind of like the idea of being more well-rounded. If I would have known that one day I'd be traveling from world to world, I never would have put all my points in Strength."

"Yeah, it's kind of pointless anyways, considering..."

He doesn't say the rest, but I get the point. I'd probably be just as strong if I hadn't put a single point in Strength.

We continue our walk to the woods, talking of how we want to build our characters going forward.

"For me," says Buzz, "it's always been about the items. "I want to have powerful items that hit hard. I don't care how slow they are. Spells are the way to go. Firebreather is kind of special, its attack is based both on my physical attack and magical powers. All those points in Intellect give me a small damage boost. It's kind of funny that you can't use magic in Steamworld, but the rayguns are powered by mana, don't you think?"

I'm distracted from Buzz's question by the sound of a horse galloping. Far in the distance, I see Ryken, the death knight, coming our way. I recognize his helm and his skull armor. This time he moves slower, and the pack of worgs that had been chasing him are replaced by zombie-like wolves. He slows down when he sees us. His orange eyes glow brightly from behind his helm. His black armor almost blends in with the night, but the bones of his horse catch the light of the moon.

He looks like such a badass on his skeletal horse. What I would give for a mount, not just for the practicality of it, but they just look awesome. I can see myself riding a large bear or a dragon, soaring through the sky.

Before I know what's happening, Buzz is screaming obscenities in his direction.

"Hey, jerkwad. What the hell was that all about? Your little doggy train got both of us killed."

Ryken lets out a laugh. It's deep and sounds like it is bouncing off the walls of a cave. He must be using a voice modifier.

"Sorry about that." He shrugs. "I was in a bit of a predicament, but it's all under control now. You know what they say, though. If you can't play with the big dogs…"

"If you can't play with the big dogs, what?" asks Buzz, a fire in his eyes. I'm almost worried he will attack Ryken. I'm certain the death knight could squash us like bugs.

Ryken sits quiet for a moment.

"I don't know, actually. Maybe I should quit saying that."

"What happened to the worgs?" I ask.

"What do you mean? They're right here." He points at the zombie wolves behind him. I focus on one of their stats.

Undead Worg. Level 57. *This reanimated worg is under the control of Ryken the death knight.*

There are five of them standing behind the fleshless horse.

"How did you—" Buzz has forgotten his anger and stands in amazement.

"One of my abilities allows me to capture the souls of the monsters I kill. I screwed up my first attempt, which is why I ran past you in the forest, but once my cooldowns reset, I was able to take them out one by one. Now that I can control each of them, I'm ready to take on the whatever it is the developers are going to throw at us."

"What do you mean?" I ask.

"You haven't heard? They are announcing the rules of the tournament tomorrow. One hundred thousand gold to the winner. I, for one, am not going to allow anyone to get in my way. You two plan on entering?"

"What's the fee?" asks Buzz.

"Not much. Just a thousand gold."

"I doubt it," says Buzz. His head drops a little. He was so excited when they first announced the tournament.

"Less competition for me then. Though, if I'm being honest, I'm not too worried. I've got the skills to pay the bills."

I find myself wishing silently that he had been killed by the worgs instead of us.

Ryken rides past us. His undead worgs bare their teeth as they walk past.

"What a tool," says Buzz. "I can't believe I ever watched that guy."

"I agree, but he has to be pretty strong to kill all those worgs and then bind them to him, don't you think?"

"Yeah. I hope I never get to the point where I say things that stupid."

I give Buzz a pat on the back. "You're already there."

We retrieve our items and spend the next few hours farming the haunted forest. By the time we leave The Haunted Forest for the night, Buzz is level seven and I am level twelve. I check my stats to decide where to allocate my new skill points.

Strength -14

Agility -1

Vitality -2

Intellect -4

Dexterity - 1
Stamina - 0

I put my two new skill points into Intellect and Dexterity. Now that I have a new spell, it seems smart to focus on my cooldowns and mana pool. I spend the rest of the night before I go to sleep scouring forums, searching for clues on the Developer's Tournament that is supposed to start tomorrow. After selling off all the loot and items I don't need, I have just over one thousand gold after everything I have spent on Buzz in the past couple of days.

As I search through dozens of posts, there's not a lot of information out there. Everyone is pretty much in the same boat as me. A lot of speculation on what it could be, but every thread is different. No one has any idea what the tournament will be. I decide to go ahead and pay my entry fee before I lose my nerve.

Just like that, almost all the gold I've accumulated over the past several days is gone. I know I'm a long shot at winning, but I don't think I can live with myself if I don't try. One hundred thousand gold is enough to save Buzz's mom.

I send Aleesia a message before I log out.

Aleesia,

Hey, I'm sure I already know the answer, but have you entered the Developer's Tournament? I just paid my entry fee. Maybe we can get a start on it together?

-Esil

. . .

It is a bold move asking for her help, but after the dungeon, I think she owes me one. I settle in for the night on the hard floor, wondering what could be in store for me tomorrow.

CHAPTER TWELVE

Notifications light up my vision when I log into Pangea the next morning. The first is from Buzz, telling me they released the announcement for the tournament. I skip over Aleesia's reply to read the official announcement.

Greetings, Esil! Thank you for entering the first annual Developer's Tournament. It will be taking place all across Pangea Online. The winner will receive one hundred thousand gold as well as a special prize to be announced at the winner's ceremony. There are three rounds of the tournament each user must complete. A new clue will be released after each quest is completed. Your first clue:

It begins at the end.
   Live or die, begin again.

. . .

Best of luck on your journey and as always, never stop leveling.
   -Pangea Online Developers

I try to piece the words together but they don't make any sense. Were the clues announced to everyone or just the entrants? If I had more time, I would spend the entire day puzzling it out, but work beckons. I open up my messages and find Aleesia's reply.

Esil,
   You bet I did. And they just announced the first clue. I have a couple of ideas of where I want to start looking. And sure, I'd love to work on it with you, as long as you are okay with a bunch of smelly dwarves following us around. Just kidding, they don't smell. Not too bad, at least. ;-)
   -Aleesia

I send her a quick reply, telling her I have to work, but I'll meet up with them once I'm off.

When I arrive at the mines, Buzz and Grayson are already there. Grayson is hard at work as usual, giving me a nod as I walk by. The green ones and zeros drift through the air past my head on their way out of the tunnel.

"Did they give out the clue in the normal announcement?" I ask Buzz.

"What clue? And what do you mean 'normal announcement'?"

I can tell Grayson is listening to our conversation because the mine is silent except for Buzz and I talking.

"I paid the fee and entered the tournament. I'm going to try and win to help your mom."

Buzz stands in silence for a moment, his face expressionless.

"Are you serious?" he asks. His voice is barely a whisper and I think he might be fighting back tears. I feel my own face grow hot in response. I'm not good with these emotional type moments. Never had many of them at the orphanage.

"I'm going to do everything I can. I'll need your help, though."

Buzz pulls me in for a hug and squeezes hard. He is so strong, it feels like my ribs might crack.

"Thank you," he says before letting me go. "So, what's the clue?"

"It begins at the end. Live or die, begin again."

"What the hell does that mean?" He taps his pickaxe with his foot as it dangles loosely in his hand.

"That's what we are supposed to find out. As soon as someone completes the first quest, I think the second one opens. I feel like I'm already behind because I have to work, but if I don't work, I lose my box and can't play anyways."

"It's okay. It will give us more time to think. You'll waste less time going to stupid worlds that you don't need to."

"I'm supposed to meet up with the princess after work. I think we're going to work as a team for now."

"Do you think that's wise?" asks Grayson. He walks over to where we are standing. "Only one person can win this thing. What makes you think she's looking out for anyone other than herself?"

I see his point. In the end, it's all about what I can do, but I've already thought this through.

"I don't. But I also know that there are going to be three quests. And there are probably hundreds, if not thousands, of other people who have entered. She won't be a problem until the third quest, so I think it's pretty smart to use all the help I can get up until that point. Don't you think?"

"It seems risky. Buzz?" Grayson wants Buzz to side with him. If there's one thing I know, though, Buzz will tell me the truth.

"I agree with Esil. We'll worry about her at the third quest if we have to."

The bell rings, telling us it is time to start work.

I'm lost in thought as I swing my pickaxe. My level is so much higher than it was a few days ago that the experience I gain offers me almost nothing compared to what a monster brings. Still, it's my job and the only thing that keeps a roof over my head.

Buzz talks to himself as we work.

"'It begins at the end.' Could mean a time travel world, or an afterlife world, or that world where the earth is flat and you have to start at the edge. There are probably dozens of worlds that fit that description. 'Live or die, begin again.' Isn't that any world you step into? If you die, you respawn where you started or last bound to."

"Yeah, that's if you die, though. Where does living make you begin again?"

"I have no idea."

Grayson doesn't say much, but I can tell he is deep in thought. Normally, his face is set as he works, but every so often I can hear him mumble a few words under his breath. I'm grateful he is looking out for me. He's been to a lot of worlds, maybe he'll remember something that can help. In order to even have a chance at this thing, I'm going to need all the help I can get.

By the time we finish work for the day, I have a list of several dozen possible worlds where the first quest could be. Word of the first clue has already spread around Pangea and the forums are abuzz with people trying to solve it. I message Aleesia to see where she is and she responds right away, telling me to come to Elysium. It's a world I've never heard of.

Welcome to Elysium! The Greek Underworld for those chosen by the gods, the righteous and heroic.

The message flashes across my vision as I step out of the portal.

Aleesia and her dwarves are waiting for me when I do.

Elysium is not like any underworld I would have ever imagined. Green grass stretches for miles in every direction. A winding stream bubbles right next to where the portal lets me out. There are no shops or towns as far as I can see, just open land, wild animals, and lots of people that are almost translucent, glowing under the bright sun.

"What is this place?" I ask.

"It's the underworld for Greek heroes," says the princess. She gives me a wild smile and then clasps her hand around my forearm. She wears her battle armor. It's silver with a hint of green in the metal. She keeps talking while I greet all the dwarves in the same manner. "We've been to several worlds today already. Based on the clue, we thought we would start with the underworlds. Both Hades and Dante's Inferno proved fruitless."

"I still can't get over the smell of the third circle of the Inferno," says Ordin. He must have a top of the line unit if it can simulate smells. He has his warhammer tossed over his shoulder and it gleams in the sun. The dwarves are excellent metalworkers.

"So what's the plan from here?" I ask the princess. I look around, but there is nothing that draws me towards it. This doesn't look like the place for the first quest.

"I'm not sure. I figure we'll know when we know," she says. "According to lore, Elysium was a place for those who lived as heroes to be rewarded with eternal glory. There must be thousands of quests just waiting for us."

"This is a cool place, but I don't think it's it."

"What do you mean?" Her eyebrow cocks at my comment.

"I feel like when we find the right world, we will know from the start."

"Then what would you have us do?" asks Nordric. He is the tallest of the dwarves, with jet black hair and a braided black beard. He carries an axe twice as big as mine even though he is half my size.

"I don't know..." I shuffle my feet. I don't really have any better ideas, so maybe I shouldn't have said anything.

"Esil, we've put a lot of thought into this." Aleesia grabs me on the arm. "Elysium is ruled by the Titan Chronus, also known as Chronos, the God of Time. Think about it. It begins at the end means the under-world, also time. Live or die, begin again. Also death and rebirth. Some of these heroes never died and were sent to the afterlife as a reward from the gods. This place has to be it."

Maybe I was wrong. It all seems to make sense.

One of the dwarves steps forward from the back. The lone female in the group. I think her name is Klink. The only difference between her and her male counterparts is the lack of facial hair, though I do spot a few wisps around her chin. She's clad in dull green leather and golden armor and holds a small warhammer in each hand. "I think I know where we should start. We need to find Chronus."

Congratulations! You have been given the quest 'Find Chronus.' Reward: Increased alliance with Dwarves. Do you accept Y/N?

I accept and join their party.

"Alright, let's find Chronus." I walk up to one of the glowing NPCs that walks through the fields. I can see through his body. It's a dull, milky white, almost like a pearl. He still wears his armor with shortsword strapped to his side. "Excuse me, but do you know where we can find Chronus?"

"Certainly, he dwells far east in the golden fields, in constant battle with the Minotaur."

Just like that, a gold dot appears on my map and we have our directions.

"That was easy enough," says the princess.

Ordin slams his warhammer into the ground and begins chanting in Dwarvish. A few moments later, we are all engulfed in a yellow shroud of mist.

Ordin has cast Breath of the Wild. Your speed has been increased by 40% when out of combat.

I can feel my legs moving faster with each step. It makes me think about putting more points into agility.

"What a great spell!" I tell him.

"Indeed, Esil. It has made our journeys easier countless times."

We travel across the great plains in quick fashion, avoiding monsters as we do. Now is not the time for leveling. Only the quest matters at this point.

I can hear the battle before we arrive. It sounds like thunder. When we come across the clearing where the battle takes place, it's easy to see why. Chronus stands tall. Some twenty feet. He swings a giant scythe through the air in a blur. The minotaur blocks the blow with its horns and throws the scythe off. The collision sounds like thunder. A long stream of steam erupts from the minotaur's nose, then the minotaur kicks at the ground, sending dirt flying through the air. Both Chronus and the minotaur are bloody, but each one wears a grin. This is truly heaven for these two. I focus on his stats.

Deity: Chronus. Level: 100. *Chronos, God of Time, Titan of the Harvest, and Ruler of Elysium.*

Chronus is barely clad, wearing only a toga draped around his waist. A large red gash bleeds freely between his ribs.

Congratulations! You have completed the quest 'Find Chronus.' Your alliance with the dwarves has grown stronger.

"So what do we do, kill him?" I ask the group.

"I fear we must," says Ordin.

"He's level one hundred," I say. "We don't have a chance."

"We don't have a choice," argues the princess. "We are

the only ones here. And that means we are the only ones who have solved the clue."

She's right, of course. Chronus will no doubt destroy us, but if we can let the minotaur do some of the damage, we might have a chance.

We prepare for the fight. The dwarves take potions and cast spells. Soon, the entire group glows in various shades of the rainbow.

The battle between Chronus and the minotaur rages on. Chronus clearly has the upper hand. He is down to fifty percent health, but the minotaur is almost dead.

"Now is the time!" yells Ordin.

We move in closer and a notification pops across my vision.

Tournament Alert! Ryken has just completed the first quest.

CHAPTER THIRTEEN

"What in seven hells?" bellows Ordin. "We're in the wrong world!"

They must have all received the same notification I did, telling us that Ryken has completed the first quest. It took him less than a day. I'm suddenly aware of just how far out of my league I am.

My message icon blinks. It's from Buzz.

"Get to Apocalyptica, now!" is all it says. I don't question him. I'm certain he's been searching the forums since the moment he got home. This quest is just as important to him as it is to me.

Should I tell the princess and dwarves about my new information? On the one hand, it might put me a few steps ahead. On the other, we agreed to help each other out.

"I just got a message saying we should go to Apocalyptica." I decide to tell them. If it is the world where we find the first quest, I may need their help.

"Yeah, we know. Apparently, Ryken left his status up

and all of his friends list could see where he was when he completed the quest. It's been posted online for a few minutes now and I bet every person who entered the tournament is on their way there right now. We better leave now if we want to have a shot at making the leaderboards."

They all begin to dissipate in front of me, teleporting back to the entrance.

I focus on the teleport icon in the bottom of my vision. Chronus and the minotaur are still locked in battle and slowly fade from my sight as I return to the portal I came in through.

I don't waste any time, immediately jumping through the portal and searching for Apocalyptica. It's another world I have never heard of, but the name sounds ominous.

When the portal empties me into Apocalyptica, I expect there to be a group of people, but instead, I am completely alone.

I stand in a clearing, a forest to my back and a ruined city in front of me. The skyline is on fire. It's late afternoon and the sun closes in on the horizon.

Something blinks on my map and I look in that direction. A gun lies on the ground. I pick it up and check the stats.

Item: M16 Assault Rifle with Bayonet. *This lightweight rifle is extremely accurate and versatile. Carries 30 rounds per magazine.*

The gun feels light in my hands. I press the stock against my shoulder and look through the sight. Everything becomes clearer as I look towards the city. Many buildings have broken windows. There appears to be several people walking the streets. Where did the princess and dwarves end up? Did they all get separated?

I open my messages to check in with them, but its grayed out and I can't get them to open. I guess part of this world's rules is no outside communication. A message flashes across my screen.

Congratulations! You have been given the quest 'Target Practice.' Do you accept? Y/N

I accept and immediately, a target range forms a hundred yards from me. Three black targets shaped like humans stand at the end. There is a bullseye on each target's head and chest.

Aim for the head.

I focus my sight on the center of the bullseye, directly where the brain would be, and pull the trigger. There is a loud boom, but very light recoil from the rifle. I miss the target entirely.

I line up the sight again, this time noticing the rise and fall of the target with each breath I take. I take a breath, hold it in, and focus on the center circle of the target's head. It steadies in front of me and I pull the trigger. This time, I hit the first target right above the ear.

I repeat this process several times until I finally hit the bullseye. I empty through the entire magazine and hit the bullseye five times out of thirty. Most of the other shots hit the target, but are not as accurate as I would like. If I had more points in Dexterity, I'm sure my aim would be better. After I fire the last shot, I receive a notification.

Congratulations! You have completed the quest 'Target Practice.' Reward: 50 gold. You have been offered another quest, 'Find the Girl.' Do you accept? Y/N

I accept and three magazines of ammo appear on the

ground in front of me, along with two grenades. What the hell could I be in for that I'm going to need grenades? My experience bar goes up slightly from completing the quest. Almost level thirteen. I add the ammo and grenades to my inventory. A pink dot has now appeared on my map.

It must be the girl. She doesn't appear to be too far away. Perhaps half a mile from my current position at the edge of the forest.

This has to be the first quest of the tournament. Why else would there be a quest waiting for me as soon as I entered the world? It's a little strange that it's a shooter, since they are far from the most popular worlds on Pangea. I've never had much interest in them myself. To me, they are very repetitive and lack the depth of most other games. Plus, when too many shooters get together, there is always a lot of teabagging and name calling.

I walk towards the pink dot on my map and it feels like I am being followed. Every time I turn around though, the world is as desolate as ever. The dot grows closer and closer on my map. I try to see if I can spot anyone up ahead, but wherever she is, she's not broad-casting her location.

The farther I walk, the dot gets closer and closer until I am practically on top of it. I'm standing next to the forest, but no one is here.

The rattle of branches in a nearby tree causes me to look up. A young girl wearing a yellow dress clutches tightly to the tree. She's scared of me, a look of terror on her face.

Congratulations! You have completed the quest 'Find the Girl.' Reward: 50 gold.

If I keep doing these small quests, I'll make back the gold I spent on Buzz in no time.

"What are you doing up there?" I ask her. For a moment, it seems like she won't talk, then the terror fades from her face.

"They can't find me up here." Her voice is barely more than a whisper.

"Who can't find you?" Besides her, the only people I've seen were far off in the city streets.

"The others."

That's spooky. Now that I've found her, there must be something that I am supposed to help her do.

"Is there anything you need from me, little girl?"

She puts her fingers to her chin as if thinking very hard. "Can you help me find my mommy?"

Congratulations! You have been given the quest, 'Find My Mommy.' Do you accept? Y/N

Of course I do. A blue square appears on my map. Her mom must be located somewhere inside it. Judging by its location, we're going into the city.

The little girl climbs down from the tree and grabs me by the hand. Her grip is strong to be so small. Now that she is in front of me, I can tell she has blonde hair and her dress is dotted with blue butterflies. She is oddly out of place in such a wasteland.

Her demeanor changes once she takes hold of my hand. She almost skips as we walk towards the burning city.

"What is this place?" I ask.

"Mommy told me to run and hide. She said she would come for me when the bad men were gone."

Who are the bad men? She called them 'the others'

earlier. This is obviously an end of the world scenario, so I could be facing renegades, rebels, or something else entirely.

The city grows larger the closer we walk. Tall buildings block out the sun as it dips closer to the horizon. I lift my rifle and look through the sight. I can see people walking through the streets. They seem to be moving without purpose.

The little girl hums beside me. I'm sure something dangerous will happen at some point and I will have to protect her. This is a classic escort mission.

I walk a little faster, aware that hundreds of other people are completing the same quest as me.

A dull roar fills the air and I realize it's coming from inside the city. The people who were walking the street have spotted me and now walk in our direction. I grab the girl by the hand and move her behind me. My rifle is raised and ready. I call out to them as they approach. I'll try for peace, first.

"Stand down. I mean you no harm. I'm trying to find this girl's mother."

They don't acknowledge my words, but press on nonetheless. The girl clings to my pants leg now that she sees the men.

"Stay behind me and we'll find your mother," I tell her. She nods, but doesn't say anything.

I look through the sight again and it stops me in my tracks. The closest man's lips are missing. He has blood caked around his mouth and down his chin and neck. He must have eaten his own lips away. Broken and chipped teeth jut out violently from his gums. His eyes are a milky white glaze. I look up and down his body at his ripped clothes and battered limbs. This man has been through hell. The others are the same.

When I try to focus on them, their stats don't show up. Whoever they are will remain a mystery for now.

I don't think there will be any talking to these people. They look crazy and murderous. Each step they take puts this girl's life in danger.

"Cover your ears," I say. Her small hands cover her ears. Our eyes lock for a moment and it feels like she may be more than an NPC.

My first shot hits the closest man in the ribs. He steps back for a moment, but then resumes his march. The noise from the rifle acts as a prod and they all move faster. I count ten. Those that weren't marching towards us certainly are now.

I take a deep breath and steady my aim. I shoot again. This time, it hits him square in the chest. In the heart. It should be enough to drop him dead in his tracks. Instead, he swipes at the air and lets out a roar.

Then I remember my training. *Aim for the head.* The man is no more than forty yards away at this point. I can make out the jagged strips of flesh that hang across his teeth.

Deep breaths.

Steady aim.

I fire.

The bullet enters his eye socket and red mist explodes from the back of his head. He falls to the ground a lifeless mess.

Now that I know how to stop them, I pick off the next few one by one. Sometimes I miss. Sometimes I graze their head or blow apart a jaw or ear, but more often than not, my aim is true and I take them down.

The last one falls to the ground and I think we are safe.

I am wrong.

The sound of the battle has brought more of them towards us. A small army, too many to count, spills around the corner of a nearby building.

I don't know if I should fight or run. The only thing I do know is that for once, I can't die. I might have only one shot at this quest for all I know. I can't take the chance that I'll die and respawn in my home portal, eliminated from the tournament. I have to win this. I have to at least beat this first quest.

They turn the corner and rush towards us. They are actually running. Their limbs flail about and it sounds like a rushing tide as their screams blend together down the city street.

I start shooting and kill a few, but at this rate, I'll never be able to kill them all. There has to be something I can do. I need to think outside the box. They'll be on us in less than a minute if I do nothing.

I have a thought. It shouldn't be possible, but I don't see any other way.

"Little girl?"

"Yes?" Her face is innocent. It makes what I'm about to ask even more preposterous.

"Can you shoot a gun?"

CHAPTER FOURTEEN

The girl smirks and holds her hand out. I place the M16 in it. She takes it, drops to one knee, and begins picking off people with pinpoint accuracy. It's like she has shot the weapon her entire life.

Congratulations! You have learned the passive 'Inspire Resistance.' NPCs in your party will fight with increased fervor.

I can't believe that worked, but I don't have time to appreciate my good fortune. A horde of crazies is fast approaching. Even with my new backup, there are so many of them that I don't know if we have a chance.

It's time to break out everything I have. I equip my axe and take off towards the mob. I cast Mud Pits and they immediately slow down. I cast Resilience on myself and jump into the fray. Their movement and attack is cut down by fifty percent while my attack speed is increased by twenty percent.

They try to bite me and I finally realize what is wrong with them. They are zombies. 'It begins at the end.' When they die, they come back again. We're in the apocalypse.

"Live or die, begin again." Whether you live or die, it's a new chance. No wonder Ryken was the first to beat this place. He's a death knight, he can control the undead. It won't be so easy for me.

I attack with everything I have, cleaving heads from shoulders and splitting them down the middle. Blood soaks through my clothes and covers my face. Pretty soon, I look no different from the zombies I am fighting.

The girl is still in position, picking off men and women who attack me from my blind side. There are so many zombies, I wonder if it will be enough.

I take my axe and spin in a harsh circle, decapitating three of them. Their heads roll along the ground and continue to bite long after they are removed from their bodies.

The funnel of zombies seems never-ending. Dozens of bodies lay in piles around me and more continue to barrage us. Through it all, the girl remains calm, almost robotic, as she fires round after round.

My stamina has dipped low and the only reason I have any at all is because of my boots. Without them, I would certainly be dead already. There is a marked difference between my fighting with both Mud Pits and Resilience active versus when they are not.

I hear a light click that cuts through the fighting. I know the sound and it sends a shiver down my spine. The M16 is out of ammo. She's run through all the ammo I gave her, some one hundred rounds.

Several dozen zombies turn the corner, but it looks like it might be the end of them for now. I tell the girl to stay back, while I try to finish them off. She stands with the rifle in her hands, obeying my command.

A zombie reaches for me and I chop off his hands. His teeth gnash together up until the moment my axe splits his face in half.

Mud Pits and Resilience both come off cooldown and I cast them. I attack in a flurry. My axe cuts through their bodies like butter. I make sure to keep the zombies in front of me. Without the girl to guard my back, I can't take any chances. I lure them towards me. They are fast and hungry, but I am faster.

I don't know what effect a single bite from them will cause and I have no desire to find out. One bite could end all of this for me. If I can help it, we're making this run clean.

Two dozen of them remain. They're as ravenous as ever as they funnel down the street towards me. Mounds of bodies litter the road, slowing their approach and funneling the zombies closer together.

I remember the grenades and take one from my inventory. I pull the pin and toss it into the crowd. The explosion is deafening. Blood and body parts erupt and rain down, taking out half of the undead horde. I'm not sure what lies ahead, so I elect to save my last grenade and take out the remaining zombies with my axe.

When I decapitate the last one and his head rolls down the street like a ball, I take a deep breath. Now we have to go into the city and find the girl's mother.

I turn around and she's not there.

In a panic, I scream for her. I call her 'little girl' because I don't even know her name. If she's gone, this is all for nothing.

A wet crunch startles me right before a heavy body pushes me to the ground.

This is it. I missed one and now I'm dead.

I expect the bite to come, but it never does. Instead, I feel a slight suction and turn around to see the girl pull the bayonet from the zombie's head.

"Uh, thanks." I don't really know what to say. I didn't expect an NPC to save my life. Was it my new ability or is she programmed to help me?

My experience bar shoots up drastically after she kills the last zombie. I hit level thirteen and put my new stat point into Dexterity. The increased accuracy will be a godsend if I can find more ammunition for the M16. It will also help with the cooldowns for my abilities. Definitely the smart choice for my current circumstances.

"I guess we go into the city now," I say, more to myself than to the girl.

The blue box telling me where to find her mother is closer now. It's only a few blocks away. Since we have no bullets, stealth is our greatest weapon going forward.

We pass the decaying bodies and enter the city. Everything is in ruins. Several buildings burn bright, fires lighting them from the inside. Broken glass litters the street and I have to choose each step carefully to avoid the crunch. Not that every zombie in the city couldn't have heard our gunfight.

Around the corner, I see a few straggling zombies. They move without purpose. Far down the street, I see a great deal more. An overturned oil tanker takes up half the road, forcing the zombies into a neat line. Our battle must have drawn their attention.

The blue box showing me our next objective is halfway between us and the zombies. With no bullets, it feels like a suicide mission to go out there. I could wait and pick them off one by one as they approach, but there is no telling how many of them are on the other side.

A thought dawns on me. I tell the girl to stay where she is, and I take off running toward the horde. Several dozen have spilled through now. When I'm close enough, I take the last grenade and throw it hard at the oil tanker.

It bounces off the metal shell and falls to the ground. For a moment, I don't know if it will explode or not. Then, a loud explosion that ignites the night sky knocks me to my feet. My vision goes red at the edges and I struggle to stand up. Charred limbs litter the street as I rush back to the girl.

When I find her, she is fixated on the fire, its flames dancing in the reflection of her eyes.

We are so close to the blue box and that is all I care about right now. I move quickly to its location. The girl follows behind, quiet as a mouse.

The blue square surrounds two buildings. One is several stories tall, and fires burn inside the lower floors. The other is an old church. The steeple has fallen off and is lodged upside down in the street. The doors to the church are chained shut.

Someone locked it from the outside.

"Which one is your mommy in?" I ask.

She doesn't say anything. Her eyes are fixed on the fire burning high in the building.

That's where we'll start.

We enter through the side stairwell. The door groans as I push it open. A burnt sofa is lodged between the door and the wall. I give it a hard push with all of my weight and it finally gives enough for us to squeeze inside.

"Stay behind me," I say. The girl nods. She still holds

the M16 in her hand. I hope she doesn't have to use it again.

The thought barely comes to mind before I hear a loud groan from up the stairs.

I creep up one step at a time. The groans grow louder with each step. I can hear someone beating on a door. Whether they are living or undead, I'm not certain.

There is a loud crack. Then, I hear running. They must have broken through the door. Dozens of thunderous stomps echo through the stairwell. I brace for a fight.

The first zombie turns the corner and dives towards me. I slice through his midsection, ripping him in half. His upper body falls behind me and the girl stabs him in the head.

I cast Mud Pits on the stairs just in time to catch the mob. Their eyes are empty, but full of rage and fury. The clatter of teeth chomping will haunt me in my sleep. I take a step closer and chop through the first zombie's head.

Not much choice at the moment, but I don't like fighting on the stairs. My feet are grounded at odd angles and I don't have the high ground.

I switch to my faithful rusty spear and begin jabbing at the zombies caught in the mud. I take out half of them before the mud pits disappear. Then I switch back to my axe.

There are five of them left.

They move with astounding speed and force me to retreat. I decapitate two and their heads roll past me down the stairs. One wraps his arms around me, catching me off-balance and sending me falling to the ground. The impact knocks the breath out of me and I gasp for air as I hold him off. His teeth continue to chomp, hungry for my flesh.

His body falls limp and I push him to the side. The girl has saved me yet again.

Before I know what has happened, the other two zombies step over my body. They don't care about me anymore. They want the girl.

Without thinking, I switch to Grappler and fire my grappling hook. It hooks one zombie through the shoulder, halting it for a moment. I equip my spear in my other hand and throw it as fast as I can. It soars through the air, impaling the second zombie through the side of his head just as his teeth are inches from the girl's face.

I jerk the other zombie hard with the grappling hook, pulling him off his feet and slamming him to the ground. With all my might, I stomp his head in and his brains splatter against the wall.

The girl's yellow dress is now stained red.

"Are you okay?" I ask. She nods and wraps her tiny arms around my leg.

"Let's go find Mommy."

We hurry up the stairs. The walls are covered in bloody handprints and streaks. When we reach the top, the door lies on the floor, broken off its hinges. A long hallway extends in front of me. Smoke billows out from under half a dozen doors.

I check my map and see a small blue dot in the room at the far end. It pulsates slowly, drawing me towards it. That must be her mother.

"Follow me."

Smoke fills the hallway by the time I reach the final room. I knock, but no one answers.

"Stand back. I'm going to kick it in."

I kick hard next to the door handle and the door flies off its hinges.

A young woman huddles behind an overturned bed. She has a sniper rifle propped against the window.

"Mommy!" the girl screams and jumps into the woman's arms.

"Kaley, I never thought I would see you again!" Tears run down her cheeks as she holds her daughter tight. "I lost you when we were taking cover and ended up trapped in this building. I came up high to see if I could see you. But then the dead found me. They've been trying to get in for days."

She puts Kaley down and walks over to me.

"Thank you for saving my baby. How can I ever repay you?"

Congratulations! You have completed the quest 'Find My Mommy.' Reward: 100 gold.

"You don't owe me anything. Is there somewhere I can help you get to?"

"No thanks. The streets are clear for the moment. If we can get out of this building, then I think we can find our way home."

I help the two of them out of the building. As soon as they exit, they disappear around the corner. A message flashes across my screen.

Congratulations, Esil! You have completed the first quest of the Developer's Tournament. Reward: 1000 gold.

A portal appears in front of me.

Holy Shit.

I'm in the thick of it.

CHAPTER FIFTEEN

"You have to wait a week for the clue?" Buzz asks. His brow is furrowed in frustration on the small video feed in the top left corner of my vision. "That's bullshit. You were the fifth one to complete the quest. Why do you have to wait?"

"I wish I knew. The notification said they would be releasing the next clue in a week. I guess with all one hundred spots being filled, they want to give us a chance to do anything we can to prepare for the next task."

Once I was out of Apocalyptica, my notifications blew up. I was the fifth person to complete the quest. Princess Aleesia was third. There were a few other familiar names in the top one hundred that I recognized as well. Two of her dwarven followers, Ordin and Klink, also managed to secure a spot. Jayce—one of our partners from steamball —made the cut as well. And of course, Ryken, the death knight, who we all have to thank for accidentally telling the world where the first quest was.

The forums are the busiest I have ever seen them. Posts pile up faster than I can sort through them as people try to predict what the next clue will be, or how each contestant completed the quest. Many famous names didn't make the final one hundred. The developers announced they would be releasing highlights of each player who successfully completed the quest the next day. I'm excited to see how everyone else managed to get the girl to her mother.

"So, what now?" Buzz asks.

"Well, tonight, I'm going to rest. That quest really took a lot out of me. And starting tomorrow, I'm going to level grind. I was lucky with the first quest that level wasn't an issue, but I can't count on that going forward. I need more spells, more weapons, and better stats."

"Okay, buddy. You earned your rest. I'm going to check out the ladies and play a little steamball. I'll catch you later."

Buzz's face disappears from my vision.

I climb out of my haptic suit and take a cold shower. The water feels good on my skin, washing away the sweat and grime caused by the stress of the past few hours. I still can't believe that I finished fifth out of everyone. Sometimes it's better to be lucky than good. And all that gold I won today, I can buy almost anything I want.

After I eat and power up my room, I browse the web for a bit. It's easy to get lost in the game of it all. An entire universe filled with worlds designed to entertain. For most people, that's all it is. I wish it was that way for me. When I think about Buzz's mom, my stomach goes in knots. I've never met her, but her life is in my hands. I've never had anyone depend on me before. Is this what it's like to have a family?

I pull up a map of The Boxes and search for a doctor. There are none in The Boxes. Those of us who can afford medical care are visited by drones. Real doctors are expensive. Luckily for me, I came into some gold today.

It's five hundred gold to arrange transport to the doctor's office just outside The Boxes. I book it. I want to hear from a real, living, breathing human what is wrong with Buzz's mom.

We won't be going in to work tomorrow. Tomorrow, I'll step out into the world for the first time in almost a year. I'll leave The Boxes for the first time I can remember.

My hands shake a little as I rip open the foil packet of my processed food. I don't know what to expect once I leave my box. I know what is outside of my window. Other boxes. Drones. That's it. I made the trip from the orphanage to my box a year ago. Even then, I saw nothing more than other boxes. My stomach churns with each flavorless bite I take.

When the vehicle that is supposed to pick us up arrives outside my door, I take a deep breath. A package enters through the airtight chute and I open it. Inside is a bright yellow mask along with a yellow wind suit that swishes with every movement. I remember wearing the mask the last time I went out. It filters the air. Makes it safe to breathe. These disposable masks last for eight hours before the filter is no longer safe. It covers my entire face aside from a piece of heavy plastic for me to see through. When I press a button on the side of the mask, it suctions to my face. It feels like my eyes are going to pop out for a moment, then it calibrates and I can breathe easy.

Once the mask is secure, the small light next to the door that is always red turns green. I press 'open' and a loud hiss fills the air as the door opens. Once I leave, the air system will flush out the entire room.

The transport vehicle is docked with my box and I am able to step directly inside. The inside is cramped and gray. I booked the cheapest transport available. No bells and whistles. It seats up to four people, two on each side facing one another. Two windows allow me to see the world around me. So far, it's nothing new.

The vehicle unhinges from my door and drifts through the air. A small screen across from me details the route to Buzz's box. Everything is already routed. A thought dawns on me.

This is the first time I will see Buzz's real face.

I arrive at his box moments later.

When the door opens, he looks just like his avatar. His dark hair is cut close, and his eyes are big and expressive. A wide grin stretches across his face. The only difference is a scar that runs down his left cheek.

"You're even uglier in person," he says before wrapping me in a bear hug. Our suits crinkle as they touch. This is the first human contact I've had in a year. It feels strange, another human body so close to mine. So warm. "This is my mom, Maria."

Even through the suit, I can see she is having a hard time walking. Her face still holds a lot of youthfulness, but her eyes tell a different story. She has the same dark hair and round eyes as Buzz, but she moves with a frailty no one her age should have.

"Thank you for this, Esil. You are a good boy. Buzz is lucky to have a friend like you." She wraps her hands around my arm. Her grip shakes slightly as she holds me.

The door closes and hisses as it locks into place. We take off and the car we are in slowly descends towards the ground. A dozen boxes pass by my window on the way down. I can't believe how many of us live our lives locked away like this, the only interaction we have taking place in a virtual world.

I search for the orphanage, but if it's there, I don't recognize it.

As we float along, several feet above the ground, something strikes me. This all seems less real to me than the worlds in Pangea. It feels less detailed. Everything is gray and bland. Has the world always felt this way?

"Thanks again for doing this, Esil." Buzz's words draw me back to reality. "I know you were wanting to level up."

"This is more important. Pangea will be there when we get back."

"I'm excited to see how you did it." Buzz changes the subject. His hand rests on his mother's leg. She stares out of the window, using the wall to support her. "I know you told me, but I can't wait to watch it. I'm going to watch everyone's and see if there is anything that might help you."

When we cross the line out of The Boxes and into Graytown, things don't change much. There are store-fronts and a few people walk the streets, but they all wear masks and are fully clothed. Nothing is exposed. Every-thing is the same gray as The Boxes. These people aren't that different from us. They just have a little more money to walk around.

We pass a man sitting on the street corner. Ragged clothes cover only parts of his body. Boils and tumors cover his skin. He doesn't wear a mask, though I'm not sure it would do much for him at this point. A cup sits in front of him on the ground, though I don't know what he hopes for. Maybe water. We haven't used physical currency in half a century.

A few moments later, we leave Graytown and arrive in Civic City. I remember studying about it in school. They are more well off than either The Boxes or Graytown, but to me, it doesn't look that different. The architecture is nicer, and the clothes the people wear are finer, but they still wear masks as they walk about. Everything is still ten shades of gray. Until we come to a stop at the hospital.

The hospital is like something out of Pangea. Tall pillars and parabolas jut into the sky, a mixture of brilliant white and glass. The brightness of the hospital contrasts starkly with everything else, including the dull gray sky.

Our vehicle takes us to a landing pad. The appointment is already booked, so the itinerary replaces the map on the screen in front of me. We will be meeting with Dr. Halfstead, who specializes in radiation poisoning.

The door hisses open and we step into a white room. A female voice tells us to remove our masks and suits. Buzz helps his mother. When we strip them down, all three of us wear the same black clothes the developers gave us when we moved into The Boxes. They fit tight against our skin and stretch as we grow.

There is another hiss as steam fills the room. A moment later, it disappears and the door opposite the vehicle opens into a lobby. It is the same blinding white as the outside of the building. The marble floors gleam, reflecting the lights overhead. It is all a lot to take in. Several drones roll past, on various missions for the hospital. People sit in white leather chairs, waiting for their appointments. This is more people in one space than I have seen since living at the orphanage. They are all absorbed in their own worlds. I can see some logged into Pangea on their mobile devices. Others watch movies or read magazines, turning the page with a wave of their hands.

A nurse sits behind the counter up ahead.

"How may I help you today?" she asks. Her red lips offer me a grand smile.

"I've scheduled an appointment for Maria Halifax with Doctor Halfstead." I lean against the counter.

The woman touches a few holographic screens that hover in front of her. She moves them around, taps them and they change before my eyes.

Another nurse appears from behind a set of double doors.

"Miss. Halifax, this way, please."

We all walk towards the door.

"I'm sorry, sir, but it's kin only," the nurse says, barring my entry.

"There's no need for that," Buzz's mom scolds the nurse. "He's as good as family."

The nurse decides not to argue. Maybe it's because Buzz's mom looks like she can barely walk through the door. Maybe it's because she knows we're from The Boxes and doesn't want to test how far we'd go to get what we want. There's a certain fear those from outside The Boxes have of us. They think we're lunatics, or contagious. Being a medical professional, she knows the second isn't true.

We walk through the door and she leads us into a room. A large metal canister sits against the wall, big enough to hold a human. There is a touchscreen on the side. The nurse points to a few chairs in the corner.

"You two can have a seat over there. Miss Halfiax, can you please step into the machine so we can take your vitals? You can leave your clothes on."

Buzz's mom steps into the giant canister. It whirs for a moment and a few lights strobe inside. The nurse has her hold up her arms. She enters a few commands into the touchscreen and then leaves after telling us the doctor will be with us shortly.

Several minutes later, a knock on the door announces the doctor's arrival. He wears a sad smile when he enters.

"I hear you wanted a second opinion on the scan our drone took?"

"We just wanted to be sure," I say.

"I'm sorry, but the scans weren't wrong." He looks at Buzz's mom. "Your body is failing you. At the current rate, you have a year. Maybe more, maybe less."

"But you can fix it, right? If we have the money. There is a cure?" I stand up, overcome with emotion.

"Look, I know where you're from. Life is hard in The Boxes. You probably spent everything you have for this visit. The procedure is expensive. Most of the people who come to this hospital couldn't afford it if they needed to. I know it's hard to hear, but that's just the way things are sometimes. I can give you medicine to deal with the pain. It'll make it all easier."

"We're not interested in that right now." I fight to

control my voice. "If we had the money... If we had a hundred thousand gold, could you cure her?"

The doctor sighs. "If you had that much gold, we'd have a very good chance of curing her."

"Then we'll be seeing you again."

CHAPTER SIXTEEN

When my highlights of the first quest go public, I become one of the most popular players in Pangea overnight. My inbox is full of message from other gamers, fans, and companies offering to sponsor me. It's a lot to process all at once. Everyone has a different opinion of my decision to ask the girl for help.

"U lucky bastard! 100% luck, nothing else. UR gonna b out n the next round."

"Wow! I never would have thought to ask the girl for help. I can't wait to see what you do next round. And only level thirteen, too."

"Congrats on completing the first mission, Esil. We at VR HaptiX, the latest and greatest in VR and haptic suits, would love to sponsor you going forward. We'll outfit you with everything you need to take your gaming to the next level. Please respond back with a time you are free to set up a meeting and we can hammer out the details."

They go on like this for quite a while. It's all a little overwhelming to be honest. To go from being a nobody to having my name plastered on forums and around the web is not something I signed up for. I just want to compete and be left alone. Even at the orphanage, I was the lone wolf, never the alpha.

I haven't had time to check out any of the highlights from the other players yet. Leveling up is my biggest priority right now. Buzz said he will give me the breakdown of any interesting tactics once he's watched them all.

The Mortican Mountains is where I spend most of my time while I level. It's an expensive world to get to, so I'm less likely to be bombarded by everyone who has watched my highlights. I turn off my gamertag as I level up so I'm less conspicuous. So far, I've gained two more levels and attributed my stat points to Dexterity and Intellect. I really want to up my spellcasting for whatever comes next.

Level 15:
  Strength - 14
  Agility - 1
  Vitality - 2
  Intellect - 5
  Dexterity - 3
  Stamina - 0

I've also gained a few new items. The rusty spear I've carried since my first day in the Mortican Mountains has finally been replaced by a beautiful Elvish Spear. It catches the light at every turn, illuminating the ground with the reflected rays of the sun.

***Item: Elvish Battle Spear. +12 attack, +15% armor pene-*tration.** It's long and strong and down to get the killing on.*

I practice with it on a few wandering bears. It's a great close combat weapon with the bonus that I can throw it from a medium range with pretty good accuracy. I alternate between it and my axe as I see fit. The spear has better stats, but nothing feels as natural as my axe.

As I continue to level up, I can't stop thinking about the offers for sponsorship. The companies would pay me to explore Pangea all day long and enter tournaments. There is no doubt I would make more than I do working in the mines. But would I be making enough to support myself living anywhere other than The Boxes? That's what I'll need to find out, because if I quit the mines, then I have to leave my box. There's also Buzz to consider. How could I ever leave him behind? Would he resent me if I did?

Still, if I could play all day, that would give me more time to prepare for the next quest. Once the next clue goes live, I can't afford to sit around all day while others make progress.

A small ding tells me I have a new message. I expect it to be another random person, since I have allowed all messages to arrive in my main inbox for the time being. I'm surprised to see it's from Aleesia.

Hey Esil,

I finally got around to watching your highlights. All I can say is wow. You really pulled that one out of your butt, huh? Only kidding. Me and a few of the dwarves are going to be at the Lion's Head Pub this evening to celebrate if you want to stop by for a few minutes. I know you're probably hard at work preparing for the next quest, but it's important to remember to enjoy the small victories. None of us are promised to make it through this next quest. Your first drink is on me. ;-)

-Aleesia

What the hell. I'm going to do it. A little relaxation might be good for me. I was the fifth person to beat the quest, for crying out loud. No one expected that, least of all, me.

I decide to kill one more monster before heading to the pub. I search the countryside, looking for the perfect monster to end with. A group of bears huddle in a nearby field. A large harpy hovers in the air to my right, reminding me of my first fight ever. A stone golem crumbles and builds itself up in perpetuity, waiting for an attack. None of these really fit the bill for what I'm looking for, so I keep walking.

The Mortican Mountains loom above me in the distance, their snowcapped peaks flirting with billowing white clouds. I press onward toward the mountains even though it takes me farther away from the pub. Once I finish the fight, I'll teleport back to the town square.

A path that winds up the side of the mountain between several pine trees catches my eye. It is almost hidden compared to the main trail several hundred feet down. Today, I'll take the road less traveled. Rocks and dirt fall behind me as I make my way up the path.

An owl stares down at me from a nearby tree. Its yellow eyes are piercing against its brown feathers. Two tufts of black feathers jut into the air on each side of its head, mimicking horns. I could kill him and gain a fraction of experience, but he looks so peaceful that I leave him be. His eyes follow me while I walk past until his head turns completely backwards. He looks strange sitting there like that. Are there still owls somewhere in the real world? The only animals I've seen in The Boxes have been rats and the occasional cat at the orphanage. I don't see many animals in my box, it's too high in the air.

I've walked half a mile when I realize I'm being followed. The owl hops from limb to limb with each step I take. When I stop, it stops.

"What do you want?" I ask.

The owl lets out a low hoot.

"I'm looking for a fight here. Why don't you go on before you get hurt? I won't be able to look out for you once the battle begins."

The owl responds with another hoot.

"Come on, now. Get going."

I pick up a rock and toss it at the owl. He jumps to the left and the rock bounces off the tree. He hoots again.

I hear a flutter of wings and notice that another owl has landed behind me. This one is snowy white with black speckles along its feathers. The two owls hoot back and forth for a moment before a third owl joins them, then a fourth. Before I know it, I am surrounded by a dozen owls. They hoot in unison. I focus on their stats. They are all level one, nothing to worry about.

I still feel uneasy by the sudden appearance of so many.

"Fine, just leave me alone."

They all hoot back in reply.

I continue walking and all around me, I hear the shake of tiny branches as each owl hops from limb to limb.

The path grows narrower the farther up the mountain I go until I am ducking between branches every few steps. The small shuffle of branches behind me lets me know the owls are still there.

Finally, the trail opens and I am in a small clearing overlooking the valley between two mountains. It is odd that I've made it so far up the mountain without encountering an enemy.

A deep mist hangs between the mountains. There has to be monsters down inside. I set off to continue my trek when a loud flurry of wings startles me.

All of the owls leave their branches and fly in my direction. They are only level one, but the action is terrifying nonetheless. The thought of a dozen talons digging into my face is not something that sounds the least bit appealing. I take a fighting stance and prepare to kill them.

They fly past me and collide together midair. There is a flash of light and then a tall, lanky man stands before me. His long brown hair is pulled into a pony tail. He carries a staff in one hand and wears a leather gauntlet on the other. When he whistles, the first owl I saw flies down from a tree and perches on his arm.

"What the hell?" is all I can think to say.

The man, who is dressed plainly in canvas robes, lifts his arm into the air and the owl flies away. I focus on his stats to see what I'm up against.

Orel. Guardian of the Hidden Pass. *Protector of the Hidden Pass of the Mortican Mountains, Orel has the sight of a thousand birds.*

Hmm, he must be an NPC because he doesn't have a

level. I bet he will drop some pretty good loot if I can defeat him, maybe even a new spell.

I clutch my spear close and take a defensive stance, but the man doesn't move. I take a step closer and he extends his arm, his staff pointed at me.

"You shall not pass."

That must be it, he's here to make sure no one goes down into the valley. Alright then, I think I know how to get this fight started. I take another step closer and lunge at Orel with my spear. Just as it is about to pierce his body, Orel disintegrates into several dozen owls and flies into the sky.

The next thing I know, a flutter of wings is the only sound I hear before I'm attacked by dozens of sharp talons. They rip at my body, painting my vision red.

This is how I die, killed by birds. But as quickly as they appear, the birds disappear and a moment later, Orel stands before me again.

"You shall not pass."

It seems that way.

With half my health gone from the attack, I search my surroundings and look for anything that can help me defeat the bird man. Nothing but trees surround us on all sides. Behind him, the mountain descends into the valley. If I could only find a way to get behind him, then maybe I could attack him by surprise. I can't turn away. This is too good of an opportunity to turn my back on and I need items and spells for the tournament.

If all I have to use are trees, then that's what I'll use. I equip Grappler in my other hand and fire at Orel. The laser beam goes directly for his heart and he morphs into his owl army again.

This time, I don't wait to be attacked. I use Grapple and shoot it into the top of the nearest tree. It catches and pulls me hard and fast into the air. Branches snap against my body as I soar higher and higher. Thirty seconds until I can use it again.

Just as I am about to come to a stop against the tree, I put Grappler back into my inventory. The force from the pull sends me soaring past the tree tops. For a moment, I can see for miles in every direction. Below me, I hear the flutter of wings.

Gravity takes hold and I begin falling towards the ground just as I see dozens of observant eyes flying in my direction. I cast Resilience and begin swiping at the owls one by one as I fall, knocking them aside. Without having me totally surrounded, it's easy to pick them off. They fall into trees and tumble to the ground. The high ground definitely has its advantages.

Suddenly, the owls turn and rush together. A flash of light and Orel is before me, falling on his back towards the ground. Now is my chance to end this. Whatever ability he was using, taking out his owls has stopped it.

We crash to the ground and I land on top of him. Immediately, I use Lunging Strike, stunning him on his back. I lift my spear and bring it down with all my might against his chest. It pierces his body and he explodes into hundreds of feathers. They float through the air like tiny sailboats on the wind and my experience bar shoots up.

I search the area for loot but find nothing.

What a waste of time.

The next thing I know, two talons grip hard on the side of my shoulder and the first owl I saw on the trail stares back at me.

Congratulations! You have unlocked a pet.

Great Horned Owl. Special ability: Flyby; The Owl can fly into enemy territory without provoking an attack. Special ability: Increased hearing and vision. *Woe befalleth the man who does not heed the wisdom of the owl.*

What? That's awesome! I've always wanted a pet. The two special abilities are amazing as well.

Suddenly, the mountains are buzzing with sounds. I can hear bugs crawling through the trees, birds in the air, and a mountain troll sleeping on the other side of the mountain. When I look out into the misty trees, I can make out branches in far greater detail than I could before. It's like my sight and hearing have been magnified tenfold.

"What's your name?" I ask.

He clicks his beak and looks off into the distance.

"I think I'll call you Merlin. Pleased to meet you."

His head turns at my words and his yellow eyes stare intently.

"What do you say we try out our new abilities?"

I will Merlin to fly into the air and he responds by kicking off my shoulder and soaring out into the valley. When I focus on him, my vision changes suddenly and I am looking down on the valley from above. I can see better than I could ever imagine. From up so high, I can make out squirrels scurrying along the forest floor and hear other gamers talking from the foot of the mountain trail. A group of lizard people wait in surprise behind a boulder for a small party of elves. My head feels like it is about to explode because it's all so overwhelming. I try to narrow my focus to one thing at a time.

There are wolves, bears, and a centaur nearby. A small

band of orcs return from a hunt of their own. Two trolls, both probably out of my league. I know I said only one more monster, but now that I have Merlin at my side, I want to test him out in battle. One more, for real this time. I continue scanning and then I spot my next opponent.

A yeti.

He's not too far up the mountain. Just where the snows begin melting away.

I focus and my normal sight returns, though I can still feel Merlin's presence as he flies above me. I'll have to be careful when switching views in the future because it leaves my body unguarded.

Half an hour later, I can see the yeti up ahead, gnawing on the bones of an elk or some other horned creature. Once I am close enough, I focus on his stats.

Yeti. Level 20. Though often solitary creatures, these fierce warriors sport natural armor and resistances. Their icy breath can freeze opponents in their tracks.

He has five levels on me, but I think I can take him as long as I don't get frozen. I clutch my spear close and prepare for battle.

As soon as I enter his range, the yeti tosses the bloody carcass to the ground and stands tall. His white fur blends in with the snowy peaks of the mountains above, but the melting snow from the trees behind him exposes his outline. I cast Resilience, upping my attack speed and move in quickly. I am able to get off three spear jabs before the yeti takes a swing at me. I roll to the right and his fist connects with the ground.

Angered, he lets out a raging howl. His icy breath

washes over me and I feel sluggish. Each step is hard to take and my spear moves slowly in my hand.

You have been hit with Frigid Breath, your movement and attack speed are cut in half.

Seven hells! The yeti moves in close and pummels me in the ribs with a hard punch. My vision goes red and I can barely breathe. One hit takes out a third of my health. If I don't get up soon, I'll be dead.

The yeti lets out a howl that echoes off the mountains. He stands over me and I can still see scraps of meat stuck between his teeth as he reaches down. No doubt he will bash my brains against a tree and have me for dinner. His hands are inches from my legs when I hear a loud screech and Merlin claws the yeti in the eyes. The yeti swats at Merlin but the owl is too quick and flies off again into the trees.

The distraction buys me just enough time to get out of the yeti's reach. Frigid Breath wears off and my speed returns. I cast Mud Pits on the angry yeti to no effect. His natural resistances nullify the ability. Lunging Strike will fare no better. My only options are brute force and my wits.

I toss my spear at the yeti and hit him in the chest, dropping him to half health. I switch to Grappler and fire the grappling hook between the yeti's legs. I focus for Merlin and he flies in, taking the gun in his talons.

"Circle the yeti," I instruct him.

I equip my axe and try to keep the yeti's attention on me while Merlin circles him.

The yeti roars and an icy blast pours from his mouth. It misses me by inches, but I can feel the cold against my skin. If I get caught in one of those, I'm done.

Merlin circles the yeti several times and the grappling hook is wrapped tightly around its legs. If I can stay alive a few more moments, my plan will be in place.

I'm not that lucky.

He howls and I'm caught again.

You have been hit with Frigid Breath, your movement and attack speed are cut in half.

I guess this is the part where I die.

The yeti tries to take a step towards me, but his feet catch in the rope of my grappling hook. It's not completely wrapped around his lower body, but it is enough to trip the yeti, sending him tumbling to the ground. He hits the mushy earth with a splash, sending melting snow and mud in every direction. Merlin drops Grappler and takes flight once more. In my sluggish state, I trudge towards the yeti and attack him with my axe. His health drops to a quarter and he roars another icy blast at me.

This time it catches me full on and I can't move.

You have been hit with Ice Blast. You are temporarily stunned.

All I can do is watch as the yeti struggles with the ropes around his legs. For the moment, he is more concerned with his freedom than killing me.

With a great display of strength, the yeti rips the ropes from his legs and tosses the frayed fibers to the ground.

My stun wears off and we lunge at each other at the same time. My axe connects with his shoulder at the same time his giant fist catches me in the jaw.

The yeti falls to the ground with zero health. My vision is ten shades of red, but I survive with a sliver of life. My experience bar shoots up almost to level sixteen. I loot the body and find another spellbook.

Item: Spellbook. Requirements: Level 15. *Activate Y/N?*

I'll wait and see what I've found when I'm not in the throes of death.

Currency: 2 gold.

I lean against a nearby tree to gather myself. My jaw throbs and my head aches. I really need to stop getting the crap beat out of me at some point. Merlin returns to me and perches on my shoulder. I pet him on the head and he nuzzles my fingers. Without him, I would have certainly died. I'm already getting attached to the little guy.

It's about time to meet up with the princess. I can heal up back at the town square, so I focus on teleporting and my body begins to dissipate before my eyes.

CHAPTER SEVENTEEN

I push the heavy wooden door open to the Lion's Head Pub. Inside, the place is packed. A bard stands on top of a nearby table, an ale sloshing in each hand, singing a song of a great battle. I spot the princess and four dwarves sitting at a table towards the back drinking. Ordin and Klink, who both made it to the next round of the tournament, sit on each side of her while Glordin and Tinker sit across from her.

Merlin rides on my shoulder, turning his head in quick succession as he surveys the room.

Several people nod at me as I walk past. I see a few shocked faces of recognition and hear the hiss of whispers. A large woman covered in platemail pats me on the back.

The dwarves stand to meet me when I arrive at the table.

"Greetings, Esil." Ordin reaches out and clasps his hand around my forearm. His red beard is braided intricately down his chest.

I do the same in turn with each of the dwarves and finally, the princess.

"I'm glad you could join us," she says. She wears a fiery dress that changes from dark red up top to a bright orange at the bottom. A pendant hangs from her neck with a tiny fire burning inside. "Who is this little guy?" she asks, reaching out to Merlin. He nibbles on her finger and gives a low hoot.

"This is Merlin. I had a stroke of luck in the mountains today."

"You seem to have a lot of that." She winks.

"So, how'd you do it?" I ask, cutting right to the chase.

"You haven't watched the highlights?"

"Haven't had a chance yet. I had things to take care of outside of Pangea."

I take a seat at the table and Merlin flies from my shoulder to the wooden chandelier above the table. Dozens of candles burn overhead, casting the room in constant dancing light.

"Apocalyptica was such a strange place for a first quest. I never would have guessed a shooter world. I guess they hoped to weed out the players who weren't as well rounded. Lucky for us Ryken gave away his location or we could have been searching for ages.

"When I finally got there and noticed the rest of our group wasn't and that we couldn't message, I got right to work. Once I found the mob of zombies, I took a risk. Not as big of a risk as you, but still, I wasn't sure if it would work. I tried to imbue my bullets and it worked. Each shot had the same effect as a spellcast. It was hard, but it all worked out in the end."

"She doesn't do herself justice," Ordin intervenes. "The

princess was accurate beyond compare. The undead never stood a chance." He bangs his fist on the table and the ale he is drinking sloshes over the side of the mug.

"And what about you?"

Ordin sits up straight and puffs out his chest.

"I brought them dwarven hell!" He laughs and raises his warhammer in the air. "It was a glorious fight. I found myself surrounded on all sides. Outnumbered. But we dwarves are a tough bunch."

"Only two of you made it through?" I counter.

"Some are tougher than others." He smirks.

Tinker takes offense to Ordin's comments.

"If I'd had a powerful warhammer, I'm sure I could have smashed the buggers around too. But I became a battle-mage so you lot would have at least one to watch your back." Tinker's gray hair falls in a mess around his shoulders. He wears large, round glasses that make his eyes seem ten sizes too large. The staff he carries is made of a vibrant silver metal and holds a blue stone at the top. "I almost made it out of there, too. If I hadn't run out of mana, I would have blasted them all to smithereens."

The others just sit back and laugh. Tinker lifts his beer mug, which is the size of my head, and drains it in one swallow.

"At least two of us are around to compete with the princess in the next round."

"Aye," the other three say in unison.

"What are your plans while we wait for the next clue?"

"Same as you, I suppose," says Aleesia. "We'll keep leveling and searching for better items. You never know what could come in handy. You're welcome to join us if you'd like." She smiles at me and I have a hard time saying no.

"We'll see. I still have to work. I was meaning to ask you, though, are any of you sponsored? I have a few offers and I've been thinking about accepting."

"It's a good way to make a little extra cash, if you like what they are offering. Nothing worse than getting stuck with a product that sucks and a contract that forces you to keep using it," says Aleesia.

Extra cash? How much money does she have if the money from sponsors is just icing on the cake? Well, her dad is a developer, so I'm sure they wipe their butts with gold coins.

"Who offered to sponsor you?" she asks.

"A lot of companies, actually, but the one I was excited about was VR HaptiX. I've heard they are the best suits around."

"That's great. I think they are the same company that sponsors Ryken. My dad uses a HaptiX suit. I'd take the money. Then you'll have more time to quest with us." The others nod in agreement.

We spend the next few hours talking about what quests could be next and all the ways the other dwarves failed the first one. It feels good to just sit, hang out, and relax, even if it is only for a few hours.

When I receive a notification saying I need to power up my box soon, I say my good-byes and head home.

In my home portal, I remember the spellbook I looted from the yeti and pull it up in my inventory.

Item: Spellbook. Requirements: Level 15. *Activate Y/N?*

I accept and the same sensation as before runs through

my body. I feel tiny vibrations throughout my being before my vision goes white.

Congratulations! You have learned the ability Haunted Earth. Cost: 100 mana. Roots spring forth from the earth, rooting your opponent in place for two seconds. Cooldown: 30 seconds.

Haunted Earth will really help me out when I'm facing monsters stronger than me. My biggest problem so far has been the hits I've taken. Now, I can root them in place and get in a few good hits before backing off. Still, I hope I get some more damage spells in the future.

The next morning, when I walk into the mines, Grayson does something he never does. He stops working. He grips my shoulder hard and looks intently in my eyes.

"You did it, kid."

I feel like he wants to say more, like there is something he's not telling me. His eyes dart away when Buzz comes clamoring down the tunnel.

"I finished watching all the highlights. You've got a lot of competition, no doubt about it, but I think you've got a real chance. A lot of them had just as much luck as you did, trying things that worked in other worlds. Some were just plain outright strong as hell and beat the zombies to a pulp. And Ryken had the unfair advantage of being the perfect role for that world."

When the bell rings for us to work, Buzz runs through details that might be of use going forward. He knows my opponents' strengths and weaknesses, what abilities they used, probably what they ate for breakfast. He will likely be my greatest asset going forward aside from my own skill. His desire for me to win is just as strong as my own.

I tell him about Merlin, my new spell, and the fight with the yeti.

"Oh, man, I've always wanted a pet. Can you imagine me riding a fire-breathing dragon? I would look so badass." He mimics riding a dragon through the tunnel.

When we break for lunch, I ask Grayson and Buzz for their advice about sponsors. Grayson is the first to answer.

"I'd think long and hard about it. Once you leave the mines, everything is on you. Food, water, electricity, a place to live. If your sponsorships fall through, if you don't make it to the next round and they drop you, what would you do then? Working here isn't the best thing, but at least you know you're taken care of as long as you go to work."

"Like they took care of my mom?" Buzz's voice shakes as he says it. Grayson and I sit in silence waiting for Buzz's next words. "You've got a real shot here, Esil. I know you're doing it for my mom and I love you for it, but this is bigger than her, you've got to see that. You're in a position to change your life forever. To never have to come back into this dirty mineshaft ever again.

"You don't owe anything to the mines. Or to me or Grayson. Hell, you don't owe anything to my mom if you don't want to. You owe it to yourself to get out of here. This is not something miners ever get a shot at. How many miners do you know who have ever made a name for themselves in the world?"

After Buzz speaks, the silence is so deafening that I hear a ringing in my ears. I know deep down that Buzz is right. If I don't take this chance now, I might not get another. I might end up like Grayson, swinging the pick every day and wondering what might have been.

"Goddammit," says Grayson, rubbing his eyes. "The boy's right."

"You should leave right now and get your sponsorship set up. Maybe you can get moved out by the end of the day if you're lucky. I'll keep researching and let you know if I find anything useful."

I'm almost out of the tunnel when I hear the shuffle of feet running to catch up. I expect to see Buzz, but it's Grayson.

"When you get settled into your new place, send me a message. There is something I want to show you."

CHAPTER EIGHTEEN

The next few days pass in a blur. I sign a contract with VR HaptiX for twenty thousand gold annually. It's enough money to buy me a small apartment in Civic City. The apartment has heat and air and hot running water. And the food, what a treat to not eat the processed mush I've been used to. Meals get delivered to me by drone and all I have to do is put them in a microwave. A few minutes later, they come out hot and delicious.

I never really knew how bad we had it in The Boxes until I got out here.

VR HaptiX sends me clothes with their logo. Living in Civic City, it's the first time in my life I've been able to freely leave and go outside. As long as I put on my mask, I can go anywhere I want. It scares me at first, the thought of just opening the door, but my apartment has a small sanitation room that fills with steam each time I enter and exit.

Part of me wonders what I'll do once this tournament

is over and I have more free time. I've never had a life before. How do I even go about being social?

Little by little, I explore the city. I don't have much time since I spend most of my days training, but for an hour a day, I walk my neighborhood. No one really speaks to me as I walk past, probably because of the masks we wear. What was the world like before all of this?

My new haptic suit is far nicer than the one I've been using. The control and immersion are so good that I notice almost no difference between my body movement in the game and in real life. The sensitivity of the feedback feels realistic when I rub my fingers together.

I log into my home portal, where Merlin stays when I'm not there. I bought him a perch and several dangly toys to keep himself occupied while I am away. As soon as I appear, he flies to my shoulder and nibbles at my ear.

Over the past few days, I have gained three more levels. I spread my new stat points into Agility, Vitality, and Intellect. My current stats are beginning to round out a little.

Level 18:
>   *Strength - 14*
>   *Agility - 2*
>   *Vitality - 3*
>   *Intellect - 6*
>   *Dexterity - 3*
>   *Stamina - 0*

· · ·

With all of my sponsorship's details finalized and my apartment set up, today is the first day I have with no constraints. I told the princess I might meet up with her later, but first, I promised Grayson I would message him when I was ready to see what he had to show me. I send him a message and a few minutes later, he responds.

Esil,

Glad to hear from you. Meet me at Pirate Bay this evening after I get off work.

-Grayson

The day passes by quickly as I explore a world inspired by old cartoons. Everything is flat and two-dimensional. Even my body is flat and when I turn my hands sideways, it looks like a piece of paper. The colors are bright, but with no shading or definition. Monsters crumble into balls of paper when defeated. I'm having such a fun time that I almost miss the alarm I set telling me Grayson is off work.

The portal to Pirate Bay lets me out onto a crowded pier. Merchants line the pier selling oysters, pearls, chests found on the bottom of the ocean, and much more. Dozens of ships float nearby at sea and others are tethered along one of the many docks. Each ship has a detailed flag hanging from the mast. Skulls, krakens, wolves, and a myriad of other colorful symbols blow in the wind. People carry boxes onto the ships, either preparing for a long voyage or quest.

Many of the people around me look weathered and dirty. Some are covered in tattoos. There are more dreadlocks than I have seen in my entire life. Large billowy shirts hang loose next to cutlasses, scimitars, and sabers.

A man with dark black hair waddles down the dock, a gun tucked into one side of his belt and a cutlass in the other. A large red parrot sits on his shoulder. The parrot squawks at me as he passes.

"Hello." The parrot's head bobs up and down.

"Hello," I reply.

"Hello," the parrot echoes again.

"Dumb bird," says the pirate. "Only knows one word." He moves in close, his golden eyes fixed on Merlin. "That's a nice owl you have there. I bet he knows when to shut up." With that, the pirate walks past me and disappears into the crowd.

I walk the pier, taking in its eclectic population. Merlin flies off my shoulder and perches upon the mast of a nearby ship. The pirates are a rowdy bunch; many of them drink rum and roll dice.

"Hey, you!" yells a man with a purple mohawk. He has a sparrow tattooed on one side of his head and an anchor on the other. "Fancy a game of dice?" Two men sit huddled next to him, a few gold coins on the worn pier.

It looks like a fun way to pass the time until Grayson arrives. "Sure, how do you play?" A wicked grin runs across the man's face and his two friends chuckle.

He picks up the gold off the dock. "It's one gold to play."

One gold is a lot for a single game. He must anticipate

taking my money. I place a gold coin on the dock and he and his two friends do the same.

"First person to roll a seven is the shooter." He hands me the dice and I toss it to the ground. I roll a six, and mohawk rolls an eight. The man next to him with dirty blond hair and gold teeth rolls snake eyes. The last man, who wears a green bandanna over his black hair, blows on the dice and rolls a seven.

"Now what?" I ask.

"Leo here is the shooter. It means he rolls the dice this round. He's going to make a bet and then we have to match it. How much are you betting, Leo?"

Leo rattles the dice in his palm. "I'm feeling lucky. Three gold."

"Now either we match it, or we lose the initial bet. So, you in for another gold?"

It doesn't really look like I have much choice. Either I pay another gold to play or I lose the gold I started with. I place another gold on the table. Mohawk and Blondie both put down a gold. Together, we have matched Leo's bet.

"If Leo rolls a seven or eleven, he wins the pot. If he rolls a two, three or twelve, the money is split up amongst us. If he rolls any other number, then that becomes his point. At that time, if he rolls the point, he wins, and if he rolls a seven, we win. Got it?"

It seems simple enough. It's just a game of probability. The first roll has the highest odds of winning or losing because there are five numbers to hit. And from then on out, only two numbers. Probability puts us all on the same playing field.

"Got it."

Leo rolls the dice and it lands on six. He mumbles something under his breath.

"Six is his point now. If he rolls it, he wins. Seven wins for us. Any other number means he rolls again. We can also take new bets on whether we think he will win or lose." Mohawk pulls a gold coin from his pocket and lets it roll across his fingers. "I think he will win. I'll bet one gold. What about you?"

"I bet one gold he loses," says a voice from behind me. "And if you try to load the dice with magic, I'll make sure he loses more than that."

I turn around and see Grayson as I have never seen him before. Not wearing his miner's clothes, he looks like a completely different man.

Grayson wears a white vest unbuttoned, exposing a roaring bear head tattooed on his chest. Several necklaces and amulets hang from his neck. A belt with a revolver sits on his hip. Two golden battle gauntlets cover his hands. His mustache curls up around the edges, almost forming a circle.

When I turn back around, the three men are no longer smiling. They seem concerned, almost worried.

"Just a friendly game of dice, Grayson."

Grayson doesn't look at me, but he places his gold coin with the others. I do the same. Leo rolls the dice and it clatters across the wood. A five. He rolls again and I can see the sweat beginning to form on his brow. A four. There's no doubt about it that they were going to hustle me. But why are they so nervous around Grayson?

It takes three more rolls before the dice hits seven. Leo is pissed, I can see it in his eyes, but he doesn't say anything. I'm up three gold from the exchange. Grayson doubles his money.

"You really ought to be careful who you get involved with, kid. Those three were going to use magic to hustle you out of your gold. By the time you knew what was happening, you would be down five to ten gold."

"Thanks for stepping in. Why were they so intimidated by you?" I ask.

"I have a bit of a history in these parts." He sets his face and looks out to sea. It's clear he doesn't want to talk about it.

"Nice threads, by the way. I never would have pegged you for a pirate."

"We all have lives outside of the mines, Esil. You know that." The necklaces he wears jingle as we walk down the pier.

Merlin swoops down from his perch and lands on my shoulder. He hoots a few times before quieting down. His head darts in many directions, taking in everything we pass.

"That's a smart bird," says Grayson. "I can see his vigilance."

"Where are we going?" There has to be a reason he brought me here in particular. He knows I need to train and level. Grayson wants me to win, so it has to be something he thinks will help me in my next quest.

"You'll see soon enough. How's life outside of The Boxes?"

I tell him about my new apartment and all the perks of being sponsored. He seems genuinely interested as we make our way out of the pier and onto a cobbled road that leads away from the nearby town.

"All Buzz does is talk about you and the quests since you've been gone. I've heard more about this damned tournament than I ever cared to."

I smile at that. "He's a good friend."

The cobbled roads turns to dirt and soon, we are far away from any other people. A dense jungle to my right rattles with the calls of thousands of insects. Sandy white beaches stretch for miles to my left. Waves roar as they crash, sending crabs scurrying back and forth as the tide retreats.

Further up the road, we come across a section where dozens of boulders, several stories high, litter the beach. The coastline here is rocky and the water that crashes against it is dark and turbulent. Several frogmen guard the boulders with spears.

Bullywug. Level 22. *These foul, amphibious creatures fight with poison and trickery.*

Grayson clinks his gauntlets together and they begin to glow a faint blue.

"They guard the entrance to a secret lair. I think it can help you if we can get there."

"Have you beaten it before?" I ask.

Grayson looks troubled when he answers.

"I tried, but there are aspects to it I haven't been able to overcome."

"No time like the present!" I switch to my elven spear. It seems like the most logical weapon to fight the bully-wugs with.

The bullywugs are half my size, but portly and angry. They have the bodies of frogs, but walk on their hind legs, holding wooden spears tipped with jagged rocks. My heightened eyesight allows me to see the liquid that coats the rocks. Poison. The largest of the bullywugs takes a defensive stance as we approach, his spear pointed in our direction.

"One more step and we will attack. You do not belong here." His voice is deep and throaty.

"That's too bad," says Grayson. He powers up his gauntlet and launches himself at the leader. His fist connects with the creature's midsection, sending it flying through the air. When it hits the ground, its HP bar is at zero.

"Holy—"

Before I can finish my expletive, dozens of darts come flying from behind the boulders. Several more bullywugs have joined the fight, using blowguns to shoot darts from far away.

"Don't let them hit you. The darts are poisoned," says Grayson. He's in the midst of the fray, sending punch after powerful punch to any frogman unlucky enough to be within his reach. His fists move with speed and preci-sion. And most of all, power.

I dodge the first volley of darts and move in closer. A bullywug croaks at me loudly and raises his spear to strike. Before the attack reaches me, I use Lunging Strike and stun him. Two hits later, he is dead.

A dart catches me in the arm and my vision goes red around the edges. Specks of green also dot my vision, letting me know I've been poisoned. I toss the dart to the ground and search for my attacker. The offending bullywag doesn't wait. He jumps at me, spear pointing down and aiming for my throat. I parry the blow and the frogman falls to the ground. My health continues to drop from the poisoned dart as he rises to his feet. He reaches into his pouch and pulls out another dart and shoots it. Not again. I spin my spear in my hands as fast as I can, like a windmill, and it catches the dart mid-flight, sending it rocketing into the ocean. He jumps at me and this time, I spear him right in the belly.

Grayson is surrounded on all sides. The bullywugs are vicious, but lack the attack of a well-trained unit. They attack at random, with no thought to taking Grayson off-guard. He parries each strike with his gauntlets, using them both as weapon and shield.

I cast Haunted Earth and roots rip through the sand, catching three bullywugs in their tangle. Next, I cast Resilience on Grayson and he attacks them in a flurry. I move up behind the others, killing them from behind.

The bodies of over a dozen frogmen lay on the sand.

"Wow. How'd you learn to fight like that?" I ask as we loot the bodies.

Item: Poisoned Dart. This dart is coated with a poison that drains 2% life per second for five seconds. *Stacks up to three times.*

"I think you know the answer." He picks up some gold coins and places them in his pouch.

My suspicions were right then. Grayson did find a Developer's Chest a long time ago.

"What next?"

He leads me between the boulders to a pool of water. The pool is clear and still, unlike the waves that crash on both sides of us. He pulls a green weed from his pocket and hands it to me.

"Eat this."

Substance: Magical Seaweed. Allows user to breathe underwater for 30 minutes.

Grayson and I both eat our seaweed. He dives into the pool and moments later, I join him. Merlin perches on the boulders, awaiting our return.

I hold my breath at first, afraid of drowning. When I can no longer hold my breath, my instincts give in and I take a mouthful of water into my lungs. I expect my haptic suit to clench around my chest and my vision to go red, but instead, my body calms. I rub my fingers across my skin and notice I have gills. I can also see clearly in the water with no blur.

It's amazing! Grayson swims ahead of me into the depths of the ocean and I receive a notification.

Grayson has invited you to a private chat. Do you accept? Y/N?

I focus on yes and I can hear Grayson's breathing in my ear.

"This is crazy," I say.

"It's a good time. Just be prepared for what comes next."

"What is it?"

"An aboleth."

I don't know what an aboleth is, but the name itself sounds sinister. I don't have to wait long to find out.

Aboleth. Level 35. Powerful tentacles and psionic attacks make this monster hard to handle. *The aboleth has sent many men to an early grave.*

A giant, tentacled monster waits for us. The monster has three large, glowing orange eyes. Its mouth is round, with a circle of sharp teeth. It's part fish, but the tentacles that hang by its side are strong and dangerous.

"Be careful," Grayson warns me. "It will try to get in your mind."

Right as he says the words, I feel an intense pressure in my head. I don't know if it is the haptic suit simulating or if the aboleth is actually finding its way into my head.

Grayson screams. "Get out!" His voice is full of rage and sadness.

In front of me, Grayson grabs at his head. He's curled up, unable to move. Whatever the aboleth is doing to him has him paralyzed. I need to stop it.

I switch to Grappler and fire a few beams at the creature. The rays cut through the water and hit the aboleth with small explosions. This is enough to distract it from Grayson. He uncurls and moves in quick, landing a hard, glowing fist into the monster's side. Its health drops by a chunk before it lets out a sonic scream that travels through the water and smashes into Grayson, slashing his health in half. It then smacks him in the side with a tentacle, dropping his health to twenty-five percent. Grayson goes limp in the water and drifts slowly to the bottom.

The creature turns its glowing eyes on me. I feel pressure building inside my head and then everything goes white.

Suddenly, I'm running through the grass. A big, black dog trots beside me. He licks at my hand. A man picks me up, hugs me, and then tosses me high into the air. I laugh, unable to control myself, and fall back into his arms.

"Again, Daddy. Again," I tell him.

He grabs me by the arms and spins me in a circle, my feet never touching the ground. His smile is warm and welcoming. His eyes are dark and powerful.

"I love you, Esil," he says.

We walk through the grass together. A woman stands on a porch. Flowers surround her. She hands the man I called daddy a glass of ice water and then bends down, kissing me on the head.

My vision goes white again and we're in a car, floating above the highway. The sky is blue like in Pangea. Hundreds of cars zoom around us. The man and woman hold hands across from me.

"I can't wait for you to see our new building, honey," he says to the woman. "It's state of the art. We're taking this company to the next level. Our family will be set for life."

The car swerves hard and we float off our designated route. It loses power and falls out of the sky. The woman screams. She's not wearing her seatbelt. Neither is the man. He tries to hold her. The car hits an embankment and I start crying. The car rolls several times, the man and woman smashing hard against the tempered glass. Blood stains the windows and seats. I keep crying.

When the car comes to a stop, they aren't moving.

"Snap out of it!" someone says.

"Dammit, Esil. Snap out of it." It's Grayson. He's screaming at me. He's also punching the aboleth and dodging the swing of its tentacles. He has a tenth of his HP, but he's not giving up. I can't shake the vision I just had. It felt so real. Was it? My entire life, as far back as I can remember, I've felt alone. In that vision, dream, whatever it was, I felt loved. Like I belonged.

I switch to my spear and move in close, casting Resilience on Grayson and watching his fists move in a flurry. The water glows and then begins to boil around his gauntlets with each punch he lands. I stab at the aboleth, drawing black blood that stains the water. I stab it in the eyes. All three of them. It hits me in the side with a tentacle and it feels like my ribs break. My visions goes a dark red. I can't breathe for a moment, but I keep stabbing. Soon, everything is black.

CHAPTER NINETEEN

The water clears and the aboleth lies lifeless on the seafloor. The vision, or dream, or whatever it was I just saw still echoes in my mind. The man. The woman. The crash. All of the blood.

A ding brings me back to reality and a silver nineteen flashes across my vision.

Grayson stands over the aboleth, looking down at its body.

"You did good, kid." His voice sounds strained in my ear. The last of the aboleth's black blood dissipates into the water.

"When that thing…when it got in your head, what did you see?" Grayson's posture is emblazoned in my mind. His huddled body bent over. His hands clutching at his head. The desperate plea for the aboleth to release his mind.

"My past."

"Was it real?" It felt more realistic than any dream I've ever had. There were feelings of…of what? Love?

"All too real," he grumbles. Does that mean that what I saw was real? Was that my family? Is that how I came to be at the orphanage?

"How does it know?"

"I don't know." He turns away from me. "Give me a moment to gather myself. Go ahead and loot the body."

I want to protest. I want answers, but Grayson was gracious enough to bring me here and he's been through a lot. I'll save my questions for later.

We loot the body and Grayson insists I take everything.

Currency: 12 gold

Item: Forgotten Chainmail. +12 armor. The relics of a ship lost at sea.

The chainmail shimmers, changing from dull green to dark blue, depending on the angle. The armor bonus is great.

Item: Staff of the Water Ancients. +20% magic damage on elemental attacks.

The beautiful blue staff has a large pearl attached at the end. It will make Haunted Earth hit a lot harder.

Substance x2: Blood of the Aboleth. Taking this substance blocks psionic attacks for 120 seconds.

This would have been incredibly useful just now. I add all the items to my inventory, excited to test them out later.

Off to the side, buried in the sand, the gold rim of a chest peeks into the water.

"That's the real prize," says Grayson. A little bit of life has returned to his voice. "Go on, open it."

I pull the chest from the sand.

Congratulations! You have found a buried treasure. Would you like to open it? Y/N

It's not a Developer's Chest, but I bet there is still something good inside. Why else have an aboleth guarding it? I focus on yes and the chest pops open. A bright light flashes and a scroll floats above me in the water.

Item: Spellbook. Requirements: Level 20. *Activate? Y/N*

I'm still one level away, but the aboleth gave enough xp that I'm already a third of the way to level twenty. If I grind a little more, I should be able to open it today.

"Do you know what it is?" I ask.

"No, but it's a new spell. I hope it can help you on your journey."

"I still need another level to open it. Thanks for all your help, Grayson."

He gives me a nod and then motions for us to surface. I want to ask him more about the aboleth. How many times has he tried to fight it? What is it he saw? How is it able to get inside our minds like that? But Grayson has put up a wall again. Whatever he saw has brought a darkness back to him.

Back on the beach, Merlin flies to my shoulder and pecks at my ear.

"I know you have things to do, but there is one more thing I want to show you, if you have time."

We walk in silence along the dirt road. Occasionally, groups of bullywugs poke out from behind boulders or trees, but we don't engage them. The scenery as we walk is absolutely beautiful. Blue skies abound for miles and miles. Dolphins jump through the water. The bright yellow sun bathes everything in light. With my enhanced hearing, I can hear the caw of seagulls far out in the ocean and the crash of waves down on the beach. A battle rages deep in the jungle to my left and I hear the last cry of a monster before it is defeated. Closer, though, is the huff of Grayson's breath as we walk along.

Eventually, the pristine beaches turn into a rocky coastline. The sands disappear and are replaced by sharp, jagged rocks that engage in constant battle with the crashing waves. Several rocks jut high into the air, earthen towers that cast shadows across the land from the setting sun. It's a place of beauty and pain. Fitting that this is where Grayson stops walking.

He leads me from the road towards the coastline. I didn't notice before, but our elevation has changed. The rocky coastline is high above the sea. It's a deadly drop to the raging waters below.

The wind picks up the closer we walk to the edge. My tunic ripples across my body like the flaps of a sail.

"Down here." Grayson points to a set of stairs carved into the rock. They lead down to the water.

I follow him and the wind continues to pummel me. The spray of saltwater coats my body until I am soaked once again. Merlin offers me an agitated hoot and tucks his head in his wings.

Midway down the cliff, the steps lead into a tunnel. A torch burns on the wall. Grayson lifts it and marches into the darkness. Is this another quest? A dungeon?

I hear a humming noise as we walk along, coming from the end of the tunnel. When he finally stops walking, we're in a cavern deep underground. There's a bubbling pool in the center. It must connect to the ocean through an underground tunnel. Several mermaids sit

along its edge, singing softly in a language I can't understand. It's beautiful though, the way their voices dance
and echo along the cave walls.

Grayson takes a seat along the edge, opposite of the
mermaids, and dips his feet in the water. I take off my
boots and sit beside him. The warm water bubbles around
my feet.

"What is this place?" I ask.

"I found out about it long ago. I think you're smart
enough to know I found a Developer's Chest similar to
yours once upon a time. It wasn't quite as nice as the one
you found, but it was good. I had a great time those first
few months. I wanted to be a great warrior in those days,
so I traveled far and wide looking for monsters to fight.
One day, I came upon this place. I told my wife about it
and brought her here. She loved it. We would sit for hours
listening to the songs of the mermaids. There aren't many
monsters this far up, so no one journeys here often. It was
our little secret."

"What happened to her?"

Grayson stares into the bubbling depths of the water.

"She died. Same thing as Buzz's mom. When she got
sick, I wanted to get her treatment, but we didn't have the
money. I started questing harder than ever before. Every
minute I wasn't in the mines, I was out in some world
fighting monsters and clearing dungeons for gold. I spent
more time leveling up than I did with my dying wife. She
died one day while I was out on a quest, completely alone.
I spent so much time trying to save her that I missed out
on her life." Grayson kicks his feet in the water, making
small splashes. His eyes are misty as he stares out at nothing. "Now I come here and sit by myself for hours and

sometimes, I can hear my wife's voice bouncing off the walls when the mermaids sing."

I reach out and grab Grayson on the top of his hand and squeeze. Just like everyone else in the mines, he has lost so much.

"I'm sorry. Is that what you saw at the aboleth?"

"Yes. Every time, I see her happy face turn to death before my eyes and know that I'm the cause. The sad thing is that I've kept going back all these years because at least for a few moments, I'm able to see her face more clearly than in my own memories."

I don't know the right words to say, but I speak from the heart.

"You can't keep holding on to that guilt. You did what you thought was best at the time and you can't change that. I'm sure your wife wouldn't blame you for what happened. We got a shitty lot in life. But you know what? At least you still have those memories of you two together in this cave. You will always have those."

I don't know what it's like to lose the one you love. It must be hard, especially to miss out on their final days while trying to save them. Grayson is a good man with good intentions. He deserves better than to wallow in his own self-pity.

"Why did you bring me here?" I ask. As beautiful and serene as this place is, there has to be more to it.

"I guess I just wanted to tell someone about Laura. And also to see where your head is at. Do you have a goal in life that is bigger than this contest? When it's all said and done, do you know what you want to do after it's over?"

"Honestly, I don't know. All I know right now is that

Buzz's mom's life depends on how well I do in this tournament. I'll figure out the rest when the time comes."

We spend the next hour or so beating down bullywugs and other local monsters. Once I hit level twenty, I immediately open my new spellbook.

Congratulations! You have learned the ability Waterfall. Cost: 200 mana. After a 2 second wait, water pours down from the sky, dealing immense damage to a singular location. Cooldown: 20 seconds.

Hell yeah! Finally, a pure damage-based ability. It'll take a little bit of strategy and guesswork for it to land, but when it does, the damage will be great. The bonus twenty percent damage from Staff of the Water Ancients will give it a heck of a punch. I put the two stat points I have from leveling up into Dexterity. The quicker I can cast my abilities, the better.

Grayson gives me a hug before leaving. It's late and he has work tomorrow. For me, though, this tournament is my life right now. I can still go for a few more hours before I need to rest. I go to my messages and reach out to the princess.

CHAPTER TWENTY

Water pours down from the sky, drenching the hill giant in the powerful stream of the waterfall. Its HP drains to zero and the giant collapses to the ground.

"Nice job, Esil," Aleesia congratulates me. My newest ability, Waterfall, does a boatload of damage. It's the only purely offensive magical ability I have right now and I can't wait for more.

The princess, along with Glordin, Ordin, Klink, and Tinker, have spent the last few hours grinding levels across the hills to the south of the Mortican Mountains. They all love this world just as much as I do, so we spend most of our time here while we wait for the next tournament clue.

My magic is a lot stronger now that I have Staff of the Water Ancients, but my mana pool isn't big enough for me to cast more than five or six abilities per battle. When I have time to rest, it's fine, but in the next stage of the tournament, it could cost me. I pick up the loot from the hill giant and add it to my inventory.

Currency: 5 gold

Item: Stone Club. +7 damage. "*Grunt softly and carry a big club.*"

Item: Benevolent Shield of Healing. +10% health. Unique ability: Double-edged shield. The next attack will be blocked and heal both attacker and defender for 5% health. Cooldown: 5 minutes.

Not a bad haul. I'm still lacking in the defense department and a good shield will really help out. I'll need to be careful with this one, though. If my opponent has more overall HP than me, I could put myself in quite the hole if I use it at the wrong time. The bonus health is a godsend, considering my lack of HP.

It's been almost a week since the first quest of the tournament, which means we should be hearing about the second quest any day now. I'm both nervous and excited at the prospect. For the most part, I've put the thoughts about my vision with the aboleth in the back of my mind. I need my entire focus on the quest, not on what might have been. If there is any truth to what I saw, there will be time for that when the tournament is over.

More giants clamor over the nearest hill. Tinker takes the lead. His gray beard blows in the wind. Even though he is old, he still has that aura of dwarvish power. He raises his staff into the air towards the giants. The blue stone on the tip glows for a moment before he brings the staff down hard to the ground. The earth rumbles for a second and I can feel it shaking beneath my feet. Then a crack opens where the staff hit and shoots out towards the hill giants, ripping the earth apart. When the canyon reaches them, rocks shoot forth and sends the giants flying into the air, taking out a chunk of their health.

Tinker gives a smirk to Ordin, who steps forward for the next attack.

Ordin strokes his red beard for a moment.

"Not bad," he mumbles.

Ordin grips his warhammer tightly. The gash in the earth has sealed itself from Tinker's attack and the hill giants roar and beat their chests, ready for revenge. Ordin's warhammer catches the light and shimmers in his hand. For a moment, Ordin doesn't move as the giants approach. He looks frozen in time. Then his warhammer glows, faint at first, then brighter until it is almost too bright to look at.

The giants are almost on him when he lifts his weapon over his head, ready to attack. The hill giant swings his club at the same time as Ordin and they meet in a violent clash of light and thunder. It's hard to see anything other than the light of their impact. A thousand splinters rain down around us.

When the light clears and we can see again, Ordin is on one knee, his warhammer halfway sunken into the earth. The bodies of three hill giants lay lifeless around him.

"Meh," scoffs Tinker. "I warmed them up for you."

"Boys…" says Klink, rolling her eyes.

Tension is high for a moment until the princess laughs. Her melodic voice causes them both to smile. I wonder if there is added tension in the group since only Ordin and Klink made it through to the next round. I remember the first time I met the princess, there were nearly a dozen dwarves. Since the first quest though, I've only seen these four. Where have the others gone? I want to ask, but I don't want to intrude.

"Where to next, Esil?" she asks me.

We've been using Merlin's Flyby ability to find the best places for leveling. The five of them surround me, each facing a different direction to protect me from attack while I merge my perception with Merlin.

From high in the sky, I can see our bodies on the ground like small ants. Far to the west is the town square. The Mortican Mountains themselves lie to the north. Several fishermen sit along the banks of a nearby stream, fishing for their dinner or perhaps to sell at the market. A lone harpy waits under a tree for her next victim. A group of giants pull trees from the earth a mile from where we stand and take turns throwing them, testing their strength. They are all around level forty, easy enough for us to tackle as a group.

I return to my body and tell them where our next battle is waiting. Aleesia walks beside me along the way. She wears cream-colored pants and a flowy blue top. How many outfits does she have? I don't think I've ever seen her wear the same thing twice. Considering how much my pants and tunic cost, her closet must be worth a small fortune.

"How's your friend's mom doing?" she asks. I've confided in her my real reason for entering the tournament. I'm not looking for pity or a handout, but the more time we've spent together, the easier it has become for me to talk to her.

"About the same, I suppose. She has medicine for the pain, but there is not much else she can do at the moment."

I haven't talked to Buzz much since moving out on my own. I get the occasional message telling me his thoughts on the tournament or any big happenings with the other contestants, but not much more than that. I know he spends a lot of time exploring worlds when he's not working or researching. With getting settled in, grinding, and the quest with Grayson, there just hasn't been much time for me to reach out. I need to make time for him soon. Maybe we can go smash some steam-powered robots or something.

The red dot in the side of my vision reminds me I'm being watched. Part of my sponsorship stipulates that I have to stream for at least an hour a day to be in good standing. I try not to talk much about Buzz's mom or my reasons for entering the tournament while streaming. Occasionally, things slip out. I don't think anyone knows that I'm a miner. Or was a miner, rather. It's still hard for me to truly believe that this is my life now. I often get messages asking me how I attack so hard, but I don't respond. I've been trying to get better with my spells so that they eventually even out with each other. My strength is a blessing, but Grayson is right. I can't rely on it solely.

Below the red dot, there is a ticker that tells me how many people are watching my stream at any given time. I have several thousand fans that log in to watch me every time I play. They must like the quiet underdog I've been labeled as. The wolf head belt buckle I wear has some calling me The Lone Wolf. I supposed as far as nicknames go, it's not so bad. I don't talk a lot as I stream, usually letting my actions take the stage. There are a few trolls here and there that send me rude messages, but I try to ignore them and carry on as best I can. Sometimes viewers from rival streams will follow along and talk shit for the duration of my stream. Ryken has a particularly nasty brand of followers who like to give death threats. The princess even has a few who get jealous when we are together. For the most part, I carry along as I would normally.

I can see the outline of the giants in the distance when a system message pops across my vision.

Greetings, Esil! Congratulations on making it through the first round of the Developer's Tournament. The fun is just getting started. The next quest will be taking place in one week. Here is a clue to help you on your way:

Faster, farther, further still.
   Daunting, dangerous, blood can spill.
   Tortoise, hare, whichever way;
   Succeed and quest another day.

Best of luck and as always, never stop leveling!
   -Pangea Online Developers

Moments after the message comes through, my viewers nearly triple. Everyone wants to know what my next move is.

"What do you think it means?" asks Aleesia. She doesn't question if I received a message. The way Ordin, Klink, and I all stopped walking at the same time was the only signal she needed.

"Some kind of journey?" I'm not sure what to make of it. I'll need to talk to Buzz as soon as I can. He has lived and breathed this tournament just as much as any of us still in it.

"Yeah, but it doesn't give any clue as to the location. Does that mean they will tell us where it is? And how is this supposed to prepare us for what comes next? Do you have any ideas?" she asks the dwarves.

I don't know what it means, but it all has meaning. Every single word is a clue. Blood can spill, tortoise, hare. All of it means something. I need to logout and clear my head.

"I need to go. I need to think about this on my own for a bit. Do you want to meet up tomorrow and discuss whatever we find out?"

We agree to meet in the morning. I call Merlin back and clasp each of my companions around the forearm in turn before teleporting back to the town square.

CHAPTER TWENTY-ONE

Buzz is talking so fast I can barely keep up with what he is saying. His hands move animatedly on the video screen in the top left corner of my vision. Merlin flies in quick circles around my home portal, all of the excitement making him antsy.

"'Blood can spill,' it has to mean it's going to be PvP," he says with a sigh. He knows as well as I that that would be bad news.

Player versus player is not something I'm looking forward to if that is how it goes down. I may have my strength bonus that no one else knows about, but I'm still way under-leveled in every other aspect of the game. At level twenty, I'm the lowest level by fifteen. Most of the other competitors are at least level fifty. PvP will be bad for me.

"But I don't think it is just a battle," he goes on. "It's some kind of journey. It sounds like all you have to do is make it through to go to the next round. Maybe if you die, you're out and if you complete it, you're through. I don't know. Could mean a hundred other things, but that's what is jumping out to me. I need to research more on the tortoise and hare and see if there is any significance there." He scratches his head, as if trying to remember some obsolete fact he learned long ago.

"Yeah, that's what I'm thinking too. It sounds like there might be some kind of bonus to completing it quicker than others, though."

"How are you feeling about all of this? Grayson told me about your quest yesterday."

"Oh, man. Grayson fights like a beast. He has these awesome gauntlets and just punches things till they die, but his outfit, he looks like he belongs on the cover of a romance novel." We both laugh. I really miss hanging out with Buzz for hours on end in the mines. It was boring, monotonous work, but we had a good time. I have more freedom now, but I miss my friend. I guess there is a cost to everything. "I don't really know what to tell you, Buzz. I'm nervous. I'm sure we all are since we don't know what is coming next. I don't care if I'm first or last, just as long as I make it through."

"We'll get you there." He winks. "You've got two of the best minds in the game on your side."

"I'll be glad to finally meet them one day," I tease.

"Yeah, yeah. See you later, bud."

"See ya." Buzz disappears from my vision and I'm left alone with Merlin in my drab, gray home portal. I should spruce the place up a bit, but what's the point? I spend most of my time out in the game worlds. I can't justify the money for something I don't need.

"Maybe when this is all over," I tell Merlin. He quits his

erratic flying and lands on my shoulder. His soft hoots are the only sound I hear aside from my breathing.

I log out and decide to go for a walk. It only takes a minute for me to scarf down a few energy bars and vitamin drink. I put on the clothes my sponsor sent me: a pair of sweatpants, sneakers, and a hoodie with the VR Haptix logo on the chest. There's no need to wear the contamination suit that I wore when I left The Boxes to take Buzz's mom to the doctor. Out here, a filter mask is all I need. I strap it on and step into the entry room for my apartment. The door slides closed and steam hisses out, filling the room. A few seconds later, the door opens and I step outside.

It's a nice evening out. The air is cool on my hands and the setting sun tints the edges of the gray sky with pink and yellow. I live in a busier part of Civic City, where people are always walking about. The strange thing is that no one ever talks. There is the shuffle of feet and the occasional blare of a car horn, but people don't speak until they are inside the buildings and able to remove their masks.

The silence is very eerie at times.

My favorite place to walk to is a park a few blocks from my apartment. Several benches surround a small pond. A few bright orange fish swim underneath the water. It's peaceful to watch them swim back and forth as the water gurgles from the makeshift waterfall that spills a constant stream into the pond. A turtle with two heads sits on a log floating in the middle.

The animals have paid the same price as everyone else.

I close my eyes and let the words of the quest run

through my head over and over until they no longer sound real.

Faster, farther, further still.
Daunting, dangerous, blood can spill.
Tortoise, hare, whichever way;
Succeed and quest another day.

What does it mean by 'tortoise, hare, whichever way?' I don't know why, but I feel like that is the key. They are both animals, but very different. Whatever connection they have, I'm not seeing it. One is a mammal, the other a reptile. One is fast, the other slow.

Wait! A memory reaches out from the back of my mind. It's fuzzy at first, but slowly comes into focus. I'm lying in bed, but I'm not at the orphanage. Bright blue walls with clouds painted on them surround me. Soft, warm blankets cover me and a lamp glows from a table beside the bed. I cling tightly to a stuffed wolf. A woman comes in, the same woman from the vision with the aboleth. She carries a book with a turtle and rabbit on the cover. It's ragged around the edges.

"My mother used to read this book to me all the time when I was your age," she says. "It's been in our family for a hundred years." Her smile is warm and welcoming as she sits down on the bed next to me and opens the book.

More pieces slowly fall into place. I remember the story of the tortoise and the hare. Of how they had a race and the hare was so far ahead that he took a nap midway through it. The tortoise kept going, slow and steady, and eventually passed the hare and won the race.

I suddenly know what the next quest will be.

It's going to be a race. And as long as I finish, I'll be

through to the next round. If I'm going to have a chance, I'll need to find a mount.

I sit up from the bench so fast that a lady nearby screams. Right now, I don't care if the memory is real or not. I need to get home.

My lungs burn and my breath fogs up the inside of my filtration mask as I run home as fast as I can. I need to tell Buzz and the others what I know.

It feels like a lifetime as I wait for the door to close and the steam to fill the room, flushing out the air from outside. When the door finally opens, I'm already naked and slip into my haptic suit faster than I ever have. I touch my fingers together, my vision goes black and then I'm in my portal.

I send Buzz a message while I simultaneously try to video chat with him. He doesn't answer, which I expected. He probably had to power up his box or check on his mom.

Aleesia answers after a few seconds and her beautiful face smiles at me from the corner of my vision.

"It's a race!" I blurt out.

"We know," she says calmly.

"What do you mean, you know?" I ask. How could they have possibly figured it out so quick?

"If you would have stayed around for another five seconds, Tinker was able to puzzle it out. His mom used to read him a book called Aesop's Fables every night before bed when he was a child. We think it's going to be some kind of PvP race. Looks like we are all finally going to have get mounts. Well, I mean I guess you don't have to, but it'll be a heck of a long race if you're on foot and everyone else is riding something."

Damn. I thought I had made a breakthrough, but it turns out anyone with a halfway decent family probably heard that story a hundred times. All one hundred of us still in the tournament should have the riddle solved by now. What is the point of making it so easy? Do they think that by letting people know, it will make the race itself more competitive?

"Cheer up, buttercup." She smiles at me. "You can come with us while we get our mounts. I'm going for a unicorn."

"That's kind of lame, don't you think?" She doesn't strike me as the girl who rides a unicorn with a rainbow tail.

"Typical. Everyone thinks that unicorns are so stupid because a bunch of little girls associate them with clouds and rainbows. Unicorns are badass. It's a horse with horn coming out of its head. They are powerful, smart, and incredibly lucky. Just you wait. You'll be impressed."

I can't help but smile at her enthusiasm.

"What about you? What kind of mount do you want?" she asks.

"Haven't had much time to think about it. I don't even know where to find one. Where are you going to get yours?"

"I'll probably buy mine." Her head drops a little. Is she ashamed to tell me? How much can a mount cost? "But if you can't afford one, then there are always quests you can do to find what you want."

I meet up with the princess, Ordin, and Klink. Glordin and Tinker have no immediate need for a mount so they decide not to come. Her merry band of dwarves grows smaller by the day.

We stand at an auction block in the Mortican Mountains town square. It's a dual world auction, meaning that people in other gameworlds will be seeing the same items as they appear on the stage in front of us. A small gnome stands on a wooden block, attempting to gather everyone's attention.

"Listen up! Listen up!" he yells to no avail. The marketplace is crowded. Apparently, word spread fast that mounts were in demand and all the local sellers showed up with their best wares.

A mist appears around the gnome and then suddenly his voice booms across the market.

"Attention!" The crowd hushes at his suddenly powerful voice. "Today is a special occasion. As most of you know, the clue for the second quest in the Developer's Tournament went live earlier today. It didn't take long for the clue to be deciphered. Due to the extraordinary circumstances, the Guild for the Sale and Development of Extraordinary Mounts and Vehicles has called a special auction to help those more well-endowed gain a foot up in the tournament." His lips curl at the edge after he speaks. This is nothing more than a money grab. Rich merchants raising the prices of mounts while those of us with little money get left behind.

"Everyone, hold onto your wallets," the gnome continues. "We have a lot of great items to get through, but first, we have five very unique mounts that might interest our higher bidders. These five mounts are one of a kind with each including a special ability only viewable to the owner upon purchase. Get ready, the bidding will start in five minutes."

"How much does a mount go for?" I ask. I haven't seen

that many in game and I've never actually seen where they sell them.

"It depends. A basic model might go for five hundred gold. Better versions cost more."

Five hundred gold! Holy shit. Maybe this tournament is designed as a plaything for the rich. If you need a thousand gold just to enter, what chance do I have in the next quest even if I do make it through this one?

The crowd chatters while we wait for the first auction item. I can see the greed in their eyes as they look around. Everyone here has money and lots of it. Everyone except me.

A hush falls over the crowd when an armored bear appears on the stage. The bear thrusts its head back and roars at the crowd. It has been outfitted with a saddle and glittering armor plating. The bear is a great mount, not only can one ride it, but it can also fight.

"Let's start the bidding at two thousand gold."

A wooden sign appears in the air above the bear. $2000 is painted on it in blue. Ordin raises his hand for the opening bid, but the sign quickly changes to $3000 and then $4000. He grunts and then walks away, mumbling something under his breath. Over the next minute, the price rises to nine thousand. Almost half of what I make in a year. More than I would make in a lifetime in the mines.

The bear finally sells for eleven thousand gold. I almost walk away from the auction. My time could be used better elsewhere.

The next item to sell is a motorcycle. The motorcycle has guns mounted to the handlebars and tires that flip in and hover. It wouldn't work in every world, but it still sells for seven thousand.

I wish I had gold for the next mount that comes up. A white wolf with bright blue eyes paces across the stage. Its sleek white fur is both beautiful and intimidating. The sun reflects off the brightness of its clean fur, making it hard to watch for too long. I can imagine it coming out of the snow, teeth bared, ready to rip an opponent apart. I have no idea what its special ability could be, but it sells for eight thousand.

"Oh, get ready!" squeals Aleesia. "This is the one I want."

"Best of luck, princess," says Klink.

I'm taken aback by how fierce the unicorn looks. Its hair is a dark gray and the horn that points out of its head is golden. It gleams in the sunlight. The creature looks anything but silly. It paws the stage and flares its nostrils. I could see a great warrior riding it into battle. The unicorn is a very fitting mount for the princess, elegant and powerful.

The bidding starts at two thousand and Aleesia raises her hand. She's outbid, but doesn't take her hand down. In a matter of seconds, the bid is at ten thousand gold. Someone else wants the mount just as much as her. Whoever it is, they're bidding from a different world, because she is the only one with her hand raised here.

For a moment, it looks like she's won the unicorn, but just as the bid is about to lock in, someone bids fifteen thousand gold.

Aleesia's hand doesn't falter for a second. How much money does her family have?

Sixteen thousand.

Seventeen thousand.

Twenty thousand.

Twenty-two thousand.

All eyes are on Aleesia now. No one even cares about the unicorn. They want to know how high will she go.

"Twenty-five thousand," she calls. More than I make in a year.

"Sold," yells the gnome and the princess jumps in the air. All the seriousness has left her face. The crowd claps and cheers at her winning bid.

"Wow," I say. I can't imagine what it would be like to just know that you could have whatever you want. There was a confidence about her that she knew no matter how high the price went, it would be hers.

"What?" she asks, her eyes sheepish.

"That was intense. You think that unicorn was worth that much?"

"Maybe. Maybe not. I guess we'll see next round. Oh wow, look at that." She points to the mount that has just taken the stage.

Another horse, except this one is black with a fiery mane, tail, and hooves. Fire explodes from its nostrils as it neighs at the crowd. The beast has a temper, that's for sure.

"This nightmare is the last of our unique mounts. Let's start the bidding at two thousand."

"You have got to be kidding me!" roars Klink, her fists clenched. "A bloody nightmare! What chance do any of us have against that thing?"

"What do you mean?" I've never even heard of a nightmare.

"They're one of the fastest mounts in the game. And

extremely rare. Only a character with an evil alignment can ride one."

While I listen to Klink rant, the price soars to fifteen thousand. No one in the crowd has bid on it, which means that someone in another world wants it really bad.

It sells at seventeen thousand.

The rest of the bids go on for a while. Ordin finally returns and buys himself a sturdy pony for a few hundred gold. It's not fast, but it's tough. Klink ends up buying some weird lizard creature that looks like a dragon without wings. It thrashes about violently as she attempts to ride it, continuously throwing her to the ground.

"I think I've made a mistake," she groans and we all laugh.

I don't buy anything.

I hang out with the princess and dwarves outside the city gates while they test out their mounts. The unicorn the princess rides is extremely fast. It bonds to her quickly. Klink, on the other hand, is tossed to the ground several times.

My message icon blinks and I see a message from Buzz.

Esil,

Sorry I missed your call, had to take care of mom. It looks like a lot has happened while I was gone. Those five exclusive mounts are bad news, but I think I might know of a place where we can find you one of your own. It'll be a long night, but if you can meet me in Asgard in an hour, I have an idea.

-Buzz

CHAPTER TWENTY-TWO

You are now entering Asgard, one of the nine worlds of Norse mythology. This is a non-technological world. All electronics have been disabled upon entering Asgard.

"How in the hell do you have a pass to Asgard?" I ask Buzz. It's not included with the basic Worldpass that I bought him. Something strange is going on.

His appearance has changed since we last quested together. He no longer wears the pinstriped steampunk clothes from Steamworld. Instead, he wears a black tunic, red pants, and a dented battle helm. He carries a large shield that could block his entire body. A black wolf is engraved in the heavy metal. A black leather cape hangs from his shoulders.

"I had a quest," he says. "Never thought I would be able to beat it on my own, so I might as well try it with you. I decided to become a tank, too. Well, a tank-mage. All those points I put into Intellect are paying off. Not to mention I still hit like a truck. I traded in all the items and clothes you bought me for some simpler but more durable items. You'd be surprised the type of shield I got for what you paid for Firebreather. I hope you aren't mad." His normal smile is gone, replaced with a look of concern. When I focus on Buzz, I can see he is now level twelve. He's been busy.

"Those were gifts. You can do whatever you want with them as long as you're happy. Now, do you want to enlighten me on why we're here?" Merlin hops from my shoulder and lands on Buzz's shield.

Buzz's smile returns and his face lights up with excitement.

"Okay, so, you know the basic Worldpass you got me allows me to travel to Midgard, the Old Norse version of Earth. Well, one day I was out trying to level up and I came upon this wolf pack. I could have killed them easily, but there was something about them, I can't quite explain it, that made me not. Probably because there was a runt with the pack. So I watched them. I sat and watched them for hours until they got up and left. Then I followed them into a cave. By not killing them, I had created an alliance with the wolves. They vowed to protect me whenever possible and asked me if I could help save their leader, Fenrir."

"Did you?"

"Did I what? Save him? God no. I would die in a heartbeat. They keep him chained in a dungeon in the heart of Asgard. Apparently, he's a total badass. He is bound in a magical chain because the gods fear that his release will bring upon Ragnarok. Basically, it's the end of their world. We'd need a whole team to make it through to him."

"I don't see how me coming here helps then. We're just two people." I don't have the money to buy a nice mount or the stats to unlock a good one. I guess I'll be stuck riding a pony or walking on foot.

"I wouldn't be so sure about that." Buzz smirks.

Right as he says it, I hear a commotion coming from the portal behind me. Grayson appears, wearing his pirate wardrobe. His necklaces jingle as he steps up to my side and grips me hard on the shoulder. Next, the princess emerges from the portal, followed by Ordin, Klink, Glordin and Tinker. Aleesia walks up to me and gives me a kiss on the cheek. She is dressed for battle, wearing a tight blue tunic. Silver bracers run down her forearms. My face burns when her lips touch my skin.

"It's time to pay you back for helping me clear that dungeon."

"You have helped us all at one time or another," says Ordin. He beats his warhammer softly against his chest, showing his allegiance. His intense stare matches the fire of his beard.

"What are all of you doing here?" I ask. None of these people owe me anything. I can understand Buzz and Grayson wanting to help, but the others, half of them have their own quest to prepare for.

"I messaged them as soon as you told me you needed a mount," says Buzz, "and they all agreed to help. No strings attached. You've got more friends than you think you do, Esil."

The city of Asgard stands before us. Carved out of stone,

the city is an elegant maze of towers and pillars that grow higher and higher into a center pillar that stretches above the clouds. Getting into the center of that city is going to take a lot of work. I hope we all have a few tricks up our sleeves.

You have been offered to help with the quest "Rescue Fenrir," do you accept? Y/N

I accept and a blue dot appears on my map. At least we know where he is. The only problem is getting there.

The gates to the city are about a mile away. Several other players walk around us, coming and going. Aside from Grayson, the rest of us look like we belong here, but even he isn't that out of place.

We walk at a brisk pace.

"What do you do with your mounts when you're not riding them?" I ask no one in particular.

The princess answers, "I'm not sure how it works, but whenever you don't need them, they just disappear into your inventory. They don't weigh you down either, which is convenient."

"Not that I'll ever master riding the bloody thing," murmurs Klink. "Whatever I was thinking buying a basilisk is beyond me." She kicks her feet against the ground, sending a cloud of dust into the air.

"A basilisk? Don't they turn you to stone if you look them in the eye?" I ask. Seems like a dangerous beast to have, especially when you can't control it.

"Mine is blind. That's why I got such a good deal on it. Figured I could guide it myself, turns out to be more work than it's worth."

Buzz leads the way up ahead. Merlin still rides on his shield. I like Buzz's new identity, I think it suits the man he has become. He's still the goofy guy I remember, but he takes things more seriously.

"This'll be fun." Aleesia walks close beside me. The memory of her kiss causes my face to grow hot.

"Yeah, thanks for helping." I try to sound nonchalant as I say it, but I fail miserably. As much as I like her, I know we could never be a couple. We are just too different. She comes from a world so far from mine that it might as well be another planet.

We pass by a group engaged in raucous laughter. One of the men has long blond hair and holds a small hammer in his hand. He is making small bolts of lightning jump out at a large green hulk of a man in front of him. The green man doesn't seem to notice he's a lightning rod. Their companion, who is as wide as he is tall, holds a keg of beer in one hand, letting it pour into his mouth and down his red beard. Merlin eyes them suspiciously as we walk by.

Inside the gates of Asgard, this city is alive with laughter, fighting, and games. Men drink and wrestle at roadside taverns. Everyone seems to be having a good time. I wish I had that sense of mirth right now. Instead, I'm worried about finding a mount for a quest that could be happening as soon as tomorrow. It's the uncertainty of it all that makes me anxious. Give me something I can fight and I'll beat it down as best I can, but not knowing, that's when my imagination runs wild.

"This way." Buzz motions. I look at my map. He is leading us away from the where the wolf is.

"What do you mean? The wolf is located straight ahead."

"You think you're just going to walk straight in and take it. Come on, Esil." He shakes his head at me.

I see a small, ragged, gray wolf disappear around a corner.

"Are these wolves seriously leading us to the quest?" asks Glordin. His battleaxe hangs from his side and his black hair is pulled into a bushy braid.

"What can I say? They like me," says Buzz. I can't help but smile. Only Buzz could befriend an entire species.

We follow the wolf down a narrow alleyway. High walls block out the sun, casting the alley in a dark shadow. It is late evening and soon the city will be shrouded in darkness.

The wolf leads us for what feels like an hour. We twist and turn from one street to another as we wind our way closer to the city's center.

The wolf looks back at us before turning the next corner. When we catch up, it has disappeared. All that stands before us is the high wall of the castle.

"What the hell?" rumbles Grayson. "We're at a dead end."

"Not quite," says Buzz. "Help me lift this sewage grate."

Hidden in the pavement, designed to look like stones, is a sewage grate that leads down into the underbelly of the city. Buzz, Grayson, and Ordin lift and the heavy metal slides to the side.

"Since we're doing this for you, you can go first." Buzz smirks.

"My pleasure." I focus on Merlin and he flies up to the castle wall. He's much more useful up there as a lookout than in the cramped pipes of an underground sewer.

I climb down a ladder attached to the stone wall into

the sewer. When I hop off, I land with a splash in the wet underbelly of the city. Everything is dark except for the stream of light from the alley. We'll need a way to see if we have any shot at finding our way through here.

Grayson is the next to join me. Soon, we're all inside.

"Anyone have a light?" asks Klink. With the grate pulled back overhead, there is even less light than before. I can barely make out the outlines of their faces.

I hear movement and then the entire tunnel is lit in a blaze of light.

Buzz holds a fireball in his free hand. He takes the fire and rubs it around the edges of his shield. It stays in place and soon his entire shield is a burning beacon.

"What the hell is that?" I ask.

"Liquid fire. Pretty neat spell I learned. It doesn't do damage, but when I coat my body in it at night in the Haunted Forest, I look badass! It also lets me craft torches and whatnot, but that's beside the point."

A pair of glowing eyes appear down the tunnel.

"Looks like we have our first challenge."

A black, hairy beast inches its way towards us, clicking its teeth together.

Giant Rat. Level 35. *Rats are the plague of humanity. Giant Rats, however, are a plague for the gods.*

It makes a chittering sound and then several more pairs of eyes glow behind it.

Four rats stand in our way.

Four big, ugly, deadly rats.

Aleesia is the first to attack. She is our only ranged physical combatant, so it's up to her to lure them in our direction. Tinker and I can both cast ranged spells, but I'd rather not waste our mana so early in this quest, not knowing what lies ahead.

"Let's try to handle them without using our mana if we can," I tell the group.

Grayson clinks his gauntlets together and steps toward the first rat. Ordin, Glordin, and Klink are right behind him.

Grayson connects with a vicious right hook and the first rat stumbles. Its health drops by half. The shocked looks on everyone else's faces tell me they didn't expect him to hit so hard. None of them know that Grayson is a miner. They've never seen Buzz fight either. By the end of this quest, I'm certain the secret will be out. I just hope I can trust them to keep it to themselves.

Klink's double warhammers glow when she collides with the same rat, taking it down a quarter. The rats refuse to sit idly by while we destroy them. They all let out a screech that carries across the tunnel. The force from the attack knocks me off my feet. Everyone takes damage, but I take the most, losing twenty percent of my health. Buzz, with his new tank setup, only loses a tenth.

For the next few moments, the tunnel is pure chaos as the rats scratch and bite in response to our attacks. I hold my shield in one hand and slash my axe with my other. Health disappears in chunks. Buzz stands to my side. We develop a rhythm of attack and defense where we both attack and then lodge our shields together to block their counter.

Buzz's flaming shield does look awesome, I'll give him that.

Grayson dishes out pain left and right. His quickness allows him to dodge many attacks with the swiftness of a great boxer. The princess stands in the back, constantly firing arrows. Tinker is the only one who doesn't fight. By his grimace, I can tell he wants to unleash hell, but his abilities will be needed in due time.

The four rats lay dead on the wet floor. I offer my spoils of loot to Buzz. Without him, I wouldn't be here. We are bruised but nothing more, and I still have over fifty percent health. Our spells would have ended the fight much sooner, but I'm glad we were able to defeat them the way we did. Mana will be a precious commodity going forward. We all take our health potions and press onward.

We clear a dozen rats before we find an exit that leads into an underground tunnel.

The stone walls of the tunnel are covered with frost. Buzz uses his liquid fire on a couple of dead torches that line the wall and passes them to Grayson and Ordin. The further we walk, the colder it gets. The tunnel ends at a set of wooden doors. A heavy iron chain holds the doors shut.

I press my ear to the door and hear an icy groan from the other side that sends chills down my body.

CHAPTER TWENTY-THREE

Grayson picks the lock and we push the frozen doors open. A thick layer of ice covers the corridor walls and deadly icicles hang from the ceiling. It shouldn't be this cold only a few feet underground. A loud, guttural scream echoes from down the hall, too far away to be seen. Buzz steps forward, his flaming shield casting light down the corridor.

I hear movement. Tiny cracks form in the ice and splinter down the corridor walls.

Glordin steps up beside me, frost covering his beard.

"It's colder than a witches ti—" Glordin starts, but a boulder twice my size rips into him. His boots and a splatter of blood are all that remain as the boulder continues tumbling down into the sewer.

"Oh, shit," says Aleesia, holding her hand over her mouth.

Two large bodies step into the light of our torches. Two blue giants with icy blue eyes look down at us like we are nothing more than ants. One carries a large battleaxe, the other a club. They speak to each other in a language I cannot understand. The giant sits his axe on the floor and picks up another frozen boulder, throwing it at us.

This time, we are ready and everyone gets out of the way.

I focus on one of the giants in front of us.

Frost Giant. Level 59. *Frost Giants have resistance to slows but take double damage to fire attacks.*

A tiny tombstone sprouts from the floor where Glordin was killed.

"For Glordin!" yells Ordin. He steps forward, his warhammer glowing with power.

"For Glordin!" echoes Klink and Tinker, thrusting their weapons in the air.

"Does anyone besides the princess have any fire spells?" I remember her fiery arrows from the dungeon.

"I wish I still had Firebreather," says Buzz. "Liquid Fire is cool and all, but it doesn't do any damage."

One of the giants steps closer. Icicles fall from the ceiling and shatter on the floor. We have to dodge in order to avoid impalement.

Tinker casts a spell, and the floor splits open. A canyon runs along the floor and rocks slam into the giants. It should have knocked them in the air, but it barely does any damage.

"Seven hells!" he shouts.

Grayson is the next to attack. He runs for the giant with the battleaxe. The giant swings and Grayson moves to the side, narrowly avoiding being cleaved in half. The frost giants are incredibly fast for being so large. While the giant recovers from the missed attack, Grayson connects a punch with the giant's ribs. It lets out a howl of pain and loses a tenth of its health.

"Nice hit!" shouts the princess. She unleashes a flaming arrow that catches the giant in the eye. It does half the damage of Grayson, even with the fire bonus. I realize I've been standing in the same place for too long. I need to join the fight.

"We need to focus on them together!" I yell. "I'm going to try and snare one of them."

I cast Haunted Earth and dozens of roots erupt from the floor, tangling around the giant's legs. I immediately follow up with Waterfall. The two-second root of Haunted Earth times out perfectly with the delay on Waterfall. Haunted Earth releases the giant at exactly the same time as Waterfall pours from the sky.

It takes out only a sliver of health.

Tinker casts spells left and right. Stones fall from the ceiling. Electricity erupts from his staff. As soon as one spell leaves, another takes its place. They do very little damage. If we're going to win, we'll need to find another way.

The princess continues to fire arrows, slowly wearing down the giant's health. The giant with the battle axe still has seventy-five percent health. The other has ninety.

Klink casts a spell on herself and her dual warhammers glow bright. She and Ordin rush at the giant with the axe. The princess casts Resilience on Klink just as her warhammers connect and she lands several hits in a fraction of a second. The giant swats her to the side and Klink tumbles into the wall, losing half her health.

Klink is slow to get up as the giant with the club swings down hard. Buzz dives forward, blocking the blow with his shield. He loses ninety percent of his health, but the blow stuns the giant. Buzz's shield must have some kind of ability.

Grayson grabs the two of them by their clothes and drags them to safety.

The giant with the battleaxe smashes his weapon into the floor. A long, icy tendril creeps along the stone floor, weaving towards us. It bypasses Grayson, Klink, and Buzz and stops at Aleesia's feet, freezing her to the floor. She struggles to move, rooted in place. Her health ticks down bit by bit, until the ice melts away and she can move again.

If we don't do something soon, the giants will kill us all. We aren't doing enough damage to take them down.

"Grayson, Buzz, I need your help. I'm going to snare this bastard. When I do, all three of us need to go in on him. The rest of you, keep the other one distracted."

"What are you doing, Esil?" asks the princess. "This is suicide."

"Madness!" says Tinker.

"Trust me," I tell them. Grayson did almost as much damage as the four of them combined. If we use all three of our miner's bonus, then we may be able to kill the giant. Assuming it doesn't kill us first.

I cast Haunted Earth again and snare the giant with the battleaxe. Next, I use Resilience on Grayson and we three move in. I make sure to stay close to Buzz. He has the lowest health of all of us, but we need his strength. If it comes down to it, I can use my shield's ability to save him.

Grayson's gauntlets move in a blur. He connects with a flurry of punches, taking out chunks of health with each hit. I equip my shield in one hand and my axe in the other and start swinging. I don't hit as hard as Grayson, but my attacks do enough. Buzz slashes with his sword, drawing blood.

"Move back!" I order as the snare disappears.

The giant is at fifty percent health. If we can do that two more times, we might be able to kill him.

Klink, Ordin, Tinker, and the princess have lured the other giant down the tunnel. All I can see is the glow of one torch and the occasional flaming arrow. If they can hold on for just a minute, we'll make it through this.

We retreat, dodging the giant's powerful swings while Haunted Earth comes off cooldown. I have enough mana for three more abilities and I know just how I want to use them.

I used Haunted Earth again, snaring the giant. We attack. The giant is wounded badly now. Blue blood has stained the stones surrounding him. When we retreat, he is down to twenty-five percent health. Once more should end it.

The giant stumbles around, swinging madly but missing. His legs are a mess of battered meat. The downside of being so tall is that all our attacks are below the waist.

I take a brief peek down the corridor and only see a faint glow. I hope they are okay.

When Haunted Earth comes off cooldown, I use it again. The giant moves so slow he has no hope of dodging it. I use the last of my mana casting Resilience on Grayson. We punch and stab and slash until the monster falls to the floor. My stamina is as low as it can be without disappearing. I am once again thankful for my dwarven boots. They might not keep me at full stamina in a fight like this, but they do enough to keep me alive.

My XP bar shoots up and a metallic green twenty-one twirls across my vision.

"We can loot the body later. We need to help the others!"

Grayson and Buzz hurry down the hall with me. The light glows brighter with each step we take.

We pass a tombstone along the way. Another person died to help me with the quest. It gives me the energy to keep going. I can't let them down.

A fiery arrow shoots through the air and I see the giant, his head pierced with arrows. He still has half his health.

The princess, Ordin, and Tinker all have less than half their health. The giant smashes his club, narrowly missing Ordin.

"Did you kill it?" he asks, huffing for breath.

"We did. I'm out of mana, though. Can any of you stun him?"

In response, the princess fires a lightning arrow. Tiny bolts fork out as it soars through the air. It hits the giant with a crack of thunder and he freezes in place. We all rush in and attack with a fury only capable by those on the edge of death. Right now, we have two options: kill the giant or die trying. I choose to survive. If we don't, Glordin and Klink gave their lives and whatever items they lost for nothing. If we make it through, maybe they get them back.

As the giant's health dips lower, I realize that this one is a woman. They are so ugly that it is hard to tell, but the lack of a beard and large chest indicate that she is female. Were they together? Who put them here? I know frost giants don't belong in Asgard. They belong on a different

Norse world. Someone put them here to stop us from getting in.

The giant has ten percent health. One more round of attacks and we're through to whatever awaits us next. I can't imagine what could upstage a frost giant.

She lashes out violently, knowing her end is near. Maybe she hopes to bring down one of us with her, but we stay back, dodging her belabored attacks.

"I'm out of mana," says Aleesia.

"Spread out then, we'll have to divert her attention."

We circle the giant until she can't turn her head fast enough to see us all. The princess shoots an arrow in her back. It's not enough to hurt, but it causes the giant to turn. Grayson runs in and punches the giant while she is turned. Buzz and Ordin follow suit. Each time she turns to her new attacker, we attack from her blindside. She lets out a scream full of rage and sadness that sinks into my bones before she falls to the ground.

If this weren't a game, we'd be monsters.

CHAPTER TWENTY-FOUR

"How did Klink die?" I ask. It might not be a real death, but the fact that she sacrificed herself and possibly lost some of her best items means a great deal.

"It was awful," growls Ordin. Blood seeps from a gash over his right eye. He leans over his warhammer.

"The giant. She ripped her in half. Worst death I've ever seen in the game," says Aleesia. Her scuffed armor is caked with a splattering of blood. She must have been right beside him when it happened.

"I owe her big time. And Glordin. I owe you all."

"What I don't understand," says Aleesia, "is how you three took down a giant that was still seventy-five percent health before we even got ours down to fifty?"

Silence fills the corridor. Ordin and Tinker want to know as well, their attention fully on me.

"And how does Grayson hit harder than I do with my fire buff? Way harder. Something doesn't add up. I remember the first time we met and how you attacked that troll. Are you all running some kind of hack?" Her brow is raised. It hurts that she thinks I might be cheating, but under the circumstances, it makes a lot more sense to an outsider than the fact that a group of us in the mines are just randomly strong.

"Aleesia, you know Pangea can't be hacked. Your dad is a developer, for heaven's sake." Pangea Online proudly boasts that it has the best defenses against hacking and cyber-attack.

"What is it then? How do you do it?"

I wish I could tell her, but it's more than just my life that would be affected if our secret got out.

I look to Grayson and he shakes his head.

"We don't know," says Grayson. The way he says it allows no more questioning.

The princess sighs. "What now then?"

"We heal and let our mana recover. Then we press on."

We all take what health and mana potions we can. The princess doesn't have enough mana to use her healing ability. I'm not even sure how effective it would be on so many of us. Over the next thirty minutes, our health returns to normal.

No one really talks as we prepare for what's next. There is a tension in the air that everyone can sense. They know that Buzz, Grayson, and I are hiding something, they just don't know what.

I need to say something to them before we leave this hall. We can't go into our next battle like this. If we do, it's a recipe for defeat.

"Guys, I wish I could tell you what the deal is, but I can't. I don't have that right. It affects more people than just us." I look each one of them in the eye in turn. I need them to understand. "It's nothing illegal. We're not cheating and we don't know how it works. I promise. I wish there was more I could say, but I can't. All of you were there when I first found out what I could do. I died over and over. I'm not some mastermind trying to cheat the game. I'm just a guy trying to help his friend's mom."

They say nothing for a moment. The princess chuckles, then the others join in. "We know you're not some mastermind. And I believe you, Esil. Only a true idiot would do some of the things you have done. We like you and we wish you the best, but we're not going to give the tournament to you. There's over ninety other players who want the same thing you do. If we ease up for a minute, they'll take advantage. You do have a little skill, though, so maybe whatever it is you have going for you might keep you alive a little longer."

"Thanks," I say. "Are we ready to find out what's next?"

"Not without me, you won't!" Glordin's voice echoes down the hall and then I see him running, his black hair shimmering in torchlight.

"You came back," I say, clasping his forearm when he returns.

"I was hoping I could get back in time to dish out a little pain." He smiles. "Plus, I lost my battleaxe when I died. Looks like you handled them just fine without me."

We're back up to seven. With a little luck, Klink might return too. Considering how she died, though, I won't count on it. I think being ripped in half might cause me to log out for a few hours at the very least.

Looking through my inventory, I still have a few mana and health potions. I don't have anything else that can really give me a buff.

The others loot the frost giant bodies. My prize still

awaits and I can't offer much other than the loot and experience of this quest. I put my stat point from reaching level twenty-one into Vitality. I have a feeling I'm going to need all the extra health I can get soon enough. I stare at my stats for a moment, taking in how far I've come.

Level 21:
  Strength - 14
  Agility - 2
  Vitality - 4
  Intellect - 6
  Dexterity - 5
  Stamina - 0

The zero in stamina is an eyesore, but with my dwarven boots, I just don't see the purpose in adding to it. They are soulbound and I'll never have to replace them. I can't imagine finding a better pair of boots that I don't have to worry about losing. It's almost like having permanent stat bonuses on my feet.

With the frost giants dead, the ice begins melting from the walls and icicles overhead. Soon, it sounds like rain as water drips down around us. At the end of the hall, two large doors block our entrance.

"I've got this," says Grayson. He leans down in front of the door and begins picking the lock.

"Why do you have a lock-picking skill?" asks Buzz.

"I used to spend a lot of time in dungeons. Thought it was a useful skill to have."

The lock clicks and the door opens with a groan.

I look at my map and realize the blue dot is in the next room. We made it. Hard to believe there were only two sets of monsters between us and such a great mount. There has to be more to it than this.

Before we cross the threshold into the next room, a notification pops across my screen.

You are about to enter Fenrir's Lair. Would you like to bind here? Y/N

I focus on yes and step forward.

I gaze into the room, searching for a trap. The circle-shaped room is lit by several torches. Two sets of stairs curl upwards around the wall and meet at a door that undoubtedly leads into the castle. In the middle of the room sits a giant black wolf. I focus on his stats.

Fenrir. Legendary wolf mount. *Fenrir is the third child of the trickster god, Loki. He was tricked and imprisoned by Tyr, the God of War, after it was prophesied that Fenrir would devour Odin, King of Asgard, and bring upon Ragnarok, the end of times. Fenrir is a loyal and powerful mount, capable of fighting when his owner is close to death.* **Ability: Fight for my master. Fenrir is able to attack and fight alongside his owner for one minute. Cooldown: 24 hours.**

Everyone watches me once we enter the room. I can feel the eyes of the wolf boring into me even as he lays against the cold stone floor, wrapped in chains.

"Go on," says Buzz. "He's yours."

I approach the wolf cautiously. His observant eyes follow me with every step I take.

I expect him to growl when I reach for the chain that holds him hostage, but instead, he lowers his head to the ground with a sigh. The chain wraps around his legs, body, and snout, making it impossible for him to move or escape. I follow the chain from Fenrir across the floor to where it begins. The chain is pierced by a sword driven deep into the floor. The silver blade shimmers, reflecting my body along its polished edges. Norse runes engrave the pommel and a large red ruby is encrusted in the hilt. The sword itself must be worth a fortune. I'll need to pull it out in order to free Fenrir.

A blue aura surrounds the sword. It could be a magical spell or enchantment designed to keep intruders from removing it or it could be the reason Fenrir hasn't escaped. Either way, I came this far and my only option is to try and free him. As long as it doesn't kill me, I can take whatever happens.

I grab the sword by the hilt and feel an energy flow through my body. It feels like I am being pulled into the sword. I try to release my grip, but my fingers refuse to let go.

Congratulations! You have reached Fenrir, legendary mount. You have two options:

1. Pull the sword from the ground and free Fenrir, binding him to you as your mount.

2. Pull the sword from the ground and kill Fenrir, taking the Sword of Tyr as your soulbound weapon.

Item: Sword of Tyr. Soulbound. Cannot be traded or discarded. +40 strength, 25% armor penetration, 1% bleed every second for five seconds, stacks up to 5 times.

No effing way! The Sword of Tyr is one of the strongest weapons I have ever seen. That, combined with my secret stat, means I could kill almost anything. I could even give Ryken a run for his money with a sword like that. Forget the strength and armor penetration, the bleed itself makes it an overpowered weapon. It would certainly give me a leg up in the tournament.

I can find another mount. What are my chances of finding another weapon like this?

When I pull the sword, it comes effortlessly out of the stone floor. It feels light in my hand. I give it a few swings and it practically whistles as it cuts through the air.

Standing over Fenrir, his eyes meet mine. There is both anger and sadness in them. How many people have stood in this exact room and chosen the sword over the mount?

Behind me, my companions look on in wonder. I'm sure each of them would do anything to be in the position I am in. They all came here to help me find a mount. What kind of person would I be to betray that? I think I'm finally beginning to understand what Grayson meant about not being able to win the tournament with strength alone.

I toss the sword to the ground and it disappears in a flash of light. I take the chain in my hands, unwinding it from Fenrir's legs, body, and finally, his mouth. When I lay the chains down beside him, he stands up and stretches, letting out a small grunt. Afterward, he licks me on the hand. I can't help but notice the size of his teeth. He's the biggest wolf I have ever seen. Bigger than the white wolf from the auction. Bigger than the worgs I saw in the Haunted Forest. As big as a horse.

Congratulations! You have chosen wisely. Fenrir will soon be bound to you for life.

Soon? What does that mean?

Congratulations! You have completed the quest 'Rescue Fenrir.' Reward: 50 gold.

I also get a good amount of experience from the quest.

"Well, are you going to ride him?" asks Buzz.

I try to focus my thoughts on riding Fenrir. It must work, because he crawls down on all fours and looks at me. I put my weapons into my inventory and climb on.

Fenrir rises to his feet. I run my fingers through his long black fur and take hold. I think about which direction I want to go and the wolf obeys. He moves with quickness, grace, and above all, power. He runs around the room and when he leaps through the air, it feels like I'm flying.

I made the right choice.

We come to a stop in front of the group and they all clap and cheer.

"Alright," says the princess. "How about we get the hell out of here and celebrate? First round is on Esil."

I can't argue with that.

As soon as we start to leave the room, the doors fly shut and the floor quakes. Fenrir bares his teeth at whatever is about to come. The door at the top of the stairs opens.

A man steps through wearing a winged battle helm and carrying the sword I just pulled from the floor. He only has one hand. The other is wrapped in bandages.

"Who dares attempt to release Fenrir from his chains?" his voice echoes through the room.

I think I know what I have to do to make Fenrir mine.

Tyr. Norse God of War. Level 75.

I jump off Fenrir and equip my battleaxe and shield.

"I do."

The sound of shuffling feet lets me know my companions are behind me. Fenrir's low growl rumbles deep within my chest. I've come too far to die now. Bring it on, God of War!

As if hearing my thought, Tyr leaps from the steps and lands on the floor in front of us with a thud. The circular room feels more like an arena now.

"I should have known better than to trust Loki to place sentries outside of the dungeon. The God of Mischief has always had an affinity for the frost giants. I gave my hand to bind Fenrir in chains. If you aim to take him, you'll have to get through me."

An arrow soars past my head. It goes straight for Tyr's face, but he slashes it away with his sword at the last second.

The battle is on.

I cast Haunted Earth, but Tyr dodges the snare. Tinker uses an ability that rains down boulders from the sky, but Tyr moves around them with ease. He is far faster than the frost giants.

Ordin runs at Tyr, his warhammer glowing bright. Their weapons connect with a flash of light and Ordin is knocked on his back. His lip drips blood when he stands up.

"Is that the best you have to offer?" goads Tyr.

I cast Mud Pits and the floor around Tyr fills with mud. Next, I use Resilience on Grayson and we move in on Tyr from opposite sides. I swing my axe and it clashes with Tyr's sword. He deflects my blow and takes out a fifth of my health just with his block. Grayson connects with a jab to his back and Tyr loses five percent health. Tyr catches Grayson in the chin with his elbow, sending a spurt of blood streaming down his chest. Grayson's health drops by a third.

The princess continually shoots arrows. Some hit, some miss, but they do relatively little damage to the god.

Tyr extends his arm and spins his blade in a circle, like a mage casting a spell, and wind whips around the room. He spins it with such speed that a wind tunnel forms and blasts across our group, knocking us all off our feet. In a flash, he glides from one of us to another, slashing his sword.

My vision goes red at the edges. For the next few seconds, my health trickles down.

We all lose twenty percent health from the attack.

"What in Odin's beard was that?" yells Glordin. "He hit all seven of us in less than a second!"

Tyr still has ninety percent of his health.

Fenrir paces back and forth. He can only attack once per day and even then only for a minute. We may need his help later, so I can't risk using him now.

Buzz steps up beside me.

"You got a plan for this?" he asks.

"Beat him till he bleeds?"

"Works for me." Buzz takes some of his liquid fire and rubs it on his battle helm and sword. "Let's show this freak what two arms can do!"

Buzz rushes into battle. I follow, along with Grayson, Ordin, and Glordin. With a swing of his sword, Tyr parries all of our blows in one swift motion. His attacks are so strong that even his deflections cause damage. Buzz is down to half health. My vision goes red again and I notice I've lost almost half my HP as well.

A screaming arrow soars past and connects with Tyr. Tiny bolts of electricity spark along his body. He's stunned.

"Attack!" I yell and we all move in. For half a second, we hack and slash and pound, until the stun wears off and Tyr swings his sword, knocking us all back twenty feet.

We took down twenty percent of his health in such a short time, but he took more from us. All of his attacks must be Area of Effect abilities, damaging anyone nearby.

Buzz leans on his shield, blood running from his nose. His health bar shows fifteen percent.

"Stand back, buddy. We'll take it from here," I say.

If we keep fighting like we have been, Tyr will destroy us. The only option I have right now is to unleash Fenrir.

I call him and he rushes to my side.

"We need your help, boy." I rub my fingers through the soft hair around his neck.

The giant wolf nods at me and then jumps into the fray. He moves as quick as Tyr, biting and clawing. Whatever history they share, it's clear the wolf has not forgotten. Tyr swings and Fenrir dodges the blow, countering by sinking his teeth into Tyr's leg. The wolf's muzzle is covered in blood.

For the next minute, the two godly beings battle. We attack when we can, but Fenrir and Tyr move with such speed that we can barely keep up. It is a beautiful chaos as they dance together, attacking and defending as they fight for their lives.

When the minute is up, Tyr only has a third of his health. Fenrir limps over to Buzz and lays down on the floor. Gashes and matted blood cover his body.

Now is our chance.

"Grayson, Ordin, and Glordin, I need you to rush in. Aleesia, I need you to get another stun. If you can, I have a plan. If not..."

The three brawlers are off running before I finish the sentence. I cast Resilience on Grayson and his hands move faster. Tyr barely blocks the punch. Ordin and Glordin follow up with attacks. The princess's arrow sails through the air and connects.

I switch to Staff of the Ancients and cast Haunted Earth. It catches Tyr in its grasp and I immediately follow up with Waterfall at the same time Tinker drops his boulders from the sky. It rains down water and rock, all the while Grayson and the two dwarves attack as fast as they can.

Tyr has ten percent health after our latest efforts. He comes unstunned and slashes madly at the three closest to him. Ordin and Glordin fall to the ground and move no more.

Grayson must know he's about to die because he tries for another punch. Tyr blocks it with his sword. The deflection is enough to take the last of Grayson's HP.

Me, Tinker, and the princess are all that's left and none of us have much HP. I cast Haunted Earth again and it misses. Without the melee distractions, Tyr swats away Aleesia's arrows like flies. Tinker's abilities have no better luck.

"I have an idea." Buzz stumbles up beside me. "We've only got one shot at this. Just be ready." Buzz puts his sword in his inventory and all he carries is his shield. Three gravestones have sprouted from the ground around Tyr's feet.

"You don't have to do this."

"Yes, I do."

Buzz stumbles toward the God of War. Tyr looks

amused as Buzz slowly approaches. One hit is all it will take to kill Buzz.

Tyr slashes down hard with his sword.

"Now," Buzz yells. The sword connects with Buzz's shield and Tyr freezes in place. Buzz slumps over, his health depleted.

I cast Waterfall.

Aleesia shoots another stunning arrow.

Tinker casts his canyon ability. The earth opens and rocks shoot Tyr into the air.

Fiery arrows explode across his chest.

Haunted Earth snares him when he lands.

Waterfall and Tinker's boulder attack smash him into the ground.

I switch to my spear and throw it at his chest as he stands from the rubble with a sliver of health.

My spear connects and Tyr hunches over before falling to the ground.

The doors to the room fly open and I receive a notification.

Congratulations! You have defeated Tyr. Fenrir is now bonded to you for life.

A gold twenty-two flashes across my vision.

Grayson, Ordin, Glordin, and Klink rush into the room. A few moments later, I see Buzz materialize at the spawn point outside the door.

"You did it!" he yells. "You bloody did it!"

"Couldn't have done it without you. Without all of you."

"You know, when this tournament is over, we'd make a pretty damn good team," says Aleesia.

Yeah, we would.

CHAPTER TWENTY-FIVE

Fenrir's powerful muscles flex between my legs as he pounces across a field in the valley of the Mortican Mountains. With each jump, we hang in the air, defying gravity, before plummeting back to the earth. I've outfitted him with a saddle that allows me better stability when Fenrir changes direction.

The developers will be announcing the next quest this evening and I have decided to take the day and really learn how to ride my mount. The more we practice, the quicker he responds to my thoughts. Merlin flies high above, keeping watch. Over the past few days, I've made myself quite the little family.

Beside me, Aleesia rides her unicorn, its charcoal coat contrasting against the golden field. The princess wanted some time with just the two of us, so the dwarves are off by themselves today.

I put my most recent stat point into Vitality again, boosting my health and regeneration a little more. As I look at my stats, I think they are finally beginning to even out somewhat.

Level 22:
  Strength - 14
  Agility - 2
  Vitality - 5
  Intellect - 6
  Dexterity - 5
  Stamina - 0

We stop at a weeping willow. Its long, droopy branches whip back and forth in the breeze. Aleesia and I take a seat in its shade while our mounts frolic nearby.

"Do you think it's strange that most of the dwarves who quested with you that first day aren't around anymore?" I ask.

She looks deep in thought before answering.

"Not really. Several of the dwarves who go questing with me were only around because of my father. They think I'm a gateway into a relationship with him or something. I didn't want to be the one to break the bad news that it was never going to happen. And having a few more helping hands with a raid never hurt either. I know a few of them, the ones who went with us to Asgard, are actually here because they like me and want to be my friends. If I ever lose favor, they'll be the ones to stay around."

I hang on every word she says. Maybe the life of the rich and famous isn't all it's cracked up to be.

She changes the subject. "I'm sorry about yesterday.

For doubting your integrity and everything. You've been nothing but a stand-up guy since I've known you. Not many people would have left that sword and taken the mount." She twirls her hair around the tip of her finger. Her pointed ears cut through the silky strands. Wow, she is beautiful.

"You don't owe me an apology. It's weird, the thing with Grayson, Buzz and I. It doesn't make sense to any of us. We're all just miners who never had a shot at anything. And as for the sword, I feel like something bad would have happened if I'd taken it. I doubt I would have been able to leave with it."

"Wait…" Her face is scrunched. "Grayson is a miner, too? He was the best fighter of any of us. I never would have suspected."

We sit in silence under the tree, watching our mounts run through the field. Did I say too much? Has she fit the pieces together? There's no way she would think that miners have a hidden stat based on that information, is there?

"You think you're ready for the race?" she asks, breaking the silence.

"Not at all, but I've got a great mount. He's fast, powerful, and if I get in a bind, he can help me out. You never did tell me what yours' special ability is."

"And I'm not going to either," she laughs. "I've got a few secrets as well, Esil."

"Oh, come on. It's gonna be like that?"

"Yeah." She grabs me by the hand. Her hand feels warm, almost like the real thing. I'm thankful it's virtual and that she can't feel the sweat on my palms. "You live in Civic City, right?"

"I do."

"I'm not too far from there by train. Maybe when this is all over, we can meet up in real life?" She squeezes my fingers.

"I'd like that a lot."

She tosses my hand aside and jumps to her feet. "Race you back to the town square!"

I log out of Pangea long enough to shower and eat. When I log back in, I have a message from the developers. My heart races as I read.

Congratulations on making it to the second round of the Developer's Tournament! Hopefully by now, you have solved the second clue and are ready for what comes next. Be at Baja Pass in Raceworld at 2300 hours.

-Pangea Online Developers

Baja Pass? Not sure what that means. I do a quick search and learn that the baja is a location in what used to be California. Back before the world got blown up and everyone had to wear masks just to go outside, it was known for its varying geography consisting of the ocean, mountains, and desert. There isn't any information on the Baja Pass in Raceworld, so it must be a new track. It will be an interesting place for a race if they incorporate all of the different elements.

The rest of the day I spend practicing with Fenrir. I

train all of my abilities and attacks while riding, getting a feel for what mounted combat is like. I'm not the greatest, but Fenrir does a lot to compensate for my lack of skill. My stream is off, because I don't want anyone knowing what I have in store for the next quest. No one knows I have Fenrir except those who were there with me and I'd like to keep it that way.

With an hour until I'm supposed to be at Raceworld, I go back to my home portal to be alone. Merlin sits on his perch and Fenrir curls up around my feet as I sit on the couch. The old timey clock I bought to hang on the wall ticks methodically, counting down the seconds until we need to leave.

At five minutes to twenty-three hundred hours, I call Merlin and Fenrir and we jump through the portal. It's time to race.

Welcome to Raceworld. Users who are not spectating must be on a mount at all times. More than thirty seconds spent on foot will result in disqualification from any race.

A wall with dozens of video screens stands before me. On each screen, there is a separate type of race. Cars, planes, animals, hoverboards; if you can ride it, there is a race for it. In the middle, there is a slightly bigger screen that reads 'Baja Pass: Developer's Tournament Stage 2- Mounts only.'

I focus on the image and a notification pops up.

Congratulations, Esil! You are qualified to compete in Baja Pass. Would you like to take your position? Y/N

I accept and the world turns to pixels around me. A few moments later, I'm behind four other people on a hilltop beside the ocean. Far ahead there is a desert, and farther still are mountains. Aleesia and Ryken wait in front of me, along with another woman and man. A pole sticks up from beside each of them, with a small flag displaying their position. There are two lines, staggered diagonally so that we aren't right beside each other. To the sides of us, there are several stands filled to capacity. I can hear the cheers of the crowd over the commotion all around me. Behind me, contestants materialize on their mounts and fill in the empty positions.

A timer appears in my vision and counts down from five minutes. I guess when it hits zero, the race will start.

My map is ablaze with a rainbow of dots that indicate all of my opponents. Along the edge of it is a diamond. It's too far away to show up on the map. That's where we'll be going.

I shake my head and try to focus on everything that is happening around me. Two spots up, the princess sits on her charcoal unicorn. She turns around and waves at me.

"Good luck!" she says.

"You too."

That's when I notice Ryken's mount. The skeletal horse has been replaced by the nightmare from the auction. Its fiery mane and tail swish back and forth. Ryken's presence is intimidating as he sits stoically on his horse. His black armor. Skull pauldrons. Helmet with curled horns of a ram. He doesn't look around. His eyes are focused on what lies ahead.

"Esil!" I hear a voice shouting my name from the stands. Buzz and Grayson sit together. They both give me thumbs up and I return the gesture.

I look around once more, taking in the competition.

The other two spots ahead of me are taken by a man on a rhinoceros and a woman riding a motorcycle. It's the motorcycle from the auction with two guns mounted to the handle bars. I'd hate to have her on my tail. The man wears a leopard vest and black leather pants, his hair falling in a mane around his neck. He carries a spear with a bone tip in one hand. The woman wears a denim jacket. Her dreaded hair falls past her shoulders and she has a machete strapped to her back.

Merlin sits on my shoulder, his head turning like a sprinkler as he watches everything around us.

Behind me, there are too many to name. I see a few familiar faces. Ordin rides his pony and shoves his warhammer into the air when he sees me. Klink wrangles with her blind basilisk, which she still hasn't tamed. Near the back, I see Jayce, our teammate from steamball, riding a mechanical horse. Steam shoots out of its ears and nostrils as it paws at the ground. Gears turn inside the massive beast's iron legs.

The bear from the auction is midway down the line, his armor gleaming in the sun. A tiny gnome sits atop the bear, making the beast look even larger than it already is. The gnome is clad in a dull green robe and a hawk sits on his shoulder. Does he have the same enhanced hearing and sight I do?

I spot a griffin ridden by a woman in a white robe with a golden staff, a dozen or so horses, a lion, a camel, a giant eagle, several motorcycles, and many others. One man rides upon a small elephant; its trunk bellows loudly from the rear of the pack.

I cringe at the spider-riding goblin. If he gets too close, I'll be the first to take him out.

When the timer hits three minutes, a woman riding a pegasus appears in front of us all. The white horse's powerful wings keep it hovering in the air. When she speaks, her voice booms over everything.

"Welcome to Baja Pass! It's a brand-new race designed specifically for the Developer's Tournament. I'm Nancy and I helped design some of it myself. But this race isn't about me. It's about you. You are here because you had the speed and cleverness to beat our first quest before everyone else, many of those sitting in the stands to both sides of you. Ninety-nine of you will be competing today. Unfortunately, one of your competitors had an out of game injury and is not able to compete. The rules are simple: finish the race. If you die, you lose. If you fall from your mount for more than thirty seconds, you will be disqualified. Both magic and technology are allowed. You are free to attack your opponents. Make it through and you advance to the next round. All third-party streams have been disabled and both viewing and recaps of the match, including live footage from every player, will be available on the official Pangea stream."

Just as I thought. I need to find a way to get away from everyone as quick as possible. I have a feeling the start of the race is going to be a bloodbath.

CHAPTER TWENTY-SIX

My hands shake and my heartbeat pounds in my ears as the timer counts down from ten. I equip my shield over my shoulder, hoping it will block anything that flies my way from behind.

The timer hits zero and a cannon blast initiates the start of the race.

For the next few moments, everything is pure chaos. Merlin leaps off my shoulder and flies high into the air. Fenrir jumps to the side and races away from the group. Something hits me in the shoulder and my vision goes red. A tenth of my health is gone.

I cast Haunted Earth and Mud Pits over my shoulder without looking, hoping to snare anyone who attempts to follow me.

Gunfire and the whir of spells fill the air. I focus on getting away from the madness, but take one last look behind me.

Shit!

I snared the princess. I don't know how. She was in front of me only moments before!

An orc riding a large boar cuts her down with a stone axe. My stomach rises and I think I might vomit.

On second glance, I realize it's not her and breathe a sigh of relief. The dead elf hangs limp, still strapped into its silver steed. In the chaos, it is hard to tell the two elves apart.

Lightning bolts down from the sky, sending bodies flying through the air in a violent explosion. The crack of thunder that follows is deafening. Several bodies lay scattered on the ground. Ryken stands among the crowd, unafraid. He raises his hands into the air and black smoke surrounds him. The mounts of the fallen competitors rise up and trample those who have been knocked to the ground.

I see Ordin's glowing warhammer just before he is overtaken by the mob.

Ryken turns and races away, a dozen undead mounts following him.

The dots of other players scatter across my map. A handful are in front of me. There is no official track or road for us to follow. Only an end goal. I plan to stay as far away from everyone else as I can.

In the top of my vision, there is a counter showing my place in the race and how many competitors are left. It said 5/99 before the race started. Now I am 11/65. Several players passed me while I ran to safety. Almost a third of our competition was wiped out at the start.

I open my messages to contact Aleesia, but they are grayed out. Obviously, the developers won't let us communicate.

Merlin flies high overhead, a speck against the blue sky. I can't risk merging with him right now, but perhaps later, I can use him to get a better view of where everyone is. We've scattered across the land and no one is visible in my immediate vicinity on my map.

Trails of dust float into the air up ahead. One of them must be the princess. Ryken is somewhere behind me. I'll need to keep an eye out for him. The bastard will murder me the first opportunity he gets.

Fenrir keeps a steady pace. The last thing I want is to tire him out early in the race. He isn't blessed with the same stamina I have from my dwarven boots. If he gets too tired, I'll have to wait for him to recover.

The first leg of the race takes place beside the sea. The ground is sandy and we pass several cacti interspersed between other prickly bushes. It's not quite a desert, but it's close. Judging by the marker on the map we are supposed to follow, the trail we're on leads away from the ocean, across the desert and towards the mountains. The desert will test Fenrir's endurance the hardest, especially if there is no food or water.

"We got this, boy." I run my fingers through the hair between his ears.

Several others have dropped out of the race. I am now 10/60.

Suddenly, we stop moving. I turn around, expecting to see someone who has snared us with a spell, but instead, empty terrain surrounds us.

I try to make Fenrir move, but he goes nowhere. When I look down, I see his feet are stuck in the sand. He struggles to move and they sink deeper.

Quicksand.

Fenrir slowly sinks deeper and deeper as he struggles to free himself. His efforts to break free only cause the sand to suck us down faster. I need to calm him.

"Easy, boy. I need you to listen. We can get out of this, but we're going to have to remain calm. Do you understand?"

The wolf's struggles cease and we stop sinking. I search for anything nearby that can pull us out. I could jump off, but then I would only have thirty seconds in which to pull Fenrir free. I doubt I could do that. I don't even have anything to pull him out with.

I search through my inventory, looking for anything that could help.

Exactly!

I equip Grappler and scan the area for a place to attach to. There are no trees nearby, only a few cacti that I'm sure would snap from the weight of both Fenrir and I. My only shot is a group of boulders some twenty feet away. If I can lodge the grappling hook between them just right, it might hold while I pull us out.

Fenrir's hind legs are fully submerged in the sand. I shoot Grappler and the hook lands a few feet past the boulders.

I pull the grappling hook carefully towards us. It lodges between two of the boulders and I tug it until it feels secure. Now comes the hard part. We are too heavy for the guns retractable feature to pull us both out. I have to pull us out without getting off of Fenrir.

I clench my legs tight around him and wrap one arm around his neck. With my other hand, I grip the rope tight and pull with all my might. We move a few inches and then I wrap the rope around my hand by twisting my wrist. I do this several times and it feels like we are escaping the quicksand.

There's a grating sound of metal on rock and then the line goes limp. The grappling hook flies loose and comes at me like a bullet, hitting me in the head. My vision goes red for a second and then we sink a few more inches into the quicksand.

"Dammit!" I yell, even though I know no one can hear me. Merlin has returned and sits upon a nearby cactus.

The important thing is to focus and make sure we get out of the bind we're in, but I can't help but notice I'm now 40/58. We have the speed to catch up, but first we have to get out.

I retract the grappling hook and fire again. It lands a few feet past the boulders and I pull until it seems like a snug fit.

"Merlin, go sit on the hook."

Merlin hoots and then hops from the cactus to the boulder.

"Make sure it's in there good."

He looks down at the hook and then moves it a small ways to the left.

"Good job."

I pull until the grappling hook is tight and try again. Inch by inch, I pull myself and Fenrir closer to the edge of the quicksand. My stamina bar hovers at one percent, never depleting, but never building back up either. My arms strain with each pull until I'm certain they will rip to shreds. My opponents continue to pass me until I'm 55/57. People keep dropping off. How many of us will make it to the next round?

Fenrir's muscles quiver when we reach the bank and

he is able to dig his paws into the earth. He lifts us both out of quicksand and shakes out his fur. I have to hold tight to keep from falling off.

Merlin takes flight again, my silent guardian in the sky.

A green dot appears on my map. Someone is nearby. I equip my axe and shield and Fenrir moves in their direction.

A small pony trudges along, slow and steady.

"Ordin!"

"Esil! Why are you so far back here?" he asks.

"Never mind that, how in the hell are you alive? The last I saw of you, you were being trampled by Ryken's undead mounts."

"Haven't you learned anything? Dwarves are hard to kill. Me and Penny here barely survived, but we made it. Been trudging along ever since. To tell you the truth, I knew I never had a chance in hell of winning the race, but finishing it, that's a different story. You best be getting along now, though. A wolf like that, you don't belong back here with me."

"You sure? We could cruise on in together," I joke.

"That's not your style. You've got something to prove whether you know it or not. I saw that since day one."

He's right. I'm going to fight tooth and nail until this race is over. If there's a chance in hell I can win, I'm gonna do it.

CHAPTER TWENTY-SEVEN

The first person I catch up to rides a motorcycle. A crossbow is hung over her shoulder, a black bandanna covers her face, and her jet-black hair whips in the wind. A painted tiger claws out from the back of her leather jacket. She is straight out of some post-apocalyptic world.

User: Polly. Level 49.

Her motorcycle roars so loud that she doesn't even hear us when Fenrir catches up to her. A swift swing of my axe depletes half her health and knocks her to the ground. The motorcycle keeps rolling until it hits a rock and flips end over end.

Polly stands up, cursing and waving her hands. She pulls her crossbow and aims it at me. The bolt fires with a crack and darts by, only inches from my head. She's a much easier target now that she's on the ground. I cast Haunted Earth, rooting her in place. Waterfall takes care of the rest. 54/56.

From here on out, if they're not my friend, they're my

enemy. Every person I let slip by into the next round is another threat down the road. I'm not going to let Buzz's mother die because I played it nice. Game on.

I pass several other players over the next hour. Most are far enough away that it would cost more time to chase them down than if I just keep riding ahead. However, I do catch a level fifty-six paladin riding a warhorse. He puts up a good fight, healing himself and damaging me to fifty percent health, but in the end, I am too much for him. 47/55.

The oceanside terrain gradually turns to desert. Plant life is sparse and eventually, even the cacti die out. It becomes a sandy wasteland. The sun bears down from overhead, causing Fenrir's stamina to wane. I lower his speed just a tad and he keeps his stamina steady.

I pass a gravestone sticking out of the sand, reminding me that I'm not the only one playing for keeps.

Sand and dust fill the air up ahead. Three people are engaged in combat. An eagle soars through the air, its rider shooting arrows at whoever is on the ground. As I get closer, the dark figures on the ground become clearer. A dark-skinned man with dreads rides a lion. He tosses spears at the other rider.

A large lizard thrashes about in the sand.

Klink!

The lion and the eagle are teaming up to take her down. I urge Fenrir to go faster and we race across the sand. By the time I arrive, Klink is down to a quarter of health. Blood drips from both her and the basilisk, turning the sand copper. I switch to my spear and throw it with as much force as I can muster. A direct hit in the lion rider's back causes him to fall from his mount. Klink climbs off the basilisk, her twin warhammers glowing red. I let her have her vengeance and focus on the eagle overhead.

The woman rider swoops down, firing a volley of arrows in my direction. One hits Fenrir in the leg, causing him to yelp.

I show the woman a gesture with my hand and switch to Grappler. I fire off a few laser beams in her direction and she soars higher in the air. With her out of the picture for a moment, I turn to help Klink. She and the dreaded man are both down to about ten percent health. They need to get on their mounts soon or they will be disqualified.

One of my laser beams hits the dreaded man in the back. I equip Grappler in my left hand and my axe in my right. Fenrir pounces next to the man and I slash down between his neck and shoulder, ripping him apart. He falls to the ground and my XP bar levels up. A metallic orange twenty-three flashes across my vision.

Klink's basilisk has run off into the desert.

"Grab my hand," I say. "I'm going to toss you."

She extends her arm as I ride by. Our hands clench together and I rocket her through the air towards the basilisk. She lands on its back and the beast thrashes even harder.

"Made it!" she bellows, a smile on her face.

The smile fades into a grimace and she falls off her mount, an arrow protruding from her back.

"No!" I scream. She killed my friend!

Anger flares through me as the eagle swoops down in my direction.

I search for Merlin and tell him without words to go for her eyes.

The eagle swoops towards me, and his talons dig into my shoulders. Red paints the edge of my vision and a timer counts down in large numbers, telling me how long I have until I'm disqualified. I slash at the eagle with my axe and he drops me.

As I fall through the air, I see Merlin clawing at the rider's face. I fire the grappling hook and it wraps around the eagle's neck. My weight takes away its balance and we both tumble towards the ground.

I hit the sand with a thud, and my vision goes red again. Twenty seconds until I'm disqualified.

The eagle regains its balance and pulls at the rope cinched around its neck.

Fenrir runs towards me out of the corner of my eye.

I take the rope in my hands and begin pulling hard. The eagle is strong, but it can't match my strength. The woman can't aim at me because I am directly beneath her. Foot by foot, I pull the eagle closer to the ground.

Ten seconds.

Five.

Fenrir comes to a stop beside me and I climb on his back. I urge him to go in the opposite direction the eagle is facing. I grab hold of the saddle with one hand and hold the rope with the other. He jumps hard and the motion pulls the eagle from the air, turning it upside-down, and slams both the bird and rider hard into the sand. Haunted Earth roots the woman to the ground. Three swings of my axe later and she moves no more. 45/50.

Merlin lands on my shoulder, hooting softly in my ear.

He feels the pain inside me of watching Klink die after trying so hard to save her.

Klink's death replays through my mind as we trek across the desert. The way her face changed from happiness to pain is etched in my memory. She may not be truly dead, but she is one less ally I will have going forward.

The desert stretches on forever. The mountains in the distance seem no closer no matter how far I ride. I pass several people, though I never see them. 37/49. Less and less of us by the minute. How many of those deaths is Ryken responsible for?

Once we make it through the desert, I take a moment to allocate my new stat point into Agility. The bonus speed boost works on Fenrir and I can feel his pace quicken.

The desert fades abruptly into rocky mountains. When I reach the peak of the first mountain, life returns. A vast array of evergreens and fog abound for miles. It's hard to see much other than the outline of the mountains. This is the last leg of the course, but there is no telling how far it stretches. If the other sections are any indicator, it will take a few hours at least.

We start our descent and I'm startled by the clop of hooves on stone. Several goats with long horns that curl back around like Ryken's helmet balance themselves along the steep incline of the mountain ridge nearby.

Mountain Ram. Level 37.

I don't want to fight them, but their leader is very protective of their territory. He rushes towards us, head bent down. Fenrir dodges out of the way at the last moment and I swing my axe.

I only take out a tenth of its health.

It should have been more.

The ram turns and charges again. I attack and again, only a tenth of his health is damaged. I use Mud Pits to slow him and then Haunted Earth and Waterfall. The combo takes out forty percent health. I switch to my spear and attack, thinking it may just be my axe, but I still only do a sliver of damage. My spells work fine, but something is wrong with my attacks.

I kill the ram after a few more hits.

I'm careful to only lure one ram away, but I need to know what is going on. I cycle through all of my weapons, and no matter what, it's like my strength has disappeared.

I don't understand what could have caused this nor do I have time to find out. We must continue.

Fenrir moves through the mountains with ease. He was built for terrain like this. He finds the quickest path, avoiding low hanging branches that might knock me off. I pass two more unseen players. 35/48. Over half us have dropped out in the first two stages of the race. At this rate, only a handful will remain by the time it is over.

I force Fenrir to go faster, depleting his stamina more and more. We climb another mountain. From the top, fog and mist hang in the valley, making it impossible to see anything. Now is the time to merge with Merlin.

I instruct Fenrir to attack anything that comes near me. He can only fight once every twenty-four hours, but I need him to keep me safe for the next thirty seconds. If he has to use the ability, now would be worth it. Hopefully, nothing shows up.

The next thing I know, I'm soaring high in the sky. The fog is only a glassy layer and I can see to the forest floor. Fenrir guards over my body at the mountain behind me. Far ahead, I see a group of people traveling together. Close to ten of them ride in a pack, the armored bear in the lead. They must have decided to group up in order to make sure they all make it through. Ahead of them, I see the princess. She is alone. It looks like she is in first place, but the group behind her is gaining ground.

To the left is Ryken. His undead horde has grown larger. The nightmare moves with great speed, cutting a diagonal path towards the large group. Does he hope to join them, or kill them? The rest of my competitors are scattered among mountains, careful to stay away from each other.

Past the mountains, there is a green valley. That must be the final leg. Several portals stretch across in a line. I bet they transport each player back to the start.

I return to my body and we take off again. With a little luck, I might be able to catch up.

Trees pass by in a blur as Fenrir sinks his claws in the ground, tossing up dirt and rocks with each thrust.

Once we're out of the mountains, I spot the first group a mile ahead. Fenrir is faster than all of their mounts. It's a balancing act between speed and stamina, but the finish line is only a few miles ahead.

Ryken's horde approaches the group from the left. A black cloud surrounds him as he moves in like the angel of death. The group must know they can't outrun him, because they turn to fight. I give them a wide berth as I approach, since I still don't know what is wrong with my attack.

I'm several hundred yards away when the two groups face off, neither one making the first move. I slow down, giving them a wide berth, but using my enhanced hearing to make out a few words from the group with the bear.

"What should we do?"

"I don't know. He's taken out so many people, he's practically his own army."

"How do you even kill a death knight?"

The nightmare neighs and a cone of fire erupts from its nose, scorching one of the horses and its rider in flames. A few seconds later, it crumbles to the ground.

The armored bear steps forward. The gnome that rides on its back holds a staff in one hand and his hawk perches on the other arm. With a wave of his hand, the hawk flies into the air. The gnome casts a spell on the hawk and it burst into flames, flying through the undead mounts and setting them aflame. The bear rears up on its hind legs and the gnome holds on tight. The bear swings with its massive paws, ripping chunks of undead flesh off anything dumb enough to approach. The rest of the group sits back in awe.

Ryken is the biggest threat in the tournament right now. Part of me wants to go help, but not knowing what is wrong with my attack and if I'd be able to hurt him at all has me hesitant. I urge Fenrir to go faster, all the while keeping my eyes on the showdown.

Ryken sends all the undead mounts at the other group. Many of them are ripped apart by the bear, some fall to other combatants, and a few make it through, taking down two men on horses.

Now, Ryken stands alone against six. He moves motions and arms spring from the earth, grabbing two of the mounts by the feet. The horses fight for freedom, but the rotting hands refuse to let go. Ryken charges and then disappears. The nightmare and Ryken are both gone, vanishing into thin air.

A moment later, they appear between two riders. Ryken's broadsword moves with speed that nothing that big should have and slashes both in quick succession before he disappears again. Is that the nightmare's special ability?

Both riders fall off their mounts.

The bear swipes at something we cannot see and when Ryken reappears, a large gash runs down the side of his mount.

Four remain against Ryken. The gnome and bear, a swordsman and a cowboy, both on horses, and a robot riding some futuristic hovercraft.

The cowboy swings his lasso and tosses it around Ryken. It glows white hot and constricts, squeezing Ryken tight. He shoots a barrage of bullets that ding against the death knight's armor. The swordsman charges Ryken at the same time several sonic beams shoot from the robot's hands.

A few feet from Ryken, the swordsman raises his sword to attack. Steam rises from Ryken's armor, the lasso cooking him alive. His orange eyes glow bright beneath his helm.

The sword is inches from hitting Ryken when he breaks free of the lasso, snapping the ends into frays. The swordsman slashes across Ryken's body, but it has no effect. The sonic beams catch Ryken in the chest, knocking him from his horse. The bear moves in, sensing his opportunity.

If they can keep him on the ground long enough, he'll be disqualified.

Ryken equips a large black shield, emblazoned with a silver skull, and thrusts it forward each time the bear attacks. The bear's claws scrape against the metal, to no effect. The four mounted warriors surround the death knight. Can they actually defeat him?

Ryken drops to one knee and places his hands against the earth. A loud buzz fills the air and the earth opens, spilling thousands of black moths from its core. They surround all four warriors, inflicting who knows what kind of pain. The cowboy falls from his mount, his HP at zero. Ryken equips his broadsword and turns toward the swordsman.

The swordsman has had enough. He turns to run, but Ryken cuts him down. Flashes of light emanate from the robot's eyes and his hands transform into blasters. He fires a volley of beams that pound into Ryken, pushing him to the ground. The nightmare attempts to return, but the bear blocks its path. Ryken must know he is nearly out of time because he runs at the bear, sword raised, and slashes hard. He finds the soft spot between the armor and a geyser of blood spurts into the air. The gnome casts several spells in Ryken's direction, but they explode in the air inches from his armor. Is he using a special ability?

The bear stumbles back and forth. The nightmare returns and Ryken climbs on seconds before he would have been disqualified.

The robot fires again, this time spraying a shotgun blast of laser beams across Ryken's chest. It barely affects him. How is it that he seems to be getting stronger as the others get weaker?

Ryken casts a spell and a blood red stream flies from his hand to the robot. The robot loses a chunk of health and Ryken's HP regenerates. Lifesteal. He waves his hand again and the robot moves in slow motion. Ryken cuts him down and electric sparks jump out before the robot's eyes go black.

All that is left is the gnome and Ryken. The gnome doesn't have a chance. Even after all of that, Ryken still has over fifty percent health.

The bear is back on all fours. He lets out a deafening roar I could hear even without my enhanced senses. The bear paws at the ground, furious. There is no way it's going down without a fight.

The two mounted warriors face each other. Ryken carries his sword over his shoulder. The gnome's staff is pointed forward. Ryken charges the bear and the nightmare's flaming mane grows bigger.

The gnome waves his staff and an electric current surrounds the bear. He swings at the nightmare and lightning shoots from its massive paws, damaging Ryken. It swings again and a second bolt connects, slowing Ryken's attack. A third blow stuns Ryken in place. The bear bites Ryken's shoulder and the death knight loses a third of his remaining health. His orange eyes glow brighter. Is it out of surprise or anger? The bear might just pull it off.

The bear swipes again, but Ryken parries it with his sword. He retreats a few feet and tosses his sword to the ground. Both of his hands touch together and a deep purple mist rolls across the ground. The earth rumbles and hands slowly break through its surface. The cowboy, swordsman, robot, and others rise up, their skin a blackish gray. No recognition registers on their faces as they turn towards the gnome.

I hesitate to turn around and engage in the battle. I'm

close enough that I could make it in time. If I snare Ryken, perhaps the bear can finish him off. In reality, I know it's a fight I can't win. I'm ahead of him and all I can do is go for the finish line.

I continue on as Ryken's horde of undead surround the bear and unleash their weapons. The bear falls to the ground.

Then Ryken turns his head in our direction.

I'm not going to die today.

"Run, Fenrir!" I yell and the wolf hustles faster. I can hear the rhythm of hooves behind me as Ryken chases us down. The portal is within sight so I put everything I have into Fenrir's speed. His stamina drops constantly and I don't know if we'll make it before he runs out, but we're pulling away from Ryken. Right now, that's all that matters.

We're only a few feet from the portal when his stamina gives out and we fall to the ground. I pull on his body, but without my strength, I'm unable to lift him. The timer ticks down in my vision. Twenty-five seconds until disqualification. Fenrir looks at me, sorrowful that we are so close. I grab around his neck and pull. We only move a few inches at a time and I can see Ryken getting closer.

If I don't do something, we are dead, and I can't die this close to the finish line. I look through my inventory—is there anything I can use to help?

Substance: Fire Whiskey. Buff: +2% attack for the next hour.

I chug the whiskey and step between Fenrir and Ryken. The death knight has his sword raised, ready to cut me down.

I take aim and cast Haunted Earth. Roots spring from the ground and catch Ryken at the perfect moment.

The buff from the whiskey doesn't reset my strength, but it gives enough that I can move Fenrir a foot at a time.

The countdown timer hits one just as I drag both of our bodies through the portal.

CHAPTER TWENTY-EIGHT

Aleesia grabs me by the arm.

"You made it!" she screams, hugging me tightly.

Fenrir begins to stir, his stamina returning. A few seconds later, Ryken appears through the portal. He looks down at me, his eyes glowing behind the darkness of his helm.

"You!" His voice is deep and cavernous. Hollow. He raises his hand and I feel the ground shaking beneath me.

Hands reach out from the earth. This is where I die. At least I made it through the second quest before he kills me.

A silver orb surrounds us and the hands crumble against it, turning to dust and falling to the ground.

"It's over Ryken. Go somewhere else!" The princess is furious. I've never seen her lose her cool before. She is vicious, her bow raised and pointed at Ryken. Her crimson face matches the fire inside her and her unicorn lowers its head, ready to attack. The shield protecting us must be from it.

"Okay, sister. We'll meet again soon." Ryken drops his sword and trots away.

Sister? What the hell?

"Why did he call you sister?" I ask.

"Because...Ryken is my brother. He's a real ass and we don't talk, not since he moved out and became obsessed with being the best. Dad cut him off to try and teach him a lesson, but by that time, Ryken was making enough to support himself, so he became an even more self-centered asshat. Are you okay?"

"Yeah, I'm fine. Fenrir ran out of stamina escaping your brother. We barely made it through."

For the first time, I look around. The stands are chaos as people cheer and yell. Competitors continue to spill out of the portal and I realize I finished seventh. The last two to emerge are Ordin and a cloaked individual riding a camel. When all is said and done, thirty-two of us make it to the next round.

Once the last person is through, my notifications go off like alarm bells. My XP shoots up and I gain another level. I have to wait to check my notifications, though, because Nancy has another announcement for us. She flies down in front of the crowd on her pegasus. Her voice echoes across the land.

"What an exciting and thrilling race! Even better than we could have hoped for. To all of you who made it to the next round, congratulations! And to those of you who didn't, I give you applause for making it this far. You all now have a better understanding of your opponents and what it will take to win. Use this knowledge wisely as you prepare for the next round. You will all be notified when the next stage is complete. Good luck and as always, never stop leveling!"

When the next stage is complete? Does that mean it's not finished yet?

"What's next for you, Esil?" asks Aleesia.

"Me? I'm going to go home and sleep."

I wave to Buzz and Grayson in the stands. They shout something at me, but I pay them no attention. I'm mentally exhausted and we can talk tomorrow. There will be plenty of time to discuss strategy then.

Merlin hoots at me from my shoulder. In the excitement of trying to escape Ryken, I didn't even notice if he made it through the portal with me, but Merlin is a smart bird.

We jump through the portal and I logout. Sleep finds me as soon as my head hits the pillow.

I wake up refreshed and ready to take on the world. Rain patters loudly outside of my apartment. I guess I won't be going outside today. After eating, showering, and stretching, I strap into my haptic suit and log into Pangea.

Merlin and Fenrir are excited to see me. It's amazing what a several hundred-mile battle-race will do to bond man and wolf.

I check my notifications from yesterday. There are messages from Buzz, Grayson, and curiously, the Pangea Online Developers. I open theirs first.

Greetings Esil,

This message is to inform you that a bug was detected in all characters whose initial class was miner from the Mines in Sector 247. The bug has been fixed and a new patch has gone through effective immediately. Have a good day and as always, never stop leveling!

-Pangea Online Developers

The next message I read is Buzz's.

Esil,

Bro, things just hit the fan. Apparently, the developers found out about our you-know-what and fixed it. We're normal now. Don't know if this message is going to reach you or not. You're about to reach the mountains as I send this. My advice if you get this: don't fight anything!

-Buzz

Grayson is not so cryptic.

Someone ratted us out. Someone who went to Asgard with us. No one else knew about our little secret, so I would watch who you trust out there. Whoever told on you obviously hopes to benefit from not having you in the race. If you see anyone, don't fight, just run. Good luck.

-Grayson

There is one more from Aleesia, dated this morning.

. . .

Esil,

> *We need to talk ASAP.*
> *-Aleesia*

That's ominous. I try to wrap my brain around one of my friends betraying my trust. I don't think any of them would do it, not even Glordin or Tinker, who didn't make it into the tournament. I risked my life for Klink and Ordin. And yet, somehow, we were reported. I know it's fair, but that was the only advantage I had going into this thing. Without my strength, I'm not strong enough to compete with the others. When Ryken can take down nine players by himself, what chance do I have of getting past him?

I send the princess a message and she replies, agreeing to meet in the Mortican Mountains.

After the second quest, my face is even more famous than before. Several people try to stop me as I make my way out of the town square.

The princess waits for me in a nearby field. I come across her battling a harpy. Her arrows soar through the air, taking down the shrieking bird-woman in a few hits. Her face drops when she sees me.

"I'm so sorry!" she says, running up to me. Tears stream down her face.

I wrap my arm around her and pull her close.

"Why are you sorry? It's not your fault. With me being so famous right now, it was bound to catch up with us."

She cries even harder.

"You don't understand. It was me."

"You? What do you mean?"

"I was asking my dad questions. If it was possible for characters to be created with hidden stats? I told him about how all of you were strong and that it didn't make any sense to me, since you worked in the mines. He said they never paid much attention to the mines, but then he looked into it and found that there was a bug. Apparently, it had been there a really long time. So, then they fixed it and that's why you lost your strength. I'm so sorry."

Her words are like a blow to the gut. It takes me a moment to find my words.

"You're the reason why I don't have a chance at winning the tournament anymore?" An anger flares up in me that I can't control. I know she didn't mean for this to happen, but it doesn't excuse it. I told her to just let it go. She should have. "You're the reason why Buzz's mom is going to die. Dammit, Aleesia. I had a real shot at saving her. Now I'm just a bug that's going to get stepped on."

I turn to walk away. I've said enough hurtful things to her already, but I know if I stay, I'll say more.

"Let me make it up to you," she squeaks.

"Make it up to me? Can you give me my strength back? Can you get me thirty levels by the time the next quest starts? I don't think so. You've done enough."

With that, I take off. I can still hear her crying as Fenrir bolts away. Merlin gives me an annoyed hoot from my shoulder. He knows I'm being unfair. Why couldn't she just keep her mouth shut?

I message Buzz and Grayson and they both agree to meet me after work.

While I wait, I travel to various worlds and level as much as I can. Even though I don't have a shot, I can't just give up on Buzz's mom. I still have to try.

Fighting is so much harder without my strength. It takes me forever to kill monsters I could defeat in seconds only yesterday. I take more damage and run out of mana more often too. So, this is what it's really like to level grind. I'm screwed.

I still have my stat point from yesterday. I look at my stats and decide to put it into Agility. If I can't hit hard, I'm going to need to be faster.

Level 24:
   Strength - 14
   Agility - 4
   Vitality - 5
   Intellect - 6
   Dexterity - 5
   Stamina - 0

We meet up at a pub in Midgard. It's Buzz's favorite world now. A burly man wearing chainmail and a leather vest pours frothy ale into our mugs as we sit down at a table near the back.

"Sausage will be out in a minute," he grumbles.

"Ah, they know me so well," says Buzz. He takes off his dented helm and places it on the table. He takes a sip of the ale and some of it runs down his black tunic. "You left in such a hurry yesterday, we didn't get to congratulate you. Or talk about you-know-what."

"Yeah, about that. I didn't read your messages until this morning."

"Any idea who might have ratted you out?" asks

Grayson. He wears his pirate clothes and the bear tattoo stares out at me between the flaps of his vest.

"I already know. It was Aleesia. She was asking questions and her dad put the pieces together. I gave her a hard time about it. I'm sorry, Buzz."

"What are you sorry for?" he asks with a full mouth, eating the sausage that had just been placed on the table. "You're one of thirty-two people who are in the final quest. I don't care if you're not as strong as you were. You're smart, and you're one of the luckiest bastards I've ever known."

"He's right," says Grayson. "You're more than a warrior. You have good spells. You might have the best mount there is. That bird's no slouch either. You may be out-leveled and outgunned, but that's how it's been our whole lives. I don't care if you moved away. You're still a kid from The Boxes. You're still a miner."

Grayson places a small box on the table.

"What's this?" I ask.

"Buzz and I got you a little something. Happy early birthday." He slides the box across the table. I almost forgot that my birthday is tomorrow. It's never really been a big deal most of my life.

"I don't know what to say. Thanks."

"Quit blabbering and open it," says Buzz.

I open the box and a small ring falls onto the table. A dark black crystal shines from the thick silver band.

*Item: **Ring of Power**. +15 attack. Unique ability: Double Ring of Power's attack bonus for 30 seconds. After the bonus is up, Ring of Power offers no bonus for 60 seconds.*

"Maybe this will help get you out of a bind one day," says Grayson.

"Thanks, guys. This means a lot." I don't know what I would do without these two in my corner.

"Don't get all emotional on us. Go out there and learn to kill some monsters."

For the rest of the day, the three of us travel across Midgard, fighting monsters and animals, laughing and having fun. I get better at fighting, adapting to a new style that blends my magic, attack, and defense into a cohesive unit. It's not as easy or as strong as before, but maybe it'll give me a shot.

CHAPTER TWENTY-NINE

I'm woken up by a delivery. VR Haptix has sent me a box of new clothes and other stuff for my birthday. I love the shirt with a level nineteen on it, but my favorite is a bobblehead of my in-game character holding an axe. Tucked in the bottom of the box, I find a picture of me pulling Fenrir into the portal with a handwritten note on the frame.

Congrats on making it to the final round! We can't wait to see what you have up your sleeve this time.

If you only knew. So far, the developers and my closest friends are the only ones who know I lost my strength. With the way I talked to Aleesia, I'm not even sure we would be considered friends at this point.

It's great that I made it to nineteen-years-old, but after talking to Buzz and Grayson, my mind is back on the tournament. I probably have the least shot at winning of anyone, but I refuse to give up.

When I log into Pangea, my notifications ding like crazy. I have messages from several people wishing me a happy birthday, including Klink, Ordin, Glordin, and Tinker. It's easy to tell when it's someone's birthday in Pangea because a little party hat appears next to their name. I respond to each of them, thanking them for their wishes. I receive a free item from the Pangea Online Developers.

Item: Birthday Party Hat. *Wear this hat to let everyone you meet know it's your special day. Expires at midnight.*

I equip the hat. It's yellow with red polka dots and a few metallic ribbons that blow around when I walk. Might as well enjoy it while I can.

There is a message from Aleesia. The subject says 'Sorry,' but I don't open it. She's the last person I want to think about right now.

Below her message, there is one from a name I don't recognize. Howard Allen. I don't know how it got through the filter that keeps out messages from anyone not on my friends list. The subject is 'Happy birthday, Esil.' My curiosity is piqued, so I open it.

Happy birthday, son,

This birthday present is eleven years in the making. Heck, I might even forget I've sent it to you by the time you open it. Right now, you're eight years old and I'm watching through the window while you play outside with Old Blue. That dog sure does love you. You'll be nineteen when you get this, which probably means you're wondering why I didn't send this to you on your eighteenth birthday, when you were first allowed to explore Pangea with no restraints. The truth is, I wanted you to be able to experience Pangea for a whole year before I gave this to you. I wanted you to make your own choices and find your way in the game. In short, to become the player you want to be.

Do you remember when you asked me what I do and I told you I made magic? You were so impressed and fascinated. You told me that you wanted to make magic when you grew up. Hopefully by now, you know that what I really do is create the magic items and abilities used in Pangea. Here's the kicker, I made one just for you. We're not technically supposed to do this, but I figured since it will be eleven years before you get this, hopefully the statute of limitations will be long passed.

I love you, son. And I look forward to seeing the man you become.

Love,

Dad

P.S. I've attached a map and a key. Let me know once you find it.

For a moment, I can't breathe. I can't move. All I can do it stare at the message in front of me. Fenrir licks my fingers, sensing my unrest.

My father was a developer for Pangea Online.

Those memories. Those dreams. They were all real. The big black dog, his name was Old Blue. That means the woman was my mother and that they both died in a car accident. Then how did I end up in an orphanage? Why didn't I have family come and take me home? My entire life has been a lie. How did no one know my family?

I log out of Pangea and search the web for any information I can find on Howard Allen.

'Howard Allen, young video game developer for Pangea Online, dies in car crash with wife. Leaves behind young son.'

'Car crashes a thing of the past? Automated vehicles were supposed to be safer. Today, a promising young life was taken when the automated vehicle drove down an embankment, killing both occupants inside.'

'Howard Allen discusses his take on magic, and why Pangea was able to win out in the entertainment revolution.'

'Son of distinguished developer disappears after parents die in car crash.'

There are several articles on my father. Many on his work as a game designer and even more on the car crash that killed him and my mother. In all of the articles, though, there is no mention of me being there. The articles say that I just disappeared. After the crash, no one could find me. I was there, though. I know I was.

I need to go to the orphanage. Maybe they can tell me how I ended up there.

I order a taxi and a few moments later, it docks with my door. I climb inside and it takes me across Civic City back to The Boxes. The rundown box that is the orphanage is just as depressing as ever. I called ahead, so they are expecting me.

When I step through the door, the room is filled with children with wide eyes.

"You're pretty famous around these parts, Esil," says Mr. Green. He has run the orphanage for years. His hair is bald down the center and two white clouds of hair surround his head. I remember him as a stern man. A stickler for the rules and swift with justice to those who would break them. "It's not very often one of our own becomes one of the most famous players in Pangea. Do you have any advice for those who want to follow in your footsteps?"

I didn't come here to give a pep talk. "Uhm, eat your veggies." Dammit, I forgot they don't get veggies here. "I mean, keep your head up and don't stop believing. Can we talk in private, Mister Green?"

He leads me down a hall into a small office.

"I never thought I would see you around these parts again. If I had a chance to get out, I'd never come back. So, what brings you here, Esil?"

"Sir, how did I end up at the orphanage? Who brought me here?"

"Ah, the question every child wants to know eventually. Why did I become an orphan?" He pauses and touches the tips of his fingers together. "We found you walking the streets. Your head was bleeding and you were mumbling something. You know how unsafe it is out there and we couldn't just leave you. It took you a few weeks before you were able to talk again. You had no memory of who you were other than your name."

"And you didn't think to find out?" My anger rises. How could they not ask questions?

"Oh, we asked around. But you know as well as I do how helpful the outside world is to those of us in The Boxes. We searched for anyone looking for a missing child. Nothing came up so the authorities left you with us. I know this isn't the easiest place to grow up, but we did the best we could."

No one was looking for me because my parents were dead.

My next stop is the Civic City Police Department. If anyone can help me, it will be them.

After an hour wait, someone finally agrees to see me.

"So you're saying that you are the missing son of this developer who died eleven years ago?" A burly woman with red hair pulled up into a messy bun stares across a plain, metal table at me.

"Yes."

"You got any proof?"

"No."

"Any family that can verify your story?"

"No."

She taps annoyingly at a pad in front of her.

"What do you want me to do, kid?" she asks.

"I don't know, point me in the right direction."

She taps at the pad some more before speaking.

"Here's the deal." She looks down at the pad as she talks, reading from an article. "Howard Allen and his wife, Isabelle, had no surviving family members. They were both only children and their parents were deceased at the time of their death. They had one child, Esil Allen, who you claim to be, but who was never heard from after the accident. Two years after their death, their belongings became property of the state and were auctioned off to the highest bidder. Even if you are who you say you are, the only thing you're heir to is a name. I suggest you drop it and carry on with the life you have." She stares blankly at me.

"So that's it then. I just let it go."

"You can go to court and attempt to prove that you're their child, but that would be a long process. And expensive. I wouldn't recommend it. If you are who I think you are, based on the shirt you're wearing and your resemblance to the character in Pangea, then I think you've got bigger problems right now. A lot of people are pulling for the underdog. You don't want to let them down."

I leave the police station and go home. Feeling no closer to solving anything than I was before I left. It all seems so hopeless.

I have a family I will never see other than the few memories that sporadically appear. Some people are just destined to be alone, I guess. The worst part is that I'm not that sad. Having never known my family, it doesn't hurt that they aren't there. What hurts is what might have been.

My only option right now is to help the family I do have. Buzz and Grayson have been there for me every step of the way and I'm not going to let them down. Buzz's mom is depending on me. I'm going to take the map and key my dad left me and I'm going to find the treasure he hid. He said it was a one-of-a-kind spell. Maybe it will help me in the tournament.

Once I am back in Pangea, I message Buzz and Grayson. I want them with me for whatever I find.

I equip the map my dad gave me and it shows up in the bottom left of my vision, opposite my normal map. I also have a physical copy I can hold in my hand. It has several handwritten notes around the edges. The map is labeled 'Greenwich Gardens,' with a five-digit code written underneath. Scribbled beside the numbers it says 'passcode'.

Greenwich Gardens is a private world. There's no cost to enter, but only those who have the code can go in.

I send Buzz and Grayson the code and focus on Greenwich Gardens as I jump through my portal. I stop at a metal door. The silver door has five digital number boxes to enter the passcode. I enter in 92095. The door hisses and then opens.

The portal lets me out in an empty street. A long strip of black pavement with dotted yellow lines stretches out in front of me. Along both sides, dozens of two-storied houses with white picket fences line the street. Each one has its own defining features. Red shutters. A flag with a lion head. A bird fountain. They are all the same, yet all different.

"What the hell is this place?" asks Buzz. He takes off his helm and holds it under one arm. His eyes scan the streets and surrounding houses.

A red dot glows on the map in my bottom left vision. We're close. This must not be a very big world.

Grayson shows up a minute later. I tell them both about the message I got from my father. About the visions and dreams, the orphanage and the police station. They both have wide eyes by the time I'm done. It's a lot to take in.

"So, you mean to tell me you're the son of some famous developer and essentially have no shot at getting anything out of it?" asks Buzz.

"It's more complicated than that," says Grayson. "Have you tried talking to Pangea? Going to their office or anything?"

"No, the policewoman made it seem like it was all pretty much hopeless. Everything they owned was sold."

"You never know, they could have stock or a percentage of the company. It's worth looking into."

"Yeah, maybe when this is all over. It's not like I have any way of proving I'm his son."

"Maybe not, but he found you somehow. I'm sure you

received a new account at the orphanage. Especially if you didn't remember who you were. There was a way for his message to find you. That might be the key."

What Grayson says makes sense, but the priority is finding this spell. Grayson's necklaces jingle as we walk down the street. We take a left on Harris Avenue, a right onto Wingfoot Place, another right onto Spaulding Avenue. Monte Vista Drive is a dead end. A sign on the sidewalk calls it a cul-de-sac. The red dot beams brightly over the house at the end.

We walk down the empty street towards the house. It's eerie how there are no people. Everything is so…empty. The house we stand in front of is white, just like the others. Flowers hang from a small porch with white railing. A tire swing dangles from an oak tree that towers over the house in the front yard. Blue shutters and yellow curtains adorn the windows. Everything about the house is quaint and beautiful.

I turn the doorknob and unsurprisingly, it's locked. I equip the key card my father gave me and swipe it through the key reader. The light glows green and we are allowed to enter.

Inside, the house is welcoming. Bright colors and family photos adorn the walls. There are photos of my mother and father…and me. I have a school uniform on in one.

I glance down at the left-hand map. It has changed to a floorplan of the house. I can see each room in detail. Squares and circles denote where chairs, tables, and appliances go. The red dot beacons in a room marked 'Esil's bedroom.'

Neither Grayson nor Buzz speak as we walk through

the house, which adds to the fact that I'm walking through a crypt of my family history. It's a history I don't remember. A history I both long for and know nothing about. I want to be sad, to miss this place, but it doesn't come.

The bedroom at the top of the stairs has my name engraved on the door. A poster of a wizard casting a spell hangs slightly askew. I twist the doorknob and step into the childhood I never had.

I'm floored by the extravagance of it all. Half a dozen stuffed animals are neatly placed on the small bed with blue blankets. A wolf, lion, elephant and many others stare at me with dead eyes. A mobile of the planets twirls overhead. There are more toys than the entire orphanage had. A computer. A holographic video projector. Gaming systems.

It almost makes me sick to look at the gluttony of it all. I see Buzz's wide eyes in my peripheral.

"Look around and see if you see a chest," I say.

We look around the room, opening drawers and emptying shelves. Searching for any clue to where the spell might be located. We find nothing.

I remember the notes on the physical copy of the map and take it from my inventory. Near the bottom, it says, 'turn on the projector.'

The projector hangs from the ceiling over the bed. I press the power button and after a few beeps, it comes to life. A blue light shines out and slowly begins to form the outlines of a man. My father.

"Hello Esil. Happy birthday!" he says with a smile. "I can't even begin to describe the excitement I feel about the prospect of you turning nineteen. You're practically a man! I hope the lack of people in Greenwich Gardens didn't freak you out. Not many people go there. It's one of several online storage areas for developers and their families. I thought it was pretty smart that I hide your present there, where only I could leave it. I'm not sure if we'll still be living there once you're grown. Hopefully, being back home brings back a few memories for you. Anyways, I'm sure you're wondering what I created for you at this point. It might not be the most powerful spell ever, but it's one of a kind. Go look in the fridge and you'll find it. And after you're done, lock the door and come see me and your mom. Love you, Esil."

Grayson puts his hand on my shoulder, a gesture I've grown accustomed to over the past few weeks. I have no doubt that the man on the hologram loved me. I'm sure I had a great life when I was younger, but when it mattered, when it really mattered, Grayson was the one I counted on.

"Thanks," I say.

He nods. Words aren't needed.

"I get that you two are having a moment, but are we going to open the fridge or what?" asks Buzz.

"Alright, let's check it out," I chuckle.

I stare at the gleaming silver fridge. The reflection of me and the two people closest to me look back at us. I still remember the first time I looked in the mirror after I had bought my green tunic. I see the little black axe that adorns the collar that just happened to spur me into buying my own axe. The silver wolf belt buckle that reminds me so much of my first day in the Mortican Mountains. Next to me is Buzz. No longer the debonair steampunker, but still the class clown. His black tunic and dented battle helm better represent the man he has become, a man of character. Behind us stands Grayson, the hardest worker I've ever known. A hard man, but also a caring one. His pirate garb reminds him of a life he once lived, and everything he lost.

I pull open the door and our figures distort.

Buzz laughs when he sees what is inside.

A tiny chest sits inside a green gelatinous blob.

"Oh man," says Buzz. "I like your dad. He put your chest in Jell-o." He bends over, clutching his stomach from laughing so hard.

"What is it?" I ask.

"It's…a…dessert." Buzz gasps for air. "He put your birthday present in a dessert."

I notice a twitch of a smile as Grayson fakes a cough.

I pull out the plate of Jell-o and sit it on the table. The gelatinous food sways back and forth like a wave that refuses to crash. It's cold and sticky as I dig my hands through and grab the chest. It's small. A fraction of the size of the developer's chest I found.

Congratulations, Esil! You have found a hidden chest. You know how this goes by now so just go ahead and open it.

-Dad

I open the chest and a piece of parchment hovers in the air before me.

Item: Spellbook. Requirements: N/A. Activate? Y/N

I focus on yes and the parchment disappears. My body vibrates all over and my vision flashes white.

Congratulations! You have learned the ability Firestorm. Ultimate Ability: Summons a tornado of fire that deals immense damage. Cost: 200 mana per second. Cooldown: 2 seconds.

CHAPTER THIRTY

The long-lost son of Howard and Isabelle Allen finally resurfaces, playing a game his father helped create, in an attempt to win the prize and save his best friend's dying mother.

I want to punch something. I don't know how they found out about my story, but I have been badgered by reporters for the past few hours. Somehow, they are able to sneak by my spam filter and send me messages asking for interviews. They are bothering me on the eve of the biggest day of my life.

It had to be someone at the police station who let it leak that I was the son of Howard Allen. This must have led to someone else figuring out my promise to Buzz.

And it couldn't have come at a worse time. Earlier in the day, the developers sent out a message telling us that the final stage of the tournament would be held tomorrow. I need a good night's rest to make sure I'm firing on all cylinders, so that leaves me with only a couple of hours to do anything.

I elect to spend the time doing nothing.

There's not much I can do to help my cause. I can spend the last few hours desperately trying to gain another level and one more stat point, or I can decompress and take stock of my situation. One more stat point isn't going to win me the tournament. The only chance I have is if I follow my instincts, and they say sit tight.

By the time the quest starts tomorrow, I might be the most famous person in it. I'm also the least likely to win. According to the odds-makers, I'm ranked sixth because of my finishes in the first two challenges, but they don't know that I lost my strength.

My story is plastered across every website I visit. It seems everyone loves an underdog.

I'm currently level twenty-four, half the level of all but one of the other thirty-one contestants.

From my home portal, I pull up my character sheet, taking stock of all the abilities I have learned since opening the developer's chest.

Level 24:
    Strength - 14
    Agility - 4
    Vitality - 5
    Intellect - 6
    Dexterity - 5
    Stamina - 0

Lunging Strike. Effect: stuns opponent for .5 seconds. Cost: 50 mana. Cooldown: 10 seconds.

Resilience. Resilience increases the attack speed of you or an ally for 20 seconds. Cost: 50 mana. 20 second cooldown.

Mud Pits. Cost 100 mana. Creates a field of mud pits, slowing your enemies attack and movement speed by 50% for 20 seconds. Cooldown: 60 seconds.

Inspire Resistance. NPCs in your party will fight with increased fervor.

Haunted Earth. Cost: 100 mana. Roots spring forth from the earth, rooting your opponent in place for two seconds. Cooldown: 30 seconds.

Waterfall. Cost: 200 mana. After a 2 second wait, water pours down from the sky, dealing immense damage to a singular location. Cooldown: 20 seconds.

Firestorm. Ultimate Ability: Summons a tornado of fire that deals immense damage. Cost: 200 mana per second. Cooldown: 2 seconds.

Not too bad, I only wish I had a larger mana pool. I have enough mana to cast roughly ten spells per battle. Or use Firestorm for five seconds. With that kind of price to use the ability, I won't be using it unless it's a life or death moment.

Next, I sort through my inventory. Making sure I have all of my best items readily available. With my strength gone, some of them aren't as useful as they once were.

Item: Meteoric Iron Axe, +10 strength. 10% armor penetration. This double-edged axe was forged from the heart of a meteorite.

Item: Elvish Battle Spear. +12 attack. +15% armor penetration. It's long and strong and down to get the killing on.

Item: Vampiric Ring. Grants 2% lifesteal per attack. To hurt thy enemy is to heal thy self.

Item: The Grappler. +7 strength. Ability: Grapple, fires a grappling hook and attaches to the first object it hits. 30 second cooldown. "You'll not get away that easy, Bucko."

Item: Forgotten Chainmail. +12 armor. The relics of a ship lost at sea.

Item: Staff of the Water Ancients. +20% magic damage on elemental attacks.

Item: Benevolent Shield of Healing. +10% health. Unique ability: Double-edged shield. The next attack will be blocked and heal both attacker and defender for 5% health. Cooldown: 5 minutes.

Item: Ring of Power. +15 attack. Unique ability: Double Ring of Power's attack bonus for 30 seconds. After the bonus is up, Ring of Power offers no bonus for 60 seconds.

Most of my items are on the physical damage side of things. The truth is, for a normal level twenty-four player, I would be pretty strong. I have great items and most of my stat points are in Strength. The problem is I'm not a normal level twenty-four player. I'm out of my league. So far out of my league that I'm playing with people who do this for a living.

I check the Market, a screen visible from my home portal where I can purchase consumable items without having to go into a game world.

I fill my inventory with as many potions and buffs as I can fit. By the time I'm done, I can outfit a small army with what I've bought. Let's just hope I stay alive long enough to use them.

For the rest of the evening, I lie in bed browsing through old articles about my father on the digital pad that VR Haptix sent me. He was very well respected for his age. Some of the ideas he created were responsible for Pangea's success among gamers. He won numerous awards and was said to be pioneering a breakthrough in game design at the time of his death.

I wake up to a steadily increasing ding, telling me it's time to get up. The pad is still in my hand, open on an article about my father.

After showering, I eat a modest breakfast and log into Pangea.

Today is the day.

A new portal waits for me inside of my home portal. Merlin hops on my shoulder and I mount Fenrir, then we jump through.

You are now entering The Maze. Please wait for further instructions.

I stand in a small enclosure with stone walls on three sides. My map is disabled. A black circle with a dot showing my position is all that shows so I focus and it disappears. An invisible barrier blocks the entryway, preventing me from leaving. Fenrir has disappeared. I feel his presence in my inventory, but am unable to call him to my side. Mounts must be disabled here. Merlin tries to fly out, but an invisible force keeps him from escaping. It's a cloudy day wherever we are. Thunder rolls in the distance, casting an ominous tone over everything. I can see glimpses of the alley in front of my enclosure. High walls run along each side, making it impossible for anyone to climb or jump over. Torches hang from the walls. My guess, it's going to get dark soon.

If I know the developers, this is more than just a simple maze. There will be monsters and challenges and worst of all, other players.

A loud voice booms from the sky overhead. The voice is surprisingly chipper.

"Welcome, challengers! It's me, Nancy, again. I can't wait to get this show started. First off, let me tell you a little about The Maze. It was designed specifically for this tournament. There are thirty-two entry points along the outer wall of the maze. At its center, a portal awaits to take you to the crowning ceremony. There will be no mounts allowed within the maze. Contestants will be staggered entry, based upon the results of the last stage. Many challenges await you, depending on the path you take. This is a PvP stage, so be aware of your fellow competitors. In five minutes' time, the first person will be allowed to enter the maze. Subsequent contestants will be permitted entry every ten seconds afterward. Your streams have been disabled and everyone across the world will be watching on the official Pangea Online stream. They can watch a montage or individual players as they choose. Good luck, challengers!"

I now see the importance of finishing high in the race. I'll be over a minute behind the first entrant, and poor Ordin, he'll be close to five minutes behind.

The timer in the top middle of my vision counts down from five minutes. I try to look out into the alley and see if there is any indication which way I should go. It all looks the same from my vantage point.

I pace back and forth across the small enclosure, waiting for my time to come.

A loud gong initiates the start of the final round.

Ten seconds later, another gong.

And another.

And another.

Feet scuffle down the alley and I catch a glimpse of the princess as she runs by to the right. Looks like that's the way I'll be going. If the princess sees me, will she take me out?

Before I know it, it's my turn. I step out into the maze. It's empty on both sides. The corridor goes in both directions for several hundred feet. A half-dozen entrances disappear further into the maze on each side of me. There is no way to know which way the princess went.

I go to the right and take a left into the first entrance.

When I turn the corner, my vision goes red and I can't move.

A tiny blue lizard hisses at me from several feet away, an electric current running along its body.

Shocker Lizard. Level 35. *These electric lizards are annoying alone, but when two or more group together, they can cause havoc.*

Luckily for me, there is only one.

Merlin swoops down at the lizard and grabs it between his talons. The lizard sparks and forces Merlin to drop it.

The stun wears off and Merlin lands on my shoulder, hooting angrily, his feathers ruffled.

I equip my spear. The little bugger is small, he can't put up that much of a fight. I use Lunging Strike and stun him in place. I pull back my spear, readying it for attack, when my vision goes red again and I freeze in place.

A second lizard appears from around the corner.

Just my luck.

Another gong makes me realize that several other people have entered the maze since this fight began.

I'm hit with a bolt of lightning and lose another chunk

of health. These two reptilian rodents have brought me down to eighty percent health. I take a potion and a Fire Whiskey and force the attack. The two lizards stand side by side, taunting me. I use Haunted Earth and root them in place, immediately following it up with Waterfall. The combo takes out half their life.

The two lizards attack at the same time, their electric bolts hitting me in the chest. It doesn't stun me, but I lose another twenty percent health.

Enough of this! I'm not going to die to the first mob I run into. They're small with no armor and probably squishy as hell. I run at the first lizard, use Lunging Strike, and attack. I might have been able to kill him with one hit a few days ago, but I'm not much of a slouch against something near my level. The first one falls over dead. The second lizard turns to run, but I throw my spear like a javelin and make lizard kabobs.

I take a mana and health potion and continue. I also use a few buffs that increase my health and defense. Half of us are in the maze now and if I don't get a move on, I stand a good chance of getting attacked from behind. Ryken won't hesitate to put his sword in my back.

A pit awaits me around the next corner. It's filled with spikes designed to impale anyone unlucky enough to fall into its trap. The pit is roughly thirty feet across to the next side, making it impossible to cross for all but the most agile of players. Lucky for me, I have just the tool for the job.

I equip Grappler and aim for the sconce holding the torch on the other side of the pit. The grappling hook catches and I hear movement around the corner behind me. There's no time to waste. I run and jump out into the pit. As soon as I am in the air, I use Grappler's retractable feature and it pulls me across. I land on the other side and slide to a stop.

On the other side, an elf mage looks back at me. His blood red cloak conceals a black staff. I give him a wave and disappear around the next corner. The maze splits again and I decide to go right.

I've been in the maze long enough that all the competitors have entered by now. Thunder roars and the patter of rain mimics the sound of a thousand footsteps. I need to watch my back. Anyone can be stealthy in this ruckus.

Rain puddles along the stone floor and I'm thankful to be away from the Shocker Lizards.

I make another right turn and I'm on the outer rim of the maze again.

"Dammit!" I yell. I have to start from the beginning with no way of knowing which path I have taken.

"Esil!" Ordin's deep and lively voice echoes down the corridor. Rain has soaked his red beard to the core. He smiles and I return the gesture, happy to see a friendly face. "What are you still doing out here?"

"Wrong turn. You?"

"I was one of the last ones out. I was hoping to find a clue as to which path to take." He looks over his shoulder. "I heard about you and the princess. Sorry for you, my friend."

"It is what it is. This is all that matters right now. Do you want to stay together and watch each other's backs?" I extend my arm to him.

"I'd be honored." He clasps my forearm and we set off down the hallway.

We decide on an entrance where the stone is covered in moss. Several turns later, we come across a giant creature with light green skin, glowing white eyes, and dark black hair.

Ogre Mage. Level 51. *Like an ogre, but with magic.*

Its skin is covered in hundreds of warts, and two rough, broken horns protrude from its head. Unlike most ogres, which are covered in the pelts of fallen enemies, this one wears chainmail and leather. One hand holds a damaged sword. The other hand glows bright blue.

It unleashes a bolt of magic and I dodge out of the way just in time. The magical bolt smashes into the wall, sending stone debris scattering across the floor.

I equip Staff of the Ancients. Time to try and beat magic with magic.

"I'm going to snare him, then you rough him up," I say. Ordin's warhammer begins to glow.

I cast Haunted Earth, but the ogre uses some sort of fire spell to burn away the roots before they grab him. Next, I use Resilience on Ordin, increasing his attack speed. I cast Waterfall, hoping my plan works and the ogre will be where I predict in two seconds, then I run towards him. A magical blast catches me in the shoulder, reddening my vision and slowing me by a fraction. Once I'm close enough, I use Lunging Strike and stun the ogre in place. Waterfall crashes down on him just before Ordin connects with his imbued warhammer. The blow sends the ogre flying into the wall with a thud, the impact stunning it again. I switch to my axe and attack. Ordin's blows take out far more than mine do, but we end the creature all the same.

My XP bar shoots up, nearly at level twenty-five. The

ogre drops a few items and some gold, but nothing note-worthy. Merlin trails behind us on foot, the rain making it difficult for him to fly in such a small space.

We come to another split in the maze and go left. Someone screams from up ahead and we run to investigate. A black minotaur stands in the way, two gravestones at his feet.

Minotaur. Level 70. With a thick hide and a propensity for stunning its opponents, the minotaur is not to be trifled with.

No thanks.

"How about we take the other way?"

Ordin nods in agreement and we retrace our steps. At least we know two of our competitors are out of the game.

For what feels like hours, Ordin and I attempt to navigate the maze. We fight when we can and turn tail when we can't. Sometimes, it's better to take the long way around than die trying. We find several more tombstones along the way, making me thankful I have Ordin by my side for the moment.

The maze is full of traps, from tripwires that cause darts to shoot out to secret tiles that change the course of the maze before our eyes.

I try to keep thoughts of Buzz and his mother at the forefront, to remind me why I am here and what I am playing for. It keeps my energy high and my concentration sharp.

The maze suddenly opens into a large room where several corridors stand empty. The sky is dark overhead. Lightning strikes and I feel my hair stand on end. Merlin softly hoots on my shoulder. Several large gargoyles are mounted on the walls. They are intricately carved, the torches that burn beneath them making the stone guardians almost look alive.

Merlin flies across the room, thankful for the extra space, and lands on one's head.

Ordin and I try to decide which route to take when I hear a flutter and then the chomp of teeth. Merlin's body falls to the floor, coated in blood. His soft, downy feathers dance through the air, slowly coming to rest beside him.

I don't understand what just happened. Merlin lays unmoving on the floor. My senses seem to be failing me. It's harder to hear and see as I rush to Merlin and pick up his small frame in my hands. He doesn't move. Flecks of stone fall on my head.

I look up and see the gargoyle's eyes are no longer stone, but a dull yellow. Its arms and legs crack and crunch as it breaks free from the wall and jumps down.

I want to curl up and cry. Merlin is dead. I hold him tight against my chest, hoping against hope that he might open his eyes and hoot. I hear Ordin's muffled voice behind me as a powerful stone hand connects with my face.

CHAPTER THIRTY-ONE

Merlin is dead.

I slam into the wall, losing a third of my health from the gargoyle's punch, but the only thing I can think about is Merlin falling to the ground covered in blood. In Pangea, when a pet dies, that's it, they're gone. Merlin is a big part of the reason why I am here in the first place.

I slowly stand up. Merlin would want me to fight. My sight and hearing have returned, but after the enhancements Merlin provided, everything seems muted.

Ordin stands in the middle of the open room while gargoyles leave their perches and land with a crash all around.

Gargoyle. Level 57. Winged stone creatures able to blend in with their surroundings, gargoyles are pure magic and turn to permanent stone in technology-only worlds.

Three gargoyles surround Ordin and one stands only feet from me. I can't think about Merlin now. I have to fight to survive.

Lunging Strike stuns the gargoyle nearest me and I run to join Ordin.

"What do we do now?" I ask.

"Gargoyles have really high magic resistances. We'll need to use our melee attacks."

Great. Four high-level monsters and I have to rely on my strength. I take a health potion and my HP slowly recovers.

"Okay, I'll stun or snare them when I can. If you can hit them into the wall, that's a bonus stun. Only attack if they can't move. Otherwise, just stay out of their way."

Ordin nods and lifts his warhammer, ready to fight.

Rain continues to pour down on us. Merlin's tiny body has disappeared. I'm sorry I never got to say good-bye to my friend. Anger rises in me again and this time, I can't control it.

Haunted Earth roots two of the gargoyles in place. I equip my Elvish Spear and battleaxe. I don't care about defending myself. In this moment, I want to make them pay for what they did to Merlin. I cast Resilience on myself and activate Ring of Power's ability, doubling its attack bonus for thirty seconds. Ordin lets out a battle cry to my right as we charge the stone monsters.

I attack in a flurry, stabbing and slashing with both arms. Ordin hits one of the gargoyles with a powerful strike, knocking it into the wall and stunning it. I switch targets and attack the frozen monster.

A powerful blast knocks me off my feet and drains my health by another twenty percent. I'm down to almost half health. Two of the gargoyles still have full HP. One is down to a third and the other has seventy-five percent health.

"Take out the lowest one first," I order.

The gargoyles shoot out magical orbs that explode upon impact. They move slow, but pack a powerful punch. One of them hits Ordin in the back, but only takes a tenth of his health. He must have great armor or defensive spells.

I run for the weakest gargoyle and use Lunging Strike. Ordin and I attack his stone hide. The bonus from Ring of Power wears off, but a glowing strike of Ordin's warhammer finishes him.

Three to go.

Stone claws rip into my shoulder and my vision goes red. The gargoyle lifts me into the air and all I can hear are the flaps of its powerful stone wings. It tosses me against the wall and my health drops like my body, down to forty percent.

I stand and one of their magical orbs hits me in the side, knocking me down. Twenty percent HP.

Ordin fights hard on the other side of the room. He still has seventy percent health. One of the gargoyles he fights is down to half.

"Equip your shield, Esil!" he yells at me. "You can be angry, but you need to live for Merlin's death to mean anything."

He's right. I need to be smart. I equip my shield in one hand and my spear in the other. As much as I love my axe, my spear has slightly better stats and I need every advantage I can get.

I cast Haunted Earth and catch the weakest gargoyle in its roots. It roars defiantly as Ordin's warhammer crashes against it in a bright flash of light. I get in one good hit before it comes unrooted and I retreat. With twenty percent health, I need to stay out of the fight.

Ordin rushes at a gargoyle and takes an orb to the face. It drops his health fifteen percent, but he is able to land a blow that knocks the gargoyle into the wall, stunning it. I cast Resilience on him, boosting his attack speed. I'm too far away to get there in time, so I toss my spear like a javelin and equip my axe.

The gargoyle's stone body crumbles to the floor.

Two left.

A gargoyle hovers in the air to the left of me. I turn to fight and with a powerful flap of its wing, a gust of wind slams into me, turning everything red and dropping my health to five percent. The gargoyle charges.

This is where I die. I came so close, too.

An electrically charged arrow cuts through the rain and hits the gargoyle in the chest. Dozens of tendrils erupt from the arrow, covering the gargoyle and stunning it mid-flight. It falls to the ground unable to move.

"Stay out of the way," orders Aleesia.

I retreat to a corner, not that I have much choice. I use my last five health potions all at once and wait for my health to restore. The princess stands in front of me, firing volley after volley at the stone creatures. Flaming arrows, electric, ice. A rainbow of arrows fly across the room, some I have never seen before. The gargoyles never have a chance once she shows up. Her arrows keep the gargoyles distracted while Ordin attacks them from behind.

When the last gargoyle crumbles, the princess faces me and extends her hand to help me up. I return the gesture and she pulls me to my feet.

"Esil, I'm so—"

"You don't owe me an apology," I cut her off. "If anyone should be apologizing, it's me. I shouldn't have been so secretive about everything and not expected you to ask questions. It's not your fault your dad is a developer." I realize I'm still holding on to her arm and let go. "Thanks for saving me."

"Don't mention it. Quite the maze though, huh?" she asks.

"Yeah, we best be getting a move on then. Want to join me and Ordin?"

A smile creeps across her face.

"I'd love to." The smile disappears as quickly as it came and she looks around the room. "Where's Merlin?"

My words catch in my throat. I'm not ready to say the words out loud.

"He didn't make it," Ordin answers for me.

"Oh, no. Esil, I'm so sorry." Her words are genuine, matching the hurt on her face.

Maybe that's why pets aren't as common in Pangea. At least in the PvP worlds. They aren't just items that can be equipped and replaced. They have personality. They bond with their owners and just like that, they can disappear forever.

We decide on a door and exit back into the maze. The rain stops for a moment and a brilliant moon shows between the clouds. Something howls nearby, making me long for Fenrir.

We wind through the maze, narrowly missing a trip-wire for who knows what kind of trap. We defeat a pair of owlbears, bears with the head and wings of an owl. They rough me up a bit, but with a few good snares, we take them down. Two of our competitors are unlucky enough to try and attack us and meet the same fate.

It feels like we've been in the maze for hours at this point, with no way of knowing if we're going in the right direction or who is closest to finding the center. We could've passed by it a dozen times without realizing how close we are for all I know.

Around the next corner, a battle rages. Three werewolves stand battling a warrior in black armor. He wears a helm with the metal horns of a ram that I'd recognize anywhere. Ryken. The three werewolves are all around half health. They take damage, then gain a little back with each hit. Their lifesteal is incredible. Ryken still has two-thirds of his health.

Something glows on the other side of their battle.

"The portal!" I say. "We can't let him get to it."

Ryken uses familiar spells against the werewolves. He calls undead hands from the ground, holding them in place. A swarm of black moths smother them. His own lifesteal heals back a portion of the damage the werewolves deal.

Then he uses a spell I've never seen before. Ryken raises both arms in the air and a black cloud forms overhead. It grows and rumbles and then two bolts of lightning jolt from the cloud, hitting both Ryken and a werewolf. Ryken loses half his health, but the werewolf dies.

"He just sacrificed his own health to kill the wolf," mumbles Ordin.

"We need to attack him while he's low," says Aleesia.

She shoots a flaming arrow that does very little

damage. Ryken is both a tank and a heavy magic dealer. He turns, finally noticing us.

"Sister," he rumbles. "How nice of you to join us."

He attacks with lifesteal and a red jet streaks across the hallway, colliding with the princess and taking twenty percent of her health and restoring it to Ryken.

The werewolves attack, their razor-sharp claws grating against the death knight's shield. He raises one hand, and a moment later, the fallen werewolf rises and attacks its brethren. Each attack raises Ryken's health bit by bit.

"Take out the wolf," yells the princess. She fires arrows at the undead wolf, dropping its health by a tenth.

Ordin runs for the werewolf, his warhammer glowing a bright yellow. Ryken tries to root the dwarf, but Ordin dodges it, his warhammer connecting with the undead creature in an explosion of light. The werewolf loses half of its health from the attack, but is on Ordin swiftly, clawing and biting.

I switch to Staff of the Ancients and cast Haunted Earth, rooting Ryken in place, and follow it up with Waterfall. His orange eyes bore into me. He loses a small amount of health, much less than I would have liked. I use my last mana potion.

Ordin does battle with the undead werewolf while the princess and I attack from a distance. The two living werewolves attack Ryken from the other side, but his health replenishes as soon as he is attacked. We're in a stalemate until someone runs out of mana.

Ordin is losing health fast. I need to help him with the werewolf.

"I'm going in to help Ordin, it's our only way," I tell Aleesia.

I switch back to my spear and move in closer. If we can take out the werewolf while Ryken's attention is away, I can run back to safety without taking any damage.

Ordin smashes his warhammer into the werewolf, slamming it against the wall and stunning it. I stab with my spear and cast Resilience on Ordin. Aleesia casts the same spell on me. All of a sudden, I can't move my feet. Undead hands hold both of us in place.

"It's over," Ryken bellows. The words reverberate in my chest.

Red tendrils of magic escape his hand and come right for me. They bypass me and crash into Ordin. He has more HP than me. It makes sense Ryken would target him. I hear a buzz and then everything goes black.

When the moths disappear, Ordin's tombstone sprouts from the ground beside me. I have almost no health, so I retreat to the princess.

"We're screwed," I say.

"Just stand behind me."

With Ordin gone, Ryken slays another werewolf.

The princess carefully approaches him from behind. She switches out her bow for her elvish sword. It's short and thin, made for fast attacks.

"Call off your dogs, Ryken. Let's settle this the old-fashioned way."

Ryken laughs. It's a deep, heartless laugh that chills me to the bone.

"Have it your way, sister. First, I'll kill you. Then I'll kill your little boy toy."

He tosses his shield aside and pulls out his

broadsword. The weapon is as long as me and must weigh several hundred pounds.

Sparks fly when their blades touch. For a blade so small, Aleesia's parries Ryken's attack with ease. The way they move, it's easy to see they might be related. They're two sides of the same coin.

The princess lets her guard down for a second and that's all it takes for Ryken to seize his opportunity and strike. His blade catches the princess in the thigh, taking a tenth of her health.

The two undead werewolves keep the living one at bay while Ryken battles his sister. With my five percent health, there is not much I can do to help. I watch, a spectator in the great match that will determine my own fate.

The princess presses the attack, forcing Ryken to defend with blazing speed for a sword so large. She attacks and then takes a step back. When Ryken moves to defend, she attacks from the opposite side and strikes between the plates of his armor. His health drops to forty percent. Ryken's eyes glow brighter with anger from deep in his helm.

He counters, but the princess is prepared this time. She blocks each blow in turn. Ryken moves just a fraction slower this time. The princess uses it to her advantage and grazes him with her sword. He's down to thirty-five percent health. He roars and slashes at Aleesia's feet. She jumps and the blade passes underneath. With Ryken off-balance, she cuts him again, bringing him to a quarter of health.

"Enough of this!" Furious, Ryken casts a spell, rooting the princess in place. The two werewolves bear down on her, covering the stone floor in a splatter of blood. There is an explosion of light and both werewolves are tossed aside. The princess crawls across the floor to me at five percent health.

"Stand up," I say.

"It's over," she responds meekly.

"Stand up and attack me."

"What?" Confusion paints her face.

"Attack me! I have a plan."

She nods. I equip my shield and activate its special ability.

She brings down her blade on my shield and the blow is blocked. Five percent health returns to both of us. It's not a lot, but maybe it will keep us alive.

"I have an ability. It's strong, but once I use it, I'll be out of mana. So it's really our only shot. It's been too big of a risk to use, but now I don't think there is any other way."

"We're going all in?" she asks.

"All in."

"Then I've got something I've been saving too."

We both stand and face Ryken. He's killed the final werewolf and now has three of the undead creatures at his back.

"Ready to say your good-byes, sister?" he goads.

His werewolves march towards us.

I equip Staff of the Ancients and cast Firestorm. A small flame forms in the middle of the hallway.

Is this some kind of joke? Did my dad pull another prank on me with this spell?

Slowly, the fire begins to grow. Wind whips around it, forming a funnel that brings the fire into the air until the storm engulfs the width of the hall. It rises above the ceiling in a monstrous tornado.

The princess casts her spell and the tornado goes dark. Lightning flares from inside it. Then bolts begin darting out in every direction. Red, then blue, then a black bolt that tears through the wall of the maze.

I look over to the princess and lose all focus on the storm. Her beautiful ivory skin has changed to a charcoal. Her blue eyes are now red. Her blonde hair, black.

"What did you cast?" I ask.

"Storm of darkness. It was the spell you gave me when we beat the lich in the dungeon. It's powerful, but in order to use it, I had to change my allegiance to the dark elves."

"Permanently?" I can't believe she would do that for a chance at victory. Or did she do it for me?

She nods.

The storm dies away. The walls of the corridor are destroyed in places. A gravestone sits amongst the charred rubble.

Ryken is dead.

The portal awaits us at the end of the hall, but how do we decide who goes through?

I feel the warmth of the princess's hand as she takes hold of mine. Together, we walk forward.

"I can't believe we did it," I say. Never in a million years would I have thought I could actually win this tournament. And I couldn't. Not by myself. It was my friends who helped me reach this moment.

"Go ahead," says Aleesia. "You earned this."

"I couldn't have done it without you. Ryken would have destroyed me." It's only fair we do this together. Hopefully, half of the prize money will be enough to get treatment started for Buzz's mom and I can earn the rest in time.

"Same time?" she asks.

"Same time."

We hold hands and prepare to jump into the portal, but then Aleesia grabs me by the neck and pulls me towards her. She presses her lips to mine. I don't care that it's virtual reality, it feels like the real thing. I close my eyes and feel her lips against mine. Then I feel a hard push against my chest and the last thing I see is Aleesia's face before I go tumbling into the portal.

CHAPTER THIRTY-TWO

Trumpets blare as I fall out of the portal. My hands reach at empty air, grasping for the Aleesia's hand. I can't believe she pushed me through. She should be here with me. We should be accepting the prize together. Hell, she probably deserves to win it more than me. I would have died twice over if not for her.

The roar of the crowd takes me by surprise. I look around into a sea of flashing lights. I'm in some kind of coliseum with giant video boards replaying my highlights of the tournament. Behind me, the screen shows the princess and I kissing, right before I go through the portal. Thousands of people fill the stands, cheering and clapping. Confetti rains down all around and fireworks ignite in the sky.

A firm hand grips me on my shoulder as a man's voice echoes throughout the coliseum.

"The first ever champion of the Developer's Tournament, Esil Allen!"

The crowd goes wild at the mention of my name. Wait, they said Allen. Does that mean—

"Ever since the news went viral, we've had everyone in our data department combing through files and records and are finally able to confirm that Esil is, in fact, the lost son of Howard and Isabelle Allen." A man wearing a black suit with blond hair neatly parted to the side steps up beside me and lowers his voice so the crowd can't hear. "We have a lot to discuss in the next few days, Esil. I want you to stop by our offices after the excitement from the tournament has died down. We're glad to have you as a part of the Pangea family. I'm just sorry it took us so long to find you."

"Uhm—" I don't really know how to respond.

"We don't have to talk now. I know you've been through a lot. I'm Benjamin, by the way. President of Pangea Online Entertainment. I wanted to be here to personally congratulate the winner. Now, let's give the crowd what they've been waiting for." He guides me over to the center of the stage.

"Many of you have been following along with Esil's journey since the first quest, when an unknown player finished in the top five. More of you came to love him when you saw his daring acts in the name of friendship and loyalty in the second quest. But how could anyone not love him once we all found out that he was playing not for himself, but for his best friend's mother? Esil, we think that what you're doing is so great that we've decided to cover any medical costs that exceed the prize winnings of the tourna-ment. But first, let's bring out the two people you entered the tournament for. They are the reason you never gave up. Let's hear it for Buzz and his mother, Maria."

Buzz steps up on the stage, his arm wrapped around his mother. He basks in the applause, waving at the crowd. Buzz was made for the spotlight. He wears a black tuxedo with a bow-tie and Maria wears a long red dress. In Pangea, she is not the weak person I rode with to the doctor. They both smile from ear to ear. Buzz wraps his arms around me once they are close enough.

"You did it!" he yells over the crowd. "I never doubted you, but, man, I can't believe it. That Firestorm though, your dad really knew how to build 'em."

"You look nice," I say.

He runs his finger between the shirt collar and his neck, trying to stretch it out. "They made me wear this. Said I needed to look 'presentable'." He mimics the last word. Buzz releases me and his mother and I embrace.

"We'll never be able to pay you back for this. I owe my life to you."

"I just wanted to do what was right. You don't owe me anything."

Buzz and Maria stand beside me and Benjamin continues talking. I tune him out as he talks about my achievements and what this tournament means to the developers at Pangea. Honestly, I just want to go home and sleep. This day has been exhausting, to say the least.

I search the crowd for Grayson and find him sitting on the front row. He gives me a thumbs up, but otherwise, his face is stern.

I tune back in when Benjamin talks about the prizes.

"Not only will Esil be winning one hundred thousand gold, he will also be receiving one of the highly sought after Developer's Chests. Even we don't know what's inside this one."

Congratulations! You have been gifted a Developer's Chest by Pangea Online. Would you like to open it? Y/N

I think I'll open this one when there aren't millions of eyes watching my every move.

"We will also be awarding prizes to the top three finishers. In second place, many of you loved to watch the feud between her and her brother Ryken, give a big round of applause for Aleesia!"

When the princess steps up to the stage, her eyes meet mine. Her dark skin and hair are so different from the girl I cleared a dungeon with so many weeks ago. I hope she doesn't regret her decision. Unless she creates a new character from scratch, she is stuck as a dark elf for as long as she has that account.

She shakes Benjamin's hand and then pushes Buzz aside to stand beside me.

"You didn't have to push me through, you know?" I say.

"I know, but I wanted to. It's not as if you could have stopped me." She smirks.

"As runner-up, Aleesia wins ten thousand gold and a Developer's Chest of her own."

The crowd cheers for the princess.

"And in third place, the little camel that could, Dantos."

The shrouded player who rode the camel in the second race moves slowly across the stage. Nothing is visible of the player under the shroud. How in the hell did he win third place?

"From last place in the second quest to third in the maze, your turnaround is nothing short of amazing. You have been awarded a Developer's Chest as well."

Brief movement underneath the shroud is the only acknowledgment Dantos gives.

"Now that we have our winners, I'd like to take a moment to acknowledge all of the developers who played a part in making this tournament a success. Many tournaments take place every day all over Pangea, but this one will always be a place for the best of the best..."

We are ushered off the stage as Benjamin honors the developers. Nancy, the host for the last two stages of the tournament, flies her pegasus through the crowd, eliciting cheers.

Our usher tells us that there will be an afterparty if we want to attend, but I'm ready to go home. I need to make the arrangements for Maria as soon as possible. He leads us behind the stage to a portal. Before I step through, Aleesia takes hold of my arm.

"I'm glad you won. You deserved it more than anyone else." The kindness in her eyes doesn't match her deadly appearance.

"Thanks. I couldn't have done this without all of you, though."

She goes sheepish for a moment. "I was wondering...if maybe you still wanted to meet up now that this is all over."

"I would love to. Actually, have you ever been to Pangea Headquarters?"

"Yeah, why?"

"I have a meeting there in a few days, maybe you could come along and show me around?"

"It's a date." She kisses me on the cheek and we step through the portal to our own destinations.

The treatment for Buzz's mom is a success. The only downside is that there is a medication she must take for the rest of her life, but Pangea Online agrees to cover the cost. Buzz is like a new man when I have them over for dinner one evening. He goes on and on about what people are saying about me in the game. In his free time, he goes from world to world, telling the story of how I overcame the odds and won an impossible tournament.

I haven't been out into Pangea since the tournament. I log in and sit with Fenrir in my home portal. Sometimes I read, sometimes I rewatch old footage of Merlin and I.

I miss Merlin a great deal. I'm sure the pain will fade eventually, but for now, in spite of all I've won, I feel a bit empty inside.

I'll be going to Pangea Headquarters in a few hours to talk with Benjamin about my father and my place at the company. It's hard to know what to expect. I don't know anything about game development.

First, though, I need to meet up with Ordin. There is something I need to give him.

A group of dwarves surround the entrance to the Lion's Head Pub. Since the tournament, Ordin has become the most famous dwarf in all of Pangea. He even has his own band that follows him wherever he goes. I notice a few familiar faces among the crowd. Glordin, and Tinker step out to say hi.

"Good to see you, Esil," says Tinker. I embrace them all around the forearm in turn. "You have been a good friend to the dwarves and you will always have our help when you need it."

He parts the others and allows me entry into the pub.

Ordin sits in the back with Klink. They both have two beautiful elf women on each side of them. Klink gives me a wink as I approach. Ordin chugs a mug of ale, some of it running down his chin.

"Esil!" he roars. "Good to see you, my friend!" He motions for the ladies to move and I take a seat across from him at the table.

"It looks like you're doing well for yourself. You too, Klink."

"Sacrificing yourself for the good of another on a stream watched by millions will do a lot for your reputation," he laughs. "What is it I can do for you, friend?"

"Actually, I have something for you." I take the Developer's Chest from my inventory and set it on the table. "I couldn't have won the tournament without you. Take it."

The dwarf's eyes brim with tears. "Esil, I can't." His voice is barely more than a whisper.

"You will. This is not a negotiation. I'm thankful for your help and I want you to have it."

He nods and takes the chest off the table.

Pangea sends a vehicle to pick me up around noon. I take a nap on the ride and don't wake until we arrive.

The vehicle door opens and I panic because I'm not wearing my filter mask. I frantically search through the car, looking for the mask. I find it on the floor and strap it to my face.

Someone laughs outside of the car.

"It's okay, Esil. The air is breathable up here."

Benjamin stands outside the door, wearing a light gray suit. His face is nearly identical to his avatar in Pangea, his blond hair is combed neatly to the side. He extends his hand and helps me out of the car. Blue skies surround us. Skies as blue as Pangea. I take off the mask and breathe in the fresh air. It cools my lungs in a way I have never felt before.

"I didn't know there were places in the world like this."

"There's a lot you don't know about the world," says the woman to his side.

I'd recognize that voice anywhere. Aleesia wraps her arms around me and gives me a hug. I bury my nose in her neck and notice the smell of—what—flowers? I don't really know what they smell like, but I imagine that's how they smell.

We let go and I take in her appearance. She is so similar to her avatar, yet different. Her ears are not pointy and her hair is darker, a few freckles line the edge of her cheeks, her eyes are a little more slanted, but there is no mistaking that it's her.

"Let's take a walk to my office and I'll show you around," says Benjamin.

Aleesia takes my hand as we walk. The outside of Pangea Headquarters is a complete mirror of the sky above. Every surface gleams, reflecting the world. Birds fly through the air, and trees blow in the breeze. Is this what the world used to be like?

We enter through a set of doors that open at our approach and walk through a lobby. Even the floors reflect my face when I look down.

Benjamin takes us to a large office. A glass table sits in the middle of the room with a large wooden chair behind it. A man in a holographic projection talks about the results from the Developer's Tournament. The nicest haptic suit I've ever seen sits in the corner. Several shelves hold books that look like they are about to fall apart.

"Collector's items," Benjamin says when he catches me looking. "Have a seat."

Aleesia and I take a seat in the two chairs across from Benjamin. He intertwines his fingers between his hands before talking.

"I heard about your visit at the police station. Unfortunately, everything they said was true. All of your parent's property was sold off by the state after two years. I'm terribly sorry for that. Lucky for you though, your father did own a piece of the company. Not a huge piece, but a piece nonetheless. Enough that after all these years, you are now a very wealthy man should you choose to sell it. However, if I were you, I would hold onto it. Sell a percentage so that you can get yourself self set up, but don't sell all of it. This company meant a lot to your father and I think he would want you to be a part of it. I can set you up with our finance department. They will help advise you on how to let your money work for you going forward." Benjamin stands up from the desk.

"As for me, I have a job offer for you. It's a brand-new division of Pangea Online, one that your father helped with many years ago. You would be the first person to try it out, report back to us and help us make changes with the product going forward."

We walk down the hallway and come to a stop in front of a door with a touchscreen lockpad. Benjamin presses his hand against the sensor and a moment later, the door hisses open.

Inside, several men and women in white lab-coats buzz around the room. In the center, there is a tall cylinder filled with a light blue liquid. A facemask and several tubes dangle in the water.

"I like to think that haptic suits are just the beginning of the user experience. Yes, you can see and hear and touch, but there is so much more to life than that. What if you could smell the flowers as you walk through a field, or smell the iron in the blood of your enemy as you cut through his armor? What if you could taste the food you eat at a tavern or the lips of a woman as you kiss her? Pretty soon, Pangea is going to give that to people and I want you to help us."

"What exactly is it you want me to do?"

"I want you to alpha test our full immersion unit."

ACKNOWLEDGMENTS

First and foremost, thank you for reading my book. I hope you loved it! If so, please leave a wonderful review. Reviews are as rare as Developer's Chests and the more positive reviews I have, the more likely it is that others will read my books as well.

Second, I should probably thank my mom. If she hadn't bought me that Super Nintendo when I was in first grade, I doubt this book would have ever happened. I spent years playing Super Mario Bros and The Legend of Zelda: A Link to the Past. Since then, I've always been a gamer. I lost years of my life to League of Legends. Super Smash Bros and Mario Kart are my go-to party games. When I discovered that that LitRPG was a genre, I knew my writing would never be the same. This book is the most fun, engaging, and challenging project I have worked on to date. And I can't wait to write more.

There's a lot of people who played a role in this book becoming a reality. First, I would like to thank Scott. You helped me craft this story in its earliest stages when I wasn't sure exactly where it was going. Caroline, thank you for your unwavering support. To my beta readers, JD, Micheal, Arthur, Ezben, Cory, Florian, Jennifer, Robert and Bas; thanks for finding the plot holes, the inconsistencies, and reading through the crap that was an unedited mess. You're the real MVPs.

I'd also like to send a big shout out to the LitRPG community. I don't know another community of readers that are as engaged and ravenous as you. If you're looking for more books similar to my own, check out LitRPG Books.

ABOUT THE AUTHOR

S.L. Rowland is a wanderer. Whether that's getting lost in the woods or road-tripping coast to coast with his Shiba Inu, Lawson, he goes where the wind blows. When not writing, he enjoys hiking, reading, weightlifting, playing video games, and having his heart broken by various Atlanta sports teams.

SLRowland.com

Patreon-For signed paperbacks, advanced chapters, exclusive short stories, art, merch, and more.

Newsletter: For updates on new releases, sales, and behind the scenes content!

Email: slrowlandauthor@gmail.com

Find out more at https://linktr.ee/SLRowland

ALSO BY S.L. ROWLAND

Tales of Aedrea

Cursed Cocktails

Sword & Thistle

Pangea Online

Pangea Online: Death and Axes

Pangea Online 2: Magic and Mayhem

Pangea Online 3: Vials and Tribulations

Sentenced to Troll

Sentenced to Troll

Sentenced to Troll 2

Sentenced to Troll 3

Sentenced to Troll 4

Sentenced to Troll 5

Path to Villainy: An NPC Kobold's Tale

Collected Editions

Pangea Online: The Complete Trilogy

Sentenced to Troll Compendium: Books 1-3